M000268169

Darkness Watches

Jason Parrish

2016

This is a work of fiction. Names, characters, places, and incidents
are the product of the author's imagination. Any resemblance to actual events,
locals, or persons, living or dead, is coincidental. All rights reserved. Except as
permitted under the U.S. Copyright Act of 1976, no part of this publication may be
reproduced, distributed, or transmitted in any form or by any means.
All quoted scripture comes from the King James Version of the bible.

Copyright © 2016 Jason Parrish

ISBN 978-0997954401

East Star Publishing, 2016

For Delia

ACKNOWLEDGEMENTS

I would like to give special thanks to some great people who helped bring this book to life. Melissa Levi (fantastic writer- check out her Mustard Seed devotionals, you'll be glad you did.). My niece, Kaitlee Riese, who kept me straight on Middle School vernacular and culture (and gave some brutally honest, but needed, feedback). Tiffney Shankles, Stacey Blaylock, Judy Camp, Susan Oates, Rachael Eldridge, and Ron Cole; who read an unpolished draft and called me out on everything from typos to serious plot and character issues. Alexis Jones, whose uncanny skill with a camera was severely tested with me as the subject. Thank you all.

Finally to Delia, my wife and first reader. Without her encouragement and patient support, these words would have died on my hard drive. Thanks for believing.

"For we wrestle not against flesh and blood, but against principalities, against powers, against the rulers of the darkness of this world, against spiritual wickedness in high places."

Ephesians 6:12

1

The Darkness watched Daniel sleep. Most mistook him for a shadow, a cruel trick the streetlight played when remnants of its glow filtered through closed shades, or a cloud passed over the full moon, shifting patterns of light and dark along the walls and ceiling. Some laid awake wondering, not certain if monsters really exist but believing in the possibility. Others thought nothing of it. Either way, he loved watching because they rarely knew for sure. Unless he chose otherwise.

***

DANIEL'S EYES FLASHED open to the red glow of digital numbers, quarter past three. He rubbed them to wipe away the fog of sleep, forcing himself from the world of dreams- bad dreams. Something wasn't right. He felt misplaced, lost, until he spotted the picture of his mom and dad. Then he remembered. They had died. This was his new room, his new house, the first night of his new life with Becky and Mike. This was now, mom and dad were before.

The hair on his arms and neck tingled to life when he sensed its stare. Evil enveloped him, seeping through his pale skin. It's here...It's really here this time. His heart, still racing from the nightmare, thundered in his

1

chest. The Superman pillowcase Aunt Becky bought him was damp and warm against his face.

Daniel clutched the sheets and pulled them close. The Darkness grew in his modest bedroom, dimming what moonlight bled through the lone window. The only images he could make out were his footboard, the dresser, and the happy picture- the picture from before. Daniel propped himself up on his elbow. He had dreamed of it, he had sensed it, but it had never manifested into his reality. It drew closer, swallowed the last of the moon's light, and thoughts of rage, hate, and murder invaded his mind. Thoughts not normal for a twelve-year-old boy.

He tracked The Darkness as it crept to his side.

"Please Jes-"

Before he could finish his plea, a grip tightened around his throat and slammed his head into the pillow. Not enough to restrict his air, but more than adequate to keep his eighty-one-pound body pinned. He thrashed his arms, desperately trying to latch onto his attacker.

Daniel struggled, lifted his head several inches, but the grip violently pinned him again, relaxing then tightening around his throat. Damp bedsheets, one of Aunt Becky's Goodwill scores, churned frantically, driven by his flailing legs. The smell of sweat and urine made him want to puke.

He tried to call out to his uncle, to God, to anyone, but his tongue failed to obey, and all he managed was a prolonged grunt. Certain he was dying, a random string of thoughts flashed through his mind. He wondered if it would hurt. He hoped Aunt Becky wouldn't tell anyone he'd peed himself like a little kid. He wondered how it would feel to meet Jesus.

As he thought The Name, hate exploded in the room. Its power ripped through Daniel with enough force to take his breath. He had never experienced emotions so strong they physically altered the surrounding air.

Fear. Hate. Fear. The feelings drummed a pulsating rhythm around him and through him.

Then it was gone.

Daniel surveyed his room; everything was in order. The only signs a struggle had occurred were the twisted pile of freshly stained sheets and a burning ache in his throat. The air no longer seemed alive. Moonlight once again revealed his worn oak dresser, "a good find" according to Aunt Becky.

His eyes filled with tears; his body trembled under the covers. Why did they have to die? He wanted his mom to stroke his hair like she did when he was little. He wanted his dad to tell him it was going to be all right, "God has a plan Daniel."

Instead, he closed his eyes, cried himself to sleep, and dreamed of The Darkness.

2

Ben Johnson jerked awake to the blare of his alarm, scowled at the numbers, and hit snooze. Five hours wasn't enough, he needed more time. Seconds before sleep embraced him once again, his eyes snapped open. The Murphy presentation. He slipped his legs over the edge, forced himself to his feet, and caught a whiff of coffee- at least Jill's watery version of it. It was going to take a lot more than her weak crap to get him through this day.

He stumbled into the bathroom, found himself in front of the mirror, and reached up to his hairline. The scar was bright pink today, a sure sign of stress. It stood out like a neon light against his shaggy blond hair, fair complexion, and blue eyes. He traced it, running his finger across his forehead, down to his right brow. Jill hated it, said it made him look like a thug. He rubbed his face, sure she'd mention three days' worth of stubble, but he didn't care, it was Monday. Then again, if he had any chance of saving his family he needed to nail the meeting, so trying for a professional image might not be a bad idea. The shave cost him time, so he skipped the shower and did the best he could with a washcloth and some hand soap. Good enough.

He was tired of the charade, tired of the lies. If she only knew how close they were to losing it all, or worse, how he'd managed to stay afloat this long, she'd leave him for sure. She didn't understand it took money to start a company. If he could make it through one more day, one more meeting, it may work out. He put on his mask, headed downstairs to the kitchen, and saw her standing by the sink.

"Morning baby," he said.

No response. She sipped her coffee, lost in the world outside the window. She was beautiful, even first thing in the morning. Not as firm or slender as when they first met, but she still turned heads. Ben grabbed a bagel and filled his travel cup with the weak brew.

"Who is she?" Jill asked, gaze fixed on the pristine colonial across the street.

"Who's who?"

She swung to him. "You know what I'm talking about."

"I have no idea."

"Don't give me that. You come to bed late every night, we haven't talked in weeks, and when we do get a couple of hours together, you're more interested in your phone than me. You never even spend time with Preston anymore." Her voice softened. "Who is she?"

"Preston's twelve. He doesn't want to spend time with me." Ben walked to her and took her hand. He didn't have time for this. Exhausting.

"Look at me Jill."

She lifted her eyes; she had been crying.

"There is no one but you. I love you as much today as I did thirteen years ago. I know I've been working a

5

lot, and we haven't spent much time together these past few weeks, but I promise I'll be home in time for dinner. My meeting is this afternoon, and once I close this deal everything will be back to normal."

"Weeks? Try months." She pulled her hand from his. "There's always another meeting, another deal, another client. Where does it end?"

She was right. There would always be another deal because that's the way the world worked. Deals pay the bills baby.

Ben drew her close. "We'll go out tonight and celebrate. Preston's staying at Tommy's, right? We'll have the whole evening to ourselves. This contract is big enough to pay off most of the loans." He planted a gentle kiss on her forehead. "Baby, I love you. We're in this together okay?" The lines around her eyes relaxed, and he thought she had softened.

"Fine," she sighed as Ben let her go. "You need to talk to him though."

"Who?"

Jill turned to the window, took a deep breath, and whirled back to him. "Who do you think? Your son."

"What's wrong with Preston?"

"I ran into Mrs. Ellison yesterday, and she told me he and his buddies have been teasing one of the new kids."

"Who's Mrs. Ellison?"

Jill rolled her eyes. He hated when she did that.

"His English teacher. That's exactly what I'm talking about."

He drew her in again and caressed her cheek. "Okay, okay. Point taken. I'll talk to him tomorrow. I promise."

She pulled away, slowly, but deliberate enough for him to understand they would revisit the talk later.

"Fine. So, where are you taking me?"

"River House Grill?" They had dined there for their first anniversary and Jill loved it.

The slightest hint of a smile settled on her lips.

"What time?"

"Be home at six."

Ben brushed the side of her mouth with a quick kiss. Had he known that would be the last time their lips touched, he would have lingered, savoring a final moment of passion before his world went bad. Instead, he hurried out the door and dumped his coffee in the bushes.

***

TRAFFIC WAS LIGHT for a Monday morning so Ben made the commute in thirty minutes. His assistant, Katie Davidson, greeted him with a fresh cup of coffee, real coffee Ben thought, when he strolled into his office at eight-twenty. Hiring Kat three months ago placed a burden on the finances, but without her he'd already be sunk. She was organized, great with the books and didn't ask many questions. And hot. Oh, was she hot. She reminded him of that Russian tennis star, blond, tall girl, Maria something. Long last name, lots of syllables. He hated tennis, but watching that gorgeous commie scamper back and forth in her little skirt had prompted him to buy a racquet. Of course Jill bought one too, and as they say, the dream was dead.

"Mr. Murphy and his team will be here at four. These are the contracts," she said, handing him the stack of folders. "I'll swing back by this afternoon and get the PowerPoint and camera up and running."

"What time?"

"Three-thirty, three forty-five."

"As long as you're here when they arrive. They need to see someone at the front desk."

"I'll be here."

"Thanks Kat. And listen, when they show up, take them in and offer coffee, water, whatever. Tell them I'm on a call, but I should be off in about five minutes. Don't hang out in the conference room, and shut the door when you leave them."

"I've got it covered. I can stick around for a bit once the meeting starts, but I've gotta run by four-thirty." She started toward the door, stopped, and glanced out the window. "You think they'll sign?"

"Yeah, I think they will."

"Ben, if he doesn't," her eyes shifted to the floor, "if he walks."

"He won't, don't worry." Ben pulled a small black box from his jacket. "I almost forgot. I bought you a gift, a thank you for what you do around here. Coming in on your vacation and all."

Kat, hands on her hips, offered a curious smile. "What's this?"

"Told you, a thank you. Not many assistants would do this."

"Hey, I'm off the rest of the week so no biggie. Besides, you're paying me, right?" With a wink, she lifted the top and pulled out the silver necklace with a white trimmed dove charm. Nice, but it didn't set him back much, which was good since he didn't have much left.

She let it dangle between her fingers. "It's beautiful. You know you don't have to get me anything." She seemed genuine.

"It's not much. Try it on."

She threw her arms around Ben's neck. "Thank you."

He watched from the window until her car pulled out of the lot, then spent the rest of the day studying the dossiers and videos of Murphy's team. They needed him, that was clear. He'd been able to break their firewall and sit in on their meetings from the comfort of his own office. Who neglected to cover their laptop cams with today's generation of hackers? Worse, who stored that kind of information in unencrypted files? Client names, Social Security Numbers, birthdates, everything an aspiring felon with minimal skills could ask for.

He dropped into the lobby sofa and reviewed his two goals for the meeting. First, land the account. They had security issues and he needed the business. Second, and this was arguably more important, find out if they knew about his intrusion.

***

THE MURPHY CONTINGENT arrived at four, and Ben watched Kat welcome them and show them into the conference room. He studied them another seven minutes, trying to identify any last minute tells that might give him an advantage. Shuffling feet, darting eyes, stiff posture, all mannerisms that hinted at a weakness. He'd learned a few tricks from his father.

Murphy was ice. Dark suit paired with a red tie, classic power attire. Dark brown eyes set above a firm jaw, a slight frown etched into his face; yet he seemed relaxed. Ben regretted skipping the shower. The woman on Murphy's right, Marlee, might prove useful. He had little on her, just her name and a few skypes to her sister in Arizona, but in the space of five minutes she'd opened and closed her folder seven times. She was anxious. So was he.

3

Pine Creek Middle School sat on Forrest Street south of Lee Square, the town's family park. The fifty-three-year-old central building anchored that side of town. Its faded brick exterior and manicured lawn mirrored the style of Pine Creek's downtown architecture. Of its four-hundred students, Daniel Palmer knew exactly two, Nichole Wilcox and Preston Johnson. Well, he recognized the names of most and had spoken to a few about trivial middle school matters, but the fate of his social status rested in the persons of Nichole and Preston.

In the two months since enrolling, Daniel learned PCMS was not much different from his old school. Both had cliques, none of which he fit into. Both had interesting teachers and boring teachers. Both were small town schools where the majority of kids had played together since kindergarten and rarely picked the new kid for a pickup game of baseball. But in Pine Creek he was the new kid. His classmates back home never voted him most popular, but at least he had friends. Back in Texas he made the cut for quick pick up games in the park, limp or not. Here he had discovered one friend, Nichole, and made one enemy, Preston.

That he and Nichole clicked wasn't a surprise. She lived with her grandmother, he lived with his aunt and uncle. One an orphan by death, the other an orphan by meth. She was beautiful, sporting shoulder length blond hair and olive skin that had yet to experience the full-fledged assault of acne, unlike many of her classmates. A natural athlete, her lean frame unencumbered by the effects of puberty, she was outgoing, smart, and loved to argue.

He had learned to avoid the doors by the library. Preston and his buddies hung out there most days before class. Certainly not because of an affection for reading; their lockers happened to line that end of the hall.

"Danny, wait up," Nichole called out from somewhere behind him. He relaxed at the sound of a friend.

"Hey." She ran up the sidewalk toward him.

"You figured out where all of your classes are?"

"I've been here two months. I think I've got the layout down."

She slugged his arm. "Smart aleck."

Daniel tried not to rub his bicep. "Maybe I am." He searched the hallway and dread swept over him. At least he didn't have to climb stairs this semester. He couldn't imagine what they might call him if they saw him drag his right foot up behind him step by step.

Nichole looked past him, toward the library end of the school. "Listen, don't let them get to you. Preston's a jerk, that's why I dumped him. Plus, you're the new kid. You're an easy target. Any day now, someone will drop their tray in the lunchroom, or trip going down the hall or whatever. Problem solved."

Daniel wished he were as confident in the laws of middle school social dynamics.

"You finish the World History homework?"

"Yeah, it was easy. How about you?"

"Um hum. Ended up two pages."

"Impressive. What did you write about?" He asked as they squeezed by a crowd of kids gathered on the steps leading up to the main doors.

"Marc Antony and Cleopatra. A story of love and betrayal," she said, throwing a hand over her heart. Her dramatic nature was one of the first things he noticed about her. She called it "living life with passion," but he wasn't so sure. "What about you?"

"I wrote about societies views on demonic possession and mental disorders in the first century."

"What?"

"Never mind, it's boring." He let the conversation drop.

They worked their way down the hall through a maze of social cliques, arriving at her locker midway down the main corridor. The first period bell would ring any minute and they still had to make it past the wannabe Goth crowd, stop at his locker near the end of the hall, and then take a right down another hallway to their classroom across from the library.

While she fished through a mountain of loose paper, notepads, and random sportswear, he checked his fly. He'd not make that mistake again.

She emerged with her *Studies in World History* book. "Got it." She hoisted it over her head. "Let's go."

13

They hurried past the few students still lingering in the common area, arriving at his locker as the bell rang. Daniel grabbed his book, a loose-leaf folder, an extra pencil, and rushed down the hall trying to keep up with Nichole. They might be a few minutes late, but at least the area looked empty. He tried to ignore the numbness in his foot, a losing battle, though it might get better by the end of the day. Sometimes it did.

"What's the hurry gimp boy?" A voice from behind.

Daniel turned his head as Preston swung his hand up, knocking the book and folder from his arm. "Morning Danny." Homework and notes floated to the floor around his feet.

Two of Preston's goons appeared from the library doors and took up position beside him. Tommy Osborne and Chase Reynolds stuck by Preston like kittens following their mom through a dog pound.

Nichole leapt between them before Daniel could respond. "Leave us alone Preston."

"That's sad," Preston said looking over her shoulder. "What kind of wuss needs a girl to protect him?"

"Maybe he doesn't need protecting. Maybe I don't like you or your toadies." She glanced at Tommy and Chase. "And FYI, you have a brown chunk of nastiness hanging on the corner of your mouth." The jab came without amusement.

Preston was twice her weight and at least five inches taller, but she faced him down without a hint of worry.

Daniel bent down and gathered his things while the stare-down continued above. "Let's go Nichole. We're already going to be in enough trouble for being late. No need to add assault to the list of charges."

14

She broke her gaze first and glanced at Daniel. "You're right. He's not worth a week of detention. Let's go." She smiled and turned down the hall toward Mr. Prescott's room.

Preston hadn't moved from beside the row of lockers, and Daniel couldn't tell if he was confused about what had happened or formulating a plan on how he would kill both of them. "You shouldn't have told him about the chocolate he was wearing. It would have hung on half the day."

"I know, I wasn't thinking," Nichole said, looked over her shoulder, then planted a kiss on Daniel's cheek. "I'll do better next time."

Preston's voice echoed down the hall. "It's not over gimp boy."

Daniel brushed his cheek, savored the evidence of her kiss, and didn't care about Preston or the nerve damage in his foot.

***

LUNCHTIME AT PINE Creek Middle determined a kid's social status for the rest of their life, at least that was the prevailing thought among students. Pockets of pre-teen princesses and pretenders camped out like tribes of ancient herdsman around their particular tables. Access to the territory was by invitation only and usually involved a lengthy initiation process, one he had endured before and had no desire to endure again. Fortunately, Nichole had intervened. Daniel knew his choices would have been limited if not for her. She rescued him from No Man's Land on his first day, snatching him from the table between the Jocks and the Gamers. He wasn't girl crazy like some of his friends in Texas, but before she died, his mom assured him things would change, and when it did they would sit down and talk. Daniel knew what that meant. He might not have armpit hair, but he was old enough to know what the talk would entail. Nichole's kiss made him think he might be sitting down with Aunt Becky or Uncle Mike before long.

He spotted her at the usual table along with some of her friends. She noticed him about the same time, waved him over, and he took the empty seat next to her.

Her friend Zach spoke up first. "Heard about that deal with Preston this morning."

Daniel cut his eyes at Nichole. She was the only one who knew, and he didn't need word to get out he was an easy target.

Nichole threw up her hands. "Hey, we were talking and I thought it was funny, you know, the chocolate and all."

Zach leaned across the table. "Yeah man, that kid's a jerk. Why didn't you just lay him out right there? I would have."

"What good would that have-" Wetness plunked Daniel on the back of his head before he could finish. He reached back and found a sticky liquid oozing down his neck.

Daniel spun around and saw Preston standing five feet away, a string of leftover spit swinging below his chin. None of the other kids had witnessed this act of aggression, save Nichole's small group and Preston's two groupies. Tommy leaned over and whispered something, obviously hilarious, to Preston.

Nichole was the first to her feet, knocking over her water in the process. "You jerk. Who do you think you

16

are?" Preston didn't respond. In fact, he did nothing but stand, feet wide and arms folded across his chest, flanked by his buddies.

Daniel knew he had to take action this time. The thought of spending the rest of middle school, maybe even his whole life, as the object of Preston Johnson's abuse was unbearable. Mustering all of the courage he could find, Daniel jumped to his feet and closed the gap between them.

Preston must have already had the awkward talk with his mom because Daniel had to tilt his head significantly upward to look him in the eyes. Groups at surrounding tables grew quiet and turned in their direction. Daniel didn't have a plan; he acted out of instinct.

"What are you going to do about it loser?"

Nichole made a move, but Daniel held up his hand. Without saying a word, he took his napkin, wiped the back of his neck, then wiped the spit hanging from Preston's chin and stuffed it in the bully's front shirt pocket. For a moment Daniel registered confusion on Preston's face. The constant static of preteen conversations ceased as a teacher, Daniel wasn't sure which one, called in their direction. The last things Daniel remembered about the encounter were a flash from his left, cold tile against his face, and a close up of Nichole's pink toenails.

***

BEN SLAMMED HIS office door. What just happened? He had them and he let them slip away. Even Marlee hammered him. Not enough experience? He was the best, better than anyone outside Atlanta anyway. He sunk into his chair and buried his head in his hands. The Murphy account was his savior, the way out. At least they didn't seem to know he'd hacked their system.

He grabbed his coffee mug and hurled it into the wall, sending several large chunks skipping across the floor. He could put the bank off for another month or two. A good lawyer might buy him three, but lawyers cost money and good ones didn't come cheap. The bank notes worried him but nothing like the fifty-thousand he owed Eddie. He never should have let Vince get him mixed up with a man like Eddie Stillwater. Sure, he had needed the money to get his fledgling business off the ground when the banks turned off the faucet, but the stress wasn't worth it. Eddie didn't care about court rulings or legal documents, and he wanted payment in full. Ben opened a drawer and fumbled for his flask. He had needed Murphy to sign. He needed money now.

The Kentucky bourbon traced a trail of warmth down his throat to his stomach, easing the knot in his neck. The faces of his family beamed back at him from the picture on his desk, one of Jill's favorites. Ben had snapped it while her and Preston relaxed on the front porch swing one evening. He didn't think it was anything special, but Jill loved it. She had bought a wooden frame and surprised him with it the day he opened his office. What would she say when he told her they might lose it all? What would she do if he told her about Eddie and the kind of business partner he'd brought into their lives?

He turned the flask up, and a single drop of Beam dropped onto his tongue. Not even a full swig to calm his nerves. Ben forwarded the phones to his answering service and closed the office early. He needed to be alone and think.

***

A STATUE OF Robert E. Lee marked the center of Lee Square, the pride of Pine Creek. The size of two football fields and lined with oaks as old as the park's namesake, it was Daniel's favorite spot in town. Moms brought their toddlers for an afternoon on the swings, high school kids ditched homeroom to come here and make out, and just recently, Daniel came on Mondays to hear Jim Monroe preach. His Uncle Mike had introduced him two months ago, the day after the move, but he was already like a grandfather to him. Mike had known Jim for years and thought the two might make a good pair. Most people around town viewed him as a mystic nut job who ran the gas station a few miles outside the city limits and held service in the park Monday afternoons. Imagine that, of the two friends he'd made here, one was a girl and the other a seventy-eight-year-old widower.

"Does it hurt?" Nichole reached over and touched Daniel's cheek. "It doesn't look like it does. Not even a black eye."

"Not really. He caught me by surprise, that's all." Preston's right hook had landed flush, and it did hurt. Not as much now, but he'd feel it for a day or two.

She rolled her eyes, but Daniel was grateful she let it drop. "Oh, I almost forgot," she pulled a card from her purse and handed it to Daniel. "Your student I.D. It must have slipped out of your pocket when Preston...you know."

"Thanks." He took it but pretended to study a squirrel scampering along the sidewalk.

19

"You never told me what happened to your foot."

"I got bit by a snake when I was five," Daniel said, wiggling his right ankle, thankful once again she had changed the topic of discussion. "Timber Rattler got me on the heel."

"And it's still messed up?"

"Yeah, they had to cut away some dead tissue, you know stuff like that. The doctor told my mom I had nerve damage."

They walked past the tennis court and picnic area, both empty. "So who is this guy?"

"A friend of my uncle. We meet up at the library every once in a while to talk about the Bible. Sometimes I come to hear him preach."

"Who does he preach to?"

"Whoever will listen I guess."

They worked their way along the sidewalk to the statue of Lee. Jim sat on the bench in front of it, Bible in one hand, cane in the other.

"That him?" Nichole motioned to Jim.

"Yep. Wonder why he's not preaching?"

Jim looked up when they got close and waved them over. "Daniel, so good to see you. Come sit."

Daniel and Nichole dropped their backpacks and joined him. "Why aren't you preaching?" Daniel had been here at least half a dozen afternoons over the past two months, and it was a first. Strands of white hair danced across Jim's leathered forehead, urged along by the light November breeze. His friend looked all of his seventy-eight years.

"First things first." Jim leaned past Daniel and offered his hand to Nichole. "Jim Monroe, and you are?"

"Nichole, Nichole Wilcox."

"Ah, Nichole, the girlfriend."

"She's not my girlfriend," Daniel said, much louder than he meant. Sure, she was pretty and he liked her, but girlfriend? He tried not to look at Nichole, but his eyes didn't listen.

"Okay, your friend. In any event, it's a pleasure to meet you Nichole, friend of Daniel who happens to be a girl."

"You too, sir."

Jim bobbed his head, obviously pleased.

"So, where is everybody?" Daniel pressed.

Jim took a few seconds to respond, and when he did, the pleased look evaporated, replaced by an exhausted one. "No interest today I guess. I don't imagine you two are up for a sermon? Got a good one ready."

Neither Daniel nor Nichole spoke or made eye contact with the preacher. Jim shook his head and let out a weak laugh. "I'm going on with you. You get enough of me already. Which reminds me, you studied up on what we talked about?"

"Yes sir. I've started at least."

"Good. Maybe your friend here would be interested in joining us sometime."

Nichole looked away and remained quiet.

"Did I say something?" Jim asked.

She turned back and forced a polite look. "No. It's fine. It's just my granny isn't into that stuff."

"What stuff? The Lord?" Jim's tone stayed calm although the surprise was obvious.

The question seemed to catch her off guard so Daniel stepped in. "Mrs. Wilcox doesn't want her around anything that has to do with...well, Jesus."

Jim took Nichole's hand, and with as much compassion as Daniel had ever witnessed him muster, asked why. Nichole shrugged.

"What about you Nichole. What do you think?"

"I don't know. I mean I've wondered but-"

"That's all I need to hear. Daniel and I meet at the library most Tuesdays. What if you just happen to show up?"

"Maybe." Her tone was pleasant but Daniel doubted her sincerity.

"Good. I'm glad," Jim said, gathering his cane and hat. "I better get on to the store. The after work crowd can get a little antsy if Betty's behind the counter. She can't seem to figure out the new register no matter how many times I show her." Jim slowly pushed himself up off the bench, stretching his back once upright.

"Front's moving in. Always know when one's coming."

4

He knew he should have driven straight home from work. That's what he had promised. He also knew he couldn't face her. Not after meeting with Murphy and his puppets. Idiots, all of them. He should have driven home and taken his wife to dinner, but he didn't and that's okay, because this place was an old friend from another life. A life before clients and bills. What he needed now was a friend.

Ben lifted the glass to his lips and peered through the haze left by countless smoldering cigarettes. A young couple, mid-twenties, huddled at a corner table laughing. An older man, who looked like he should be teaching a community college economics class, sat at the bar shifting his feet on the stool, eyeing a blond thirty years his junior. A clean cut business type with slick dark hair sat within earshot, glancing at his designer watch every few minutes. Slick's probably waiting on a date that isn't coming. Idiots, all of them, Ben thought, and finished the last of his drink.

His phone buzzed for the fifth, or was it the sixth time since he had sat down. Jill. What time was it, eight-thirty? Nine? Maybe he should call her back and let her know he was okay. Ben reached for his phone then hesitated. Bad idea. Arguing with Jill worked best face to face. He'd call a cab and beg her forgiveness the instant he walked in the door. He would tell her everything; the money, Eddie Stillwater, the disaster with Murphy. He would lay it all out to her, and she would forgive him. That was the plan.

"Hey Ben." His head jerked up at the sound of Kat's voice. "What's up?" She still wore the charm necklace.

"I'm just..." He was in no condition to explain the series of events that had brought him to Top Shelf Lounge on a Monday night. "I was headed home. Calling a cab. What are you doing here?" He fought the urge to reach for her hand.

"Celebrating the real start of my vacation, but I'm getting out of here too. Gray toupee over there is giving me the creeps." She signaled toward the professor. The cute blond. How did he not recognize her?

"You okay?"

"Yeah, I'm fine. A little tired, that's all," he said.

"You're more than tired. Grab your stuff and let's go. I'm driving you home."

Ben thought about his conversation with Jill that morning and her hormone induced accusation. "Not a good idea." He twisted the gold band on his left hand.

"And why not?"

Kat proved a sharp assistant but remained blissfully naïve about the intricacies of long-term relationships.

"It's just not Kat. Jill accused me this morning of having an affair, and I think her seeing you drop me off, after I stood her up for dinner tonight, would be a very bad idea. I'll call a cab."

Ben was frustrated. Not with Kat, she was great. She was more than great, she was beautiful. She was witty. She was... He didn't know what she was, but he knew he loved his wife, even if his actions tonight weakened his position for that particular argument.

Kat reached out and touched his arm. "Listen, we've known each other for a while. We've worked long nights together. We talk and text all day. It's natural for a woman's mind to wander down that path. I think it's time I met Jill, so we can clear the air. Besides, I'm going your direction, I haven't had a drink all night, and I won't charge you by the mile."

"We lost the deal with Murphy."

Kat's eyes softened, and she sat down in the chair across from him. "I'm sorry. What happened?"

"I don't know. It doesn't matter, I'll figure it out."

"Look, if you ever need to talk I'm here. You know that don't you? I may not give the greatest business advice, but I can listen with the best of them."

She stood from the table, digging in her purse while she talked. "If you'd rather call a cab that's fine, but my offer stands."

Ben watched Kat glide to the bar to say her good-byes. He felt a pang of guilt for watching her, but she was stunning- and he was a man. Halfway across the floor, she glanced back and flashed a coy smile. He couldn't read the intention behind the gesture, but he didn't care. He decided Kat was taking him home. Sure, nothing would happen between them. They would ride and talk, twenty minutes together tops. Then he would say goodbye, go inside, and deal with Jill. They would talk, she would cry, he would apologize, then they would go to bed. That was the plan.

Ben gathered his satchel and left a hundred on the table. He started toward her when a voice from his left caused him to pause.

"Choices are a funny thing."

For a moment Ben thought the words were meant for someone else, but when he glanced toward the table, Slick's eyes were focused on him.

"Excuse me?" Ben asked. More of a reflex than anything else.

"Choices are a funny thing," Slick repeated, with a slight grin and tilt of his head.

Ben had no desire to engage this particular idiot in any type of conversation.

"Yeah, thanks. I'll remember that." He turned back to the bar in search of Kat.

"You see Ben," he stopped cold upon hearing his name, "some choices are insignificant while others have irreversible consequences."

"How do you know my name?"

The man considered him with no expression other than that condescending grin. For a moment Ben wondered if Slick had missed the question.

"That's what your friend called you isn't it?"

He relaxed. This wasn't one of Eddie's men tailing him. He could be a lonely psychiatrist, or a wacko undercover bible thumper looking for sinners like him to give soul saving wisdom about drinking and loose women. Ben didn't care which, he was ready to go with Kat and get home to Jill.

"Listen man, I appreciate your concern, but I don't have time for a lecture."

Slick dipped his head, a gesture Ben understood to mean the conversation would not continue.

Wacko, Ben thought as he brushed past.

He spotted Kat among a group of twenty-somethings and pushed his way into the middle of the crowd.

"You ready?"

"Sure thing," she said, and slipped her arm through his.

They weaved their way to the door, and instinctively, he glanced over his shoulder. Professor Gray Toupee didn't look happy. Serves him right. He didn't have a chance with a girl like Kat. Ben smirked when she pulled him closer to her side, and they squeezed through the crowd gathered near the entrance.

When they crossed the threshold leading to the sidewalk the air cleared. The nicotine fog and confusion of a hundred conversations no longer assaulted his senses. Outside, a light mist fell in the autumn night and a single car idled at the red light down the street, while the distant hum of traffic from the highway three blocks north provided the soundtrack to the scene. The contrast struck Ben as profound. On this side of the window, peace, refreshment, a friend. On the other side, a stinging haze, chaos, a weird old man, and...Ben almost lost his balance. Slick was staring at him, grinning and mindlessly strumming his fingers on the table. "Pathetic idiots, all of them," Ben murmured to no one in particular, and they walked arm-in-arm toward Kat's car.

***

THE RIDE HOME with her proved uneventful. Ben talked Kat out of coming in and explaining the situation to Jill as they pulled into his driveway. He was thankful she wasn't her usual persistent self; part of what made her an excellent assistant and would serve her well when she moved into sales at some point. At least that was his plan. With her personality and body, she'd make him a killing selling his firm to pale faced computer trolls, tucked safely out of sight in their basement offices.

He spent most of the ride home carrying on two conversations; one with Kat about why this would not be the best night to introduce herself to Jill, and the other with himself, trying to formulate the exact wording for the upcoming encounter with his wife. He spent the majority of time involved in the second, which seemed to annoy Kat.

"Are you listening to me? I said I'm a woman and I know how women think. Ben. Ben!"

Her words barely registered.

How truthful should he be with Jill? Not enough and she would know he was hiding something. However, if he were to confess the whole story, Eddie included, she might leave. Thanks for the good times babe, but mama's gotta roll. Oh, and by the way, my attorney will be in touch about mama's half.

Kat pulled into his cobblestone driveway, and Ben dreaded the fight he knew was coming.

She hadn't left the porch light on, but anyone could see it was a beautiful home. He and Jill bought it last year, two months before he went out on his own. It was more space than the three of them needed but exactly what he wanted. His was the nicest house on a street of

28

nice houses. It didn't have the splendor of the homes on White Oak Way, but it had the charm of a grand heritage. That's why he preferred his street. New Money people lived on White Oak Way. He thought the Old Money crowd better suited his tastes.

He and Jill spent the better part of that first year making the old Victorian their own, "putting their stamp on it," New Money might say. They worked hard, refinishing the oak floors, meticulously refurbishing the crown molding that accentuated the nine foot ceilings, and a whole list of other weekend fixes. Jill's favorite project was the bench swing that hung on the far end of the porch, the one from the picture. She wasted many mornings lounging, reading, sipping coffee, in that swing. "The perfect spot," she had once told him. Typical Jill.

Ben could remember a time not too long ago when they were happy, a regular Mayberry family, complete with picnics and homemade ice cream. Which glacier did the ship hit? Lack of attention? Jealousy? Long hours at the office unraveled marital vows all over the world, but getting his company off the ground was an investment in his future, in their future. She had to understand, and if she didn't, he'd make her.

Or, maybe he was attracted to Kat and Jill sensed it. Women can smell competition like a shark smells blood. Jill was his soul mate though, and he loved her despite their differences. Paint was peeling off the swing's armrest and one chain showed a hint of rust. Jill had not sat on that swing in at least three months, curled up, lost in one of her mystery novels. He missed those days.

"Sure you don't want me to come in with you?" Kat asked one final time as he opened the passenger door.

"No, really. Thanks for the ride though. See you next week and rest up because we'll hit it hard when you get back." Ben made it to the edge of his walkway, thankful she hadn't pressed the matter. He prayed that since it was dark, Jill wouldn't recognize that a woman sat behind the wheel.

"Oh, I almost forgot." Ben flinched at the shout, frustrated to hear the car idling in the middle of the drive. "You got a message while you were in your meeting."

He continued toward the porch. "It can wait. Shoot me an email." Too loud, he thought. Much too loud.

"It sounded important. Some guy named Vince wanted me to give you a-"

Unfortunately, he never heard the rest as the front door closed behind him. If it was Vince, he knew what it was about, and he wasn't in the mood. Looking back, weeks after the carnage had swept through his life, he wondered what might have happened had he chose to stop and listen.

***

BEN FLIPPED THE foyer light and walked through the double French Doors into the Great Room. Jill called it the Family Room, but he thought Great Room fit the house's character. She tended to lean toward a more pedestrian outlook on life. An irritating trait he endured with a grin.

"Jill, baby I'm home." When she didn't respond, Ben deduced two things. One, she turned in early, which by itself might mean nothing, but coupled with the dark porch and foyer, she was obviously in no mood to talk. The second conclusion was that tomorrow morning would be bad.

Wondering how to play his hand, he walked to the quaint oak writing desk, turned on the lamp, and noticed an overturned picture on the end table. The image brought a wave of memories. He thought of the vacation and how Jill and Preston had argued about standing on the steps of The Cathedral of St. John the Baptist, in the heat of a Savannah August, while he tried to find the best angle for the shot. That was a good trip.

Thirsty, and feeling the effects of his evening at the bar, Ben meandered back through the foyer toward the kitchen. The second floor looked dark, but he called out anyway. "Jill, you up?"

A shimmer of light bounced off of the hardwoods. Perplexed, he reached down and picked up a piece of glass. Its origin didn't register until he noticed the wooden frame under the sofa table. He immediately recognized the picture of he and Jill at her parents' Christmas party from a couple of years ago. Several feet away, leaning against the dining room wall, he spotted another busted frame. Ben's heart raced. He took the stairs two at a time, flung open his bedroom door and saw the empty bed. Back down the stairs and a quick check of the garage confirmed she was gone.

He grabbed his phone and pulled up her number. "Come on baby pick up. I'm so sorry baby pick up." No answer.

Preston.

Ben dialed his son. Stay calm.

"Hey dad, what's up?"

"Just checking in kiddo." Ben wasn't about to burden his only child with the marital problems of his parents, but he struggled to maintain his composure. "You and Tommy having a good time?"

"Yeah. Hanging and playing some Madden. Why are you out of breath?"

Tommy cursed his quarterback in the background. "Moving some boxes. You talked to your mom tonight?"

"Yeah, I called and asked if I could stay at Tommy's tomorrow night too. She said it's okay since we've got Fall Break the rest of the week. Tommy's mom said it was okay."

"That's fine. I had to work late and need to get in touch with her. She must have her phone off. No big deal, but did she say where she was going?"

"Nope." More muffled cursing. "Got to go dad, fourth and three. Tell mom I love her."

He sat on the sofa and debated his options. If the pictures were an indication of her mood, he'd reached the limit of her patience. She didn't pitch this big of a fit two years ago when he had forgotten her birthday. He closed his eyes, and for a moment, imagined himself a bachelor, unconcerned with the messiness of relationships and boundaries of marriage, but the thought didn't linger. Tonight he'd clean and tomorrow they would talk. This time he would listen.

It took Ben a full two hours to sweep every sliver of glass, rehang and reset the pictures, and repair three cracked frames. Exhausted, both physically and mentally, he hauled himself upstairs to the master bath and flipped on the light. Written on the mirror in Jill's red lipstick, three words. TIME TO PAY.

His mind couldn't process the sweeping red letters that filled the wall in front of him. This wasn't Jill, couldn't be. Murphy didn't make sense. Besides he hadn't picked up anything hinting they knew about the files. Not from the meeting or the intercepted emails and skypes. No, it wasn't Murphy. Ben slumped onto the edge of the tub. Eddie, it had to be. Kat said Vince had left a message for him. Ben grabbed his phone and called.

"Hey, this is Kat. Leave a message."

"It's me. Call me back, I need to know what the message was from that guy Vince. I need his number, a way to get in touch with him. It's an emergency. Call me." He cursed and threw the phone across the room.

5

Daniel sat alone on the steps of Pine Creek Public Library and watched the line of cars in front of the school grow. Jim would come pulling in almost any minute, but he'd hear Doris before he saw it. Daniel laughed. Doris and Freedom, Jim's rides. He was a strange old man, but Daniel hoped these occasional Tuesday afternoon library meetings turned into a regular event. He could talk to Jim about things, dark things his Uncle Mike or Aunt Becky wouldn't understand.

Several minutes later, the familiar rumble of a sputtering engine sounded his arrival. Daniel waved as the truck pulled into the handicap spot by the sidewalk but didn't stand. He knew from experience it would be a few minutes before his friend managed to will his bones to the bottom of the steps. He'd made the mistake of offering assistance once, and Jim responded with a cane to his shin.

The Head Librarian, Mrs. Walsh, peered up from her desk when they entered but didn't speak. Not prone to small talk or excessive joy, she offered a dry smile as they passed. No one else seemed to notice them, which was fine with Daniel. He fared much better when he blended into the background. Some kids were wolves, others lambs. He strove for a chameleon lifestyle.

They found their spot, a round wooden table in the far corner, onto which he unloaded several books from his backpack. They had an hour before Mike would pick him up for a quick trip to the lake.

"So, did you study the verses we talked about last time?" Jim sorted through the stack of books, examining each thoroughly before tossing it aside.

A few weeks ago Daniel had told him about the dreams and finally, after some prodding, the attack his first night in Pine Creek. Most adults would have tried to explain the encounter away, unwilling or unable to accept an evil they couldn't see or touch. Not Jim though. Jim believed him.

"Ephesians 6:10-20, read through them several times." Daniel knew the verses. As a preacher's kid he knew most of the popular verses.

"And?"

"And Paul was writing about the Armor of God, spiritual warfare."

"Yes, yes. I know that and you know that, but what did you learn?" Jim tapped the side of his head with a boney finger.

Daniel didn't know how to respond so he waited, hoping Jim might elaborate. He didn't. "Here's the short version. There is a reality beyond what we can see, and it's in that realm where Christians fight the real battle."

"Good, good. But not just Christians, all battles are fought primarily in the spiritual realm. Go ahead finish."

Jim wagged his hand at him like he was shooing away a fly.

"Paul said we don't fight against flesh and blood, but against, then he lists several titles which I assume are types or ranks. Am I on the right track?"

"You're doing great. Now, when you say fight, what did Paul mean?"

"He said wrestle."

"Which means?"

"I looked it up and it means hand to hand combat."

"Do you see where we're going with this, Daniel?"

He did. When The Darkness had gripped his throat, he believed it allowed him, permitted him, to lift his head before pinning him again.

"It was testing me wasn't it?"

Jim rested his arms on the table, and his look turned serious. "No, not testing. I don't think that's the right word. I believe he was challenging you."

The thought unnerved Daniel. What had he done to draw the attention of a monster? "Why me?"

"Why you? Why me? Why any of us?" Jim leaned forward. "The reason is simple, it hates."

Daniel expected a more profound statement from the man that, from what he'd surmised, the whole town considered a modern day Christian Shaman- if such a thing existed. Everyone knew of his dreams, visions, and other supernatural encounters. He enjoyed sharing the details, so most people gave him plenty of room on the sidewalk or grocery aisle. Except for Uncle Mike. None of Jim's eccentricities seemed to bother Mike at all, which Daniel thought odd since Mike shied away from anything concerning God.

"Is that it? It hates?"

"Oh, there's so much more, I wish we had time. For now, remember this, you won a victory that night."

Daniel wasn't sure he understood. In his recollection of the encounter, he'd been so terrified he had peed himself. He didn't know the rules in Georgia, but back in Texas, you wet your crotch, you lost the fight.

Jim continued. "Think about it. You told me images, thoughts, flashed through your mind. Do you remember?"

A girl about his age sat down at the table next to them and took out a textbook. She didn't take notice of them, but Daniel thought he recognized her from English class. Not as pretty as Nichole but cute in a cheerleader sort of way.

Daniel nodded his response to Jim.

"What were they?"

Daniel gave a quick shake of his head, discreetly pointed to their new neighbor, and Jim got the hint. "Okay, what was the last one?"

Daniel leaned even closer, "I thought about what it would be like to meet Jesus."

Jim's eyes lit up. "There you have it my boy. Your first lesson of warfare, they are terrified of Jesus." He said it loud enough for the girl to jump in her seat and shoot them a wary look.

Heat rushed to Daniel's cheeks.

"Well Danny, sorry I've got to cut it short, but I've got to get to the store. Betty's leaving early so I'm closing it down tonight. What time's Mike coming to get you?"

Daniel looked up at the clock on the wall. "He should be here in fifteen or twenty minutes. He's taking me fishing."

Slowly, Jim pushed away from the table and fumbled for his cane and hat. "The lake?"

"Um hum...I mean yes sir."

"Stop by and I'll set you up with some homemade peanut brittle. Fish love the smell of peanut butter." Jim laughed and slapped his leg, prompting cheerleader to swing in her chair fast enough to almost tip over. "Now come on and help an old man to his truck. I got one more thing to show you." Jim held out his arm and Daniel took it, surprised by the invitation to assist. "Invite your friend Nichole again. I got a feeling God's calling to her. Maybe next week she'll come."

Daniel helped Jim navigate the three steps down to the parking lot, taking care not to stumble himself. A whirlwind of leaves skated across the asphalt, several coming to rest against Doris' front tire.

"I got it from here," Jim fished for his keys, "give me a second." Jim's upper half disappeared into the Chevy and emerged a moment later with a balloon. Wind pulled the string taut. "Okay here we go."

"A balloon?" Daniel's foot ached from the trip down the stairs.

"Yep. Now tell me what you think of when you look at it?"

Daniel eyed it, then Jim, and finally back to the balloon. Yellow and plain with no design or text, it bobbed against the breeze. "I don't know, a party?"

Jim wrapped the string around his hand and the balloon inched closer. "No, no, no. Deeper."

Daniel wasn't sure what he wanted, but Jim's wisdom rarely came easy. Always a great destination, but you had to take the scenic route. He watched Jim take the string for another run around his finger, and the balloon jerked against a gust. Before Daniel could answer, Jim let the line uncoil, catching it an instant before the string left his hand.

"Have you ever watched a child with a balloon Daniel? At the County Fair maybe."

"Yes."

"Ever watched one get away? Float up into the clouds while little Johnny cries like he lost his best friend?" Jim paused, looking from his hand, up the string, to the yellow bubble floating above his head. "This balloon is your fear. We hold it tight because we're conditioned to not let it go. We think fear keeps us safe, but it doesn't. You see, we know not to stick a screwdriver in an electrical outlet, because if we do we'll get a shock. Now, are you afraid of electrical outlets?"

"No."

"How about screwdrivers? You afraid of them?"

"No."

"Then how do you know not grab one and jab it in?"

"I don't know. I guess I'm afraid of what will happen if I do."

"Deeper Danny. Go deeper. How do you know what would happen? Is it fear that keeps you safe or is it more? Do you follow?"

Daniel wasn't sure but said yes anyway.

Jim let out a long breath that seemed to come from way down in his chest. "No you don't. Think about it like this; a rattlesnake bit you when you were little. Are you afraid of snakes?" Jim didn't give him time to answer. "It's okay, your uncle told me the story when I asked about your limp."

"No, not anymore." It was the truth. For several years after the bite, every time he saw a snake on TV he cried. Then his dad took him to Caldwell Zoo in Tyler. Before the trip they read all about the snakes that lived in Texas. Before long, Daniel began identifying them on flash cards. By the time they walked into the Herpetarium, he knew more about snakes than anyone in his class. He held his dad's hand, and together they walked to the Timber Rattlesnake enclosure. He wasn't afraid, and even pressed his nose to the glass.

Jim held the door frame as he knelt down in front of Daniel. "Why weren't you afraid anymore?"

He had never thought about the question. "I guess because I knew something about them. I know what they can do, but I learned how to protect myself from them."

Jim's eye's gleamed. "Yes, yes, and what else? What else eased your fear?"

"Because my dad was with me the whole time." Daniel's voice cracked when he spoke.

"Good Daniel, very good." Jim held the string over his head. "What if we let go of the fear? What if we gave the balloon to God?" Jim closed his eyes and lifted his face to the sky. "You see; we fear what we don't understand. We become so used to fear, we forget God's with us the whole time, longing to give us understanding and ready to protect what is his." He released the string. "We're afraid to let it go."

Daniel watched the balloon shoot up over the cab of the truck, through the trees, and into the late afternoon sun.

***

ALONE IN THE parking lot, Daniel watched Jim drive off toward his store. He thought about heading back into the library and out of the wind -it had picked up giving the air a distinctly Fall quality- but sat down on the steps instead. Jim's balloon had drifted out of sight, but the lesson remained.

A man's voice from behind caught him off guard. He hadn't even heard the door open.

"Mind if I have a seat?"

Daniel's heart quickened, and his initial instinct was to run. The man looked normal, respectable even. Mid-thirties, expensive suit, dark hair slicked back with some sort of mousse, gel, or whatever rich people use to make themselves look important. But he wasn't normal. The man flashed a mouth full of sugar white teeth and sat.

Daniel struggled to speak but found his voice. "I know who you are."

The man's smirk somehow grew wider, but he said nothing.

Panic crept up on Daniel, and he moved to stand. He had to get away from The Darkness that had somehow commandeered the man sitting beside him. A cold hand on his shoulder forced him back onto the step.

"Daniel, please. Give me some credit. I only want to talk. A civilized conversation. Can you do that?"

Daniel couldn't think. His head swam with the impossibility of the moment.

The man seemed to sense his difficulty. "Don't worry, I'll do most of the talking. Do you think you can listen?"

Again, Daniel wanted to run, but he remained glued to the step as if a backpack filled with cement blocks held him in place, and despite his fear, yielded.

"Good boy. I take it you know who I am?"

Daniel's head moved slowly up and down.

"Of course you do. We wouldn't be having this conversation if you didn't." The man extended his hand. "You can call me Richard if it helps."

Instinctively, Daniel reached out to him, then jerked his hand back and stuffed it in his pocket. "Okay."

"I would like to clear the air if I may. Please don't take our first meeting personal. I had no intention of harming you your first night in this lovely town, nor do I intend to harm you today." Richard cocked his head and waited.

Daniel didn't speak, and after an uncomfortable silence, Richard continued. "In fact, I'm here to make you an offer."

Daniel tried silently praying but couldn't concentrate. His thoughts ran together like someone had dumped them into a blender and pushed puree.

The corner of Richard's mouth curled up into a half grin. "Occasionally my presence has that effect on humans. Call it a gift. Now, we're almost out of time so let's get down to business."

Daniel's eye's darted past the parking lot searching for his uncle, but the streets were empty.

"Here is my offer. You have a powerful gift. The ability to see through the veil of this world and into the spiritual one is rare. Experience has taught me those with your gift will either help me or hinder me. I will teach you to harness that gift in ways you could never imagine. No more bullying at school, real friends, popularity, everything a teenager could ask for." Richard paused and searched the boy's eyes before continuing. "But that's just the beginning. Oh, it's fine for now, but when you're older the real fun will begin. You can't imagine how far you'll go if you allow me to guide you, mentor you. Daniel, the world can be yours." He spread his arms like a gameshow assistant introducing the grand prize, and for a moment the thought intrigued him. No more teasing from Preston and his buddies, friends he could play ball and Xbox with, it all sounded good.

"What's the catch?" He couldn't believe he was allowing the conversation to continue, but he couldn't stop. The man's words called out to a desire rooted deep within him.

"You'll break off any connections with those who profess to be followers of The Author. I understand that will be difficult with your aunt, but you're smart and your uncle really could use an ally. The situation is ripe for manipulation."

"Jim too?"

"Yes." Richard's eyes flashed solid white when he spoke. "And you'll instead meet with me to begin your tutoring."

He didn't hesitate. "No. I know what you are."

Richard seemed to take this in stride. "Again, we wouldn't be having this conversation if you didn't, so let me sweeten the deal." He leaned close to Daniel. "I understand your mom and dad died not too long ago. You must miss them."

The mention of his mom and dad brought an immediate swell of emotion to the surface. He missed them so much it hurt even thinking about it. His biggest fear was forgetting. Losing even the slightest detail of their faces, the smell of his mom's perfume, the sound of his dad's voice. In spite of the monster asking the question, Daniel managed a weak yes.

"What if you could continue your relationship with them? Talk to them, laugh with them, and maybe one day, if your gift is strong and you're willing to submit to my direction, you'll see them."

A car sped by, but Daniel hardly noticed. In his spirit he knew the truth, this thing sitting beside him was wicked, pure evil, but the temptation was over-whelming. In spite of his love for The Author, a powerful craving drew him to Richard and his promises. Daniel thought he would give anything to feel his mom hug him one more time.

"The feel of her touch is the first thing you'll forget. I'll bet that memory is already fading." Daniel wanted to ask Richard how he knew, then remembered whom he was talking to. "Before you decide, there is one thing you must consider." Still inches from his face, he took Daniel's chin and gently lifted his head. Daniel gasped as the color drained from Richards eyes, leaving nothing but lifeless white marbles. "If you refuse, I will have you exterminated, but not before dismantling your life piece by piece. If you will not help me, you will hinder me, and that is unacceptable. I know it seems unfair, such a complex dilemma for a boy your age, but that is the offer." Daniel tried to jerk his head away from the sight, but Richard's grip tightened. "I need you to comprehend what I'm saying. Piece by piece. Nod if you understand."

When Daniel nodded, the grip relaxed, and the details of Richard's dark brown eyes returned.

"Is that a yes?"

Daniel didn't have to think. The answer came from deep within him. A place he didn't know existed until the power of Richard's temptation revealed its presence.

"No."

Daniel expected the fury of hell to unleash on him right there on the library steps, but Richard simply dropped his hand and leaned back.

"Not the answer I had hoped for, but in time you may reconsider. We'll talk again soon. Until then, I hope you are willing to live with the consequences."

Daniel spotted a flash of red down the street, and relief swept over him when he realized it was Uncle Mike. He turned to Richard, who was already standing. "Get away from me."

The monster reached down and caressed Daniel's head. "Piece by piece." Then he was gone.

***

DANIEL AND HIS uncle pulled into Monroe's Kwik-Shop at 5:25 Tuesday afternoon. Mike promised him an hour or so of feeding the fish, and the word around town was Jim had the stuff Crappie liked. The run down building sat on Highway 27, the main road through Pine Creek that snaked its way the length of the state all the way to the Florida line. Daniel liked the simplicity of Monroe's. No smoothie bar in the corner or fast food restaurant at the other end like the big name convenience stores closer to town. It had gas, snacks, cold drinks, and night crawlers in the cooler by the window. The Farmer's Almanac Calendar that hung behind the counter hadn't been updated since Coach Dooley ran the show between The Hedges.

Jim looked up from behind the register when the bell above the door sounded their entrance. Perched on his stool, he resembled a wrinkled owl, outfitted with a Fedora and over-sized metal glasses. The place was empty except for Jim, which didn't surprise Daniel. According to his uncle, people passed through Pine Creek, Kwik-Shop included, on their way to somewhere more exciting.

Jim waved and put down his book when they walked in. "Well, ain't seen you two in a while."

"Hey old timer."

"Seventy-eight ain't old young buck, eighty-eight maybe, but not seventy-eight. Got me at least ten more years till you can call the old people home. Ask that young fella there. I've still got a few things left to teach this world." Jim winked at Daniel.

"What you need is to find yourself a woman and settle down. Quit all that running around and partying. I hear Mrs. Walsh might have a thing for you."

"Ain't too many ladies can handle a fella like me," Jim said, laughing so hard he nearly toppled off the stool. "Especially the proper type. Mrs. Myrtle Walsh included."

Daniel thumbed through the weekly Pine Creek Trader while the adults amused themselves. It amazed him what people tried to sell. 21" PUSHMOWER. NO

WHEELS. $50 CASH. SERIOUS INQUIRIES ONLY. Daniel tossed the paper aside and glanced out to the parking lot. The sky had gotten dark. He wouldn't have even looked outside if not for the sudden drop in sunlight creeping through the front windows. Thunder rumbled far in the distance, maybe as far away as Longview, ten miles to the north. He hoped the rain would hold off until after the fishing trip. With the lake still two miles south, the storm might miss them.

Mike pointed to the wall behind Jim. "You've got a point old timer. Grab me a roll of snuff will you? We're going to grab some crawlers."

"Daniel said you were taking him fishing, get the fresh ones from the bottom, the ones with the red lid."

"Thanks, we're kicking off a few days of Fall Break. It'd be nice if the rain holds off so the boy could hook one."

"I hear you. Oh, by the way, I about got Freedom's tranny doctored up. You going to take her up to the bluff with me in a couple weeks?"

"You don't need to take that thing anywhere near those roads. You'd lose it around the first curve, and that's a long drop. What about Doris? Throw some new tires on her and she'd look good."

"I don't know how many more trips around town Doris can handle," Jim said, and looked out to his old truck. "Much less how she'd climb those roads."

Lots of people named their cars, or trucks if you lived in a place like Pine Creek, but Jim took special care when selecting titles for his wheels. The green Chevy that sat in the parking lot rolled off the assembly line around the time another Georgia native walked the halls of the White House. It was also around that time Jim's wife, Doris, walked out on him a day after their fifteenth anniversary. The name was practical. The truck was loud, she was loud. He'd bought the Trans-Am six months later- a car his ex never would have agreed to.

Daniel and Mike turned down the aisle at the far end of the store and worked their way around unopened boxes of baked beans and Spam. Daniel heard the clank of the bell over the front door, but didn't turn toward it as Mike dug a couple of worm cups from the floor cooler and handed them to him. Out of his peripheral vision Daniel saw Jim talking with a young man. It didn't feel right. The shadows were all wrong. Wrong place? Wrong shade? Just wrong.

Mike grabbed their drinks, and the pair headed back toward the front. When they reached the end of the aisle, the stranger swung around and leveled a pistol at Mike. They both dropped their cargo and froze.

Daniel noticed Jim's hands shaking, an odd thing to focus on with a gun pointed at you, but that's what stuck out.

The stranger invited them to move behind the counter and they complied.

"What you got?" He asked Mike. "Give it up. Slow."

Mike slid his wallet out of his back pocket and tossed it by the register. Daniel prayed silently as Jim fumbled for the last few bills in the cash drawer.

"Hurry up old man," the stranger said, resting one arm on the counter while keeping the hardware pointed directly at Mike.

Daniel tried to focus. He snapped a mental picture of the stranger and the scene so he would be ready when the police asked him to help with a lineup. A man, no more than twenty or twenty-five, five-ten, hundred and fifty pounds or so. Short cropped blond hair and wearing an Alabama hat, Roll Tide printed across the front. Old, Baby Blue car in the parking lot, one of the muscle car types, though Daniel didn't know the name. Lots of acne on his face, looks like a microwave pepperoni pizza. You know the kind I'm talking about officer, the cheap ones with little chunks instead of slices.

Jim handed the money over and stepped back.

"Unload that shelf of menthols into this," he said, handing Jim a paper sack from the pile by the register.

Jim's hands shook violently enough that he couldn't open the bag, so Mike took it and loaded the smokes.

"I said menthols. Don't mix any of that other-"

The sound of a siren wailing in the distance cut the strangers command short. Daniel guessed an ambulance, but the man froze and snapped his head toward the road. Jim glanced at Mike, then toward the gun, now pointed at his midsection.

The wail grew louder, but the curve a quarter mile up hid the source. The stranger peeked at Jim and Mike before turning his attention to the road again. Jim lowered his eyes back to the gun and dipped his head. Daniel thought Mike would take advantage of the distraction. He towered over the guy and had a clear angle. Instead, he did nothing.

The ambulance screamed past the store and out of sight, and Tide Fan turned back to the trio behind the counter. "Now fill it up."

The hair on Daniel's neck bristled at the look on the man's face. It was casual, almost serene, as he leaned against the counter, tapping out a rolling tune with his fingers.

Mike handed off the overflowing sack, spilling several packs in the process. Without saying a word, the man took it, left the rejects, and walked toward the door. Before he reached it, he turned around, looked directly at Daniel, and sauntered back to the counter.

"I almost forgot. I have a message for you."

For an instant, Daniel thought he might be the target of one of those hidden camera TV shows. Gotcha Daniel Palmer! Look right there and wave at your friends.

It was a fleeting hope.

He watched the stranger smile, lift the gun, and squeeze the trigger. Daniel experienced the senseless act in slow motion. Jim's head snapped back as the explosion thundered in his ears. He tried to scream, but the only sound he heard was a painful, high pitch ringing. Jim crumpled to the floor, smacking his chin on the counter when he fell. The impact broke his upper dentures and sent them skidding into Daniel's shoe. His eyes locked on the stranger, and through a light pink mist, he read the man's lips. Piece by piece. Then without another word, Tide Fan strolled out the front door, got into his car and pulled onto the highway.

***

BEN SAT AT the kitchen table and watched heavy drops of rain pelt the window and slide down the glass in waves. Longview and areas north were getting the worst of it, but he didn't care. Let it flood like it did with that guy from the bible.

He still hadn't heard from Jill. Not this morning when he had called and left another message. Not at lunch when he had texted before calling her again. Not since he'd closed the office an hour early and left two more messages on the way home. All day he had tried to concentrate on finding a solution to his financial problems, but with Kat on vacation and worrying about his wife, the emails and spreadsheets didn't come easy.

The rain intensified, and he rose and walked to the sink. Through sheets of water rolling down the window, the old colonial across the street looked like an oil painting, brought to life by an artist who would never pay the bills with a brush and canvas. Mr. Gilligan, a widower, lived there alone. No children, no siblings, wife gone more than a decade- run down by another old woman while checking the mailbox. Ben heard the Lexus SUV had drug poor Mrs. Gilligan over a hundred feet before finally swerving off the road and into the ditch. Jill had passed the story along to him one night over coffee. She'd heard it from another neighbor who claimed to have witnessed the whole thing.

The siren of a single ambulance blasted along the main road outside his subdivision, slowly fading as it sped towards the outskirts of town. He picked up his phone, checked for missed calls or texts, and double-checked the ringer. Nothing from Jill, volume on high. He sat back down and waited.

Five minutes passed, then ten. More sirens screamed through town. Several this time, all headed the same direction as the first. Ben wondered if someone had drowned at the lake, or maybe a bad wreck out by old man Monroe's store. He tried to think of a reason Jill would be out that way. She had a couple of friends around town, Megan from the gym and the chunky girl from the bank, both single. Megan lived with a roommate in a two-bedroom apartment somewhere between Pine Creek and Longview. Chunky lived in her mom's basement with a parakeet. No address or phone number for either. She also talked about a Becky. Last name Hill, or was it Gill? Didn't matter. All he knew about Becky was that she was married and taking care of her nephew. Crazy world when aunts and uncles have to raise somebody else's kids.

From the table, his phone chirped to life.

AT MEGAN'S. B HOME 2MORROW.

Ben grabbed the phone and called. It went to voicemail.

A few seconds later another chirp, another message.

U DON'T WANT 2 TALK 2 ME RIGHT NOW. 2MORROW.

***

DANIEL AND MIKE walked into the Hill house around nine, three and a half hours after Jim Monroe's murder. Daniel had called 911, and sheriff's deputies arrived a few minutes later. They found Mike passed out against the wall, Daniel crying by the window, and Jim sprawled out in a growing pool of blood. The Farmer's Almanac, wet with gore, was lying by his feet. "Most God awful crime scene I ever seen." Detective James Hodge told the reporter from the Wilson County Enquirer. Paramedics checked Mike out and decided that other than emotional trauma, he was fine. Same with Daniel.

They took statements from he and his uncle. Daniel gave the best description he could, answering every question as honestly as he thought the detective could handle, which meant omitting his talk with the man in the suit and the last words of the murderer. Yes sir. No sir. Short blond. I don't know. One officer told them it was "of utmost importance they describe the event in its entirety owing to the lack of surveillance video." Daniel worried his uncle would deck that one. Mike agreed to make himself available for any follow-up questions and promised to call if either of them thought of anything else. They drove home in complete silence.

"Mike, sweetie, are you okay?" Becky asked, running up to him and grabbing him in a bear hug.

"I'm fine honey, just a little tired."

She let go of Mike then bent down to Daniel. "Honey, I'm so sorry."

"Do you want to talk about it?" Becky looked at Mike, but Daniel thought the question might be an open invitation to either of them.

"No, not right now. Maybe later," Mike said.

Becky smacked Mike on the arm hard enough for him to flinch. "I was so worried. Why couldn't you call sooner?"

"How? Tell the police 'hang on a second, I need to use the phone' then jump over Jim's body to get to it?"

"I've told you and told you that you need a cell phone."

He started to protest, but she cut him off. "Don't give me that mess about people snooping into your business or tracking you from some stinking satellite. I was worried."

"I know, and I'm sorry."

Becky took Mike's hand and led him to the sofa. Daniel fell into the recliner. He admired them. Mike and Becky were going on eleven years together and had been through a lot; losing their only child, a bankruptcy, and the deaths of both of their fathers to name a few. Through all of this, they made it work.

"I'm going to put on some coffee." Then to Daniel, "and I'll make you some hot chocolate if you're up to it?"

Daniel shook his head and closed his eyes. He heard Mike and Becky talking for a while, but wasn't listening. The words floated through his head like background noise from a faraway radio. All he could think about was the look on his friend's face when the stranger turned around and smiled. I have a message for you.

***

MIKE LET HIS head sink back into the pillow and closed his eyes while Becky started the coffee. Was this really happening? Why would anyone want to kill Jim?

Becky returned with two cups and sat down beside him.

"You sure you don't want to talk about it?"

"Yeah, but I ain't going to be sleeping anytime soon. You brew a whole pot?"

"I did." Becky pulled a knitted throw over their legs and leaned against his chest. "So, what do you want to talk about?"

"Anything you want as long as it's you doing most of the talking."

Becky gave him a wary look, as if she were deciding whether or not she should proceed.

Mike closed his eyes again and patted her hand. "It's fine honey. Anything to get my mind off tonight."

"Okay. Remember me talking about my friend Jill?"

Mike mumbled a yes.

"Honey are you sure you don't want to go on to bed?"

"No, go on. I'm listening."

"If you're sure."

Mike nodded, and she continued. "Her and her husband are having some issues."

"What kind of issues?" Mike asked, eyes still closed.

"She called this afternoon crying and carrying on. It's a long story, but the short of it is, she thinks something's going on with another woman. He didn't come home from work last night."

"She try and call him? Maybe he was working late and forgot to let her know."

"Of course she tried to call. Six times as a matter of fact." Her voice had the familiar tone it reached right before she went off on one of her dramas. "He promised to be home at six and take her to dinner, and when he didn't show up or answer his phone she got worried."

Becky lowered her voice to its normal octave. "After the sixth try she went looking for him."

"Hmm." Mike listened, but his thoughts drifted to the stranger and that smile. He smiled then shot the old man. Shot him right in the face.

"Are you listening?"

Mike opened his eyes and tried to clear his mind. "I'm listening."

"Well, she headed down to Jefferson, that's where her husband works, has some kind of computer company, and saw him standing on the sidewalk arm in arm with some floozy."

Floozy was one of Becky's favorite words. That floozy at the dollar store charged me a dollar fifty. That floozy in front of me pulled out a hundred coupons. According to Becky, every woman in Pine Creek is, was, or will be a floozy. Lord please don't let me smile.

"What did she do?"

"What do you mean 'what did she do'? She went to her friend Megan's apartment and cried her eyes out, that's what she did. Then she called me today, told me the story, and cried some more."

"What did you tell her?"

"I told her I would help her find that floozy and hold her down while she smacked the truth out of her. And wipe that grin off your face, this is serious."

"That all?"

"I invited her to stay with us since Megan's place is one of the studio setups. Not much room in those. She said thanks but she's good for now. Her boy, I can't remember his name, was staying with a friend, so it was just her. If it turns into something more serious, I told her they could stay in Emily's room for a while. As long as they needed."

Hearing her name still hurt. Emily died three years ago, three and a half if you count the time from when she stopped being his vibrant little girl. The doctors told them the tumor was growing fast, they couldn't operate. Had to do with the type and where it was in her brain. The only words he heard that day were "inoperable" and "three to six months." She died six months, fourteen days later, shortly after her twelfth

56

birthday. For a while he and Becky leaned on one another for support, but that didn't last. She blamed him for not taking Emily seriously when she started complaining of headaches. Said he was more worried about running out of whisky than the health of his daughter. He blamed her for spending too much time during those last days at church. They dealt with it in their own way. He self-medicated with his buddy Jack, she self-medicated with her buddy from the Big Church in the sky. Looking back, Mike could see they were both angry. He was angry with himself for not listening to his little girl, and Becky was mad at God for not listening to her prayers. For a while he thought they might split up, but things had gotten better between them over the past year. They weren't in the same place relationship-wise as they were before Emily died, but they were healing. They were together, and Mike was thankful.

"That's fine honey." Mike turned to her. "I thought he was going to kill me."

Becky broke down. She rested her head on his chest and let the tears flow uninhibited. They cried and talked about Emily, their wedding, Daniel, good memories and bad, for over an hour. Struggling against the weights pulling his eyelids shut, Mike took her hand and planted a light kiss on her ring finger.

"I think I want us to have a baby." He was too tired to talk anymore, but he let her continue without interrupting. "Having Daniel here over these past couple of months has been amazing. I think of..." She paused and drew a breath. "It makes me miss Emily even more. I know we haven't talked about it, and I don't mean to spring this on you now, but ever since Daniel moved in,

I can't quit thinking about how it would feel to hold a little one again."

Mike stroked her head but didn't respond. What could he say? He wasn't ready? Didn't know if he'd ever be ready? That he didn't want another kid because, truth be told, they couldn't afford the one fate shoved on them?

"Mike, are you listening to me? I'm serious about this."

Mike barely heard the words as he drifted off to sleep.

"Yeah honey, we'll see."

Then nothing but darkness.

***

MIKE WOKE SOMETIME after three, still in the living room. Becky slept curled up, head in his lap, snoring softly. He eased himself out from underneath her, rolling his neck hoping to release the knotted muscles causing his head to ache. He dreamed of Emily, of Jim Monroe, of blood and flashing lights. The dream wasn't cohesive, not like a movie playing start to finish. Instead, images flashed as a series of random pictures. A still shot of Emily blowing out candles at her eighth birthday party, the one where they had rented inflatables and invited all of her friends. The terror on Jim's face when the stranger turned around and walked back to the counter. A rundown gas station fenced in by yellow tape. A pizza faced kid with cold eyes and a casual smile staring at him.

He'd give anything for a drink.

Deciding sleep was out of the question, he grabbed a blanket from the hall closet and a pillow from the lounge chair. He covered Daniel, who was still curled up in the recliner, with the blanket, then pulled the throw up to Becky's chin. He eased the pillow under her head, taking care not to wake her.

Mike slipped out the front door and set off walking down the path that led to the pond near the edge of their property. It was time he got answers from God, if He was there.

6

Sleeping in on a Wednesday felt strange. The last thing he remembered was drifting off in the recliner while Mike and Becky talked. He was in his bed now but didn't remember how he got there. It didn't matter. Wrapped in blankets that smelled like the dryer sheets Becky kept over the washer, he yanked his pillow over his head and tried to doze back off. Finally, the smell of bacon trumped fresh cotton, and the sound of pots and pans clanging against one another drew him from the protective cocoon of his covers.

"Daniel, breakfast's ready," Becky's voice boomed from down the hall. "Come on before it gets cold."

The ache in Daniel's stomach told him she was right. When was the last time he'd eaten? Yesterday at lunch?

"Coming," he called back.

By the time he trudged into the kitchen, Mike and Becky were already seated and filling their plates with scrambled eggs, bacon, biscuits, and gravy.

"Look who decided to join us." Becky loaded a spoon-ful of eggs onto an empty plate and patted the seat next to her. "You sleep okay?"

"Yes ma'am. All I remember is falling asleep in the living room."

"Your uncle carried you to bed early this morning. I was worried you might end up with a crick in your neck the way you were all hunched over on your side."

Mike asked Becky to pass the salt, which she did, albeit reluctantly. After shaking a generous portion on his gravy, he took one bite and pushed the plate away.

"Still not hungry?" Becky asked.

"No."

Becky turned back to Daniel. "Your friend Nichole called this morning. She sounds cute. You two got a little romance going on?"

Daniel could tell his aunt was trying to lighten the mood, but he almost choked on his biscuit. "No. We're friends."

"Oh honey, with eyes like yours, you're going to have a lot of pretty friends. Every time I look at them I see your mama. Your uncle got plain old brown, she got...well those."

Daniel couldn't count the times people had com-plimented him and his mom on their eyes, amber with a hint of blue in the center. No mistaking, he was his mother's son.

"Just friends. I promise."

"Sure sweetie, sure. Me and your uncle were just friends too. That's what we used to tell your mama when we first met. She was mighty protective of her little brother." Becky smacked Mike on the arm. "What do you think? You think the little man is growing up?"

Mike took a sip of coffee and shrugged.

She turned back to Daniel. "Anyway, she said to give her a call this morning. You ought to invite her to church. Her parents too."

"I don't know if I'm in the mood to talk to anyone."

"Honey, I know you're hurting, but it's times like this that you need to talk. Give her a call and see what she wants. I'll bet if you asked, she'd come to church with us this weekend."

"She lives with her grandmother, and I don't think Mrs. Wilcox would come if we paid her. She might not even let Nichole go."

Becky looked surprised, even offended. "Oh really?"

"Really. She's into a lot of crazy stuff." Daniel wished he could snatch the words back the second they rolled off his tongue.

"Crazy stuff? Like what?"

"I don't know. I know she goes to psychics and reads about spells and stuff."

Becky laid her fork on the table, pushed her plate away, and turned to face him. "And how do you know all that?"

"Nichole told me."

"Is she into that kind of stuff?"

"No ma'am."

Mike sat his coffee down and studied Becky, an annoyed expression on his face.

"You sure? I don't want you running around with a girl that's into Voodoo."

"I'm sure. I think her parents were Baptists." Daniel wasn't sure about that particular fact, but he figured it couldn't hurt.

He was wrong. "Where are they? Why's she living with her grandmother?"

"I don't know much, just that her dad left a couple of years ago and her mom's in jail for drugs. She has an aunt in Knoxville, but I think that's it besides her grandma."

"Drugs? I thought you said they were Baptists."

"Um, I think they used to be. I don't know for sure. She said she went to Vacation Bible School when she was little." Daniel took another bite of his biscuit, hoping to buy some time.

"I don't know if-"

Mike cut her off. "Go easy on him. He didn't say she did drugs."

"I want to meet this young lady, romance or not. You invite her to dinner next week. Tell her to have her grandma call if she wants."

Becky turned her attention from Daniel to Mike. "What time did you come to bed last night?"

"I don't know, maybe five, five-thirty."

"You okay?" She reached across the table and rested her hand on his. Then looking at Daniel, "are you both okay?"

"I don't know. Lot of things on my mind." Mike didn't acknowledge her hand but didn't withdraw his.

"Either of you want to talk about it?"

"No, not right now." Mike said.

Daniel remained silent and no one pressed him.

"It's okay. I couldn't imagine going through what y'all did." There was a tenderness in her voice Daniel hadn't heard since he'd moved in. "I love you," to Mike, then to Daniel "I love you too." She paused, nodded to each of them. "I know y'all have some things you're working through, will be for a while I imagine. All I'm asking is that we work through them together as a family." Daniel wondered if she meant the last comment more for Mike than him but rolled with it anyway. Family was a good thing.

Mike glanced at Becky. He opened his mouth to speak but didn't. A few seconds later it came out anyway. "I talked to God last night. Or at least I tried talking to God, I don't know if He heard."

"He heard. I'm sure of it," Becky said, her face suddenly glowing.

Mike got up from the table without responding. "Maybe I should go on into work. No sense in moping around here all day."

"You've already got plans."

"Plans?"

"Yep. You're going fishing with Pastor Middleton in an hour."

***

SHE TOLD MIKE the story while they washed dishes. Becky had arranged the afternoon of fishing before he woke up. She thought it might be a good idea to give Pastor Middleton a call after last night's tragedy- that's what she called it, a tragedy. She told Mike that's what pastors do. They listen and help you see things the way the Lord sees them.

Mike resisted even though he knew her simple logic was often hard to overcome. He told Becky he liked the preacher well enough, but couldn't see himself wetting a hook with a man of the cloth. "What if I lost a big one and went to cussing? Besides," he argued, "the man's eighty years old. Ain't no way he can get down the bank to my honey hole without slipping and breaking a hip."

She told him, hands on her hips, finger jumping up and down, "He's seventy-eight and can still run the aisles and preach hell hot and heaven sweet. If he can jump up on a pew, he can get to your honey hole-whatever that is." Case closed.

***

MIKE DUG THROUGH the brown paper bag full of potted meat, saltines, and bologna sandwiches Becky had put together. He found the napkins and handed one to the preacher.

"Thank you," John Middleton said, and wiped a bit of mayonnaise off his face. "Not biting today are they?"

"No they ain't preacher."

"Becky told me about y'all being in the store with Jim yesterday." John wadded up the napkin and sat it down in the grass beside him. "That couldn't have been easy."

"No sir it wasn't. There wasn't no reason for that punk to shoot him. He was a good man, preacher."

"He was," Middleton agreed. "How's Daniel?"

"Okay I guess. Little shook up."

Preacher Middleton looked out over the lake. "Your sister's boy right? Been here what, about two months?"

"Something like that."

"I was sorry to hear about the accident. I know what you two have been through over the past few years."

Mike hoped the preacher wouldn't press the matter, and for a while he didn't. The two of them sat on the bank for another ten minutes in silence.

"You doing okay? You want to talk about it?"

No, I'm not doing okay preacher. As a matter of fact, I'm not okay at all. I saw a friend get shot in the face. Little chunks of his brain landed on my arm. How do you think I'm doing?

"I'm okay," Mike said.

The preacher cleared his throat and gazed back out over the lake.

"Mike, what do you think happens when you die? Do you believe in an afterlife?"

The question caught Mike off guard. "What?"

"Do you believe in an afterlife? Or do we snap into non-existence?"

Mike looked out over the water and didn't answer for several seconds. Then, with a long exhale, "I don't know preacher. I just don't know."

"I think there is," the preacher said, taking another bite of his sandwich.

"I hope you believe that or you're in the wrong business."

"You'd be surprised at how many people in my business don't believe. Some lost their faith and continue on giving out the gospel because it's all they've ever done. Others never believed at all. Guess they figured standing behind a pulpit for a living sure beat working in a mill. I know at least one of each pastoring churches in town now."

Mike dug through his tackle box and wondered how the conversation had made such an ugly turn.

"My point is, the existence of an afterlife isn't dependent on whether or not you believe. Either it is or it isn't. Make sense?"

"Sure," Mike said, trying to will the man from continuing down this road. It didn't work.

"It's the same thing with God. People can believe anything they want, but what they believe has no bearing on the truth. Still with me?"

Mike clipped a spinner to his lead and tried to think of some way out of this. Leave it to a preacher to ruin an afternoon on the lake. "I'm with you."

"Good. Now tell me when you stopped believing."

Mike dropped the lure and looked up without turning his head toward the pastor.

"I don't think I want to talk about it right now if it's all the same."

The preacher offered an understanding smile. "My wife used to tell me I talk the same way kids go swimming, not easy down the ladder, just jump right in like hornets was chasing them." He turned the crank on his rod. "Enough serious talk. What do you say we pack it up and grab a milkshake back in town? I'm buying."

Mike reeled in his line. "I like it preacher. Just need to find a tree to hide behind for second. Gotta take a whiz." Then, after a pause, "Sorry, I didn't mean to sound so crass. My papaw used to say that to me."

Middleton laughed and waved him off. "No need to apologize, I've heard and said much worse in my time. One thing though, I'm going to play heavy handed and invite you to church while we're enjoying those milkshakes. Thought I'd give you fair warning since I'm buying."

Mike hurried toward the tree line to do his business while the preacher gathered the gear. Once inside the relative privacy of the thick pine cover, the smell of rancid meat assaulted him. Something had met its demise, unpleasant but not unusual. Another day in the woods. He thought of another one of his papaw's sayings. "Only two things you gotta worry about if you drop your britches in the woods, Poison Oak and Copperheads. It's a bad day if either of those get in on whatever business you're doing." Amen papaw. Amen.

He unzipped his pants and a faint sparkle, ahead and to his right, caught his eye. His first thought was that a Copperhead was indeed about to get in on his business. Painful as it was, he held off the call of his bladder until he could be sure. The tall trees didn't allow much sunlight through, only a shifting patch of light here and there. He held his breath and tried not to panic; his eyes searched the ground for any sign of movement.

He knew he was being paranoid, he'd grown up in the woods, but for some reason he couldn't get past the thought of a snake curled up amongst the dead leaves and pine needles. And that smell- ripe. Whatever it was would feed the buzzards tonight. Finally, the stabbing pain in his bladder forced the decision, and with great relief, he started and finished without company.

The rustling of leaves from behind made him jump. He whirled around and saw a crow standing on a log, with a twig in its beak. Mike had once witnessed a chicken pick up his uncle's discarded cigarette and take off through the yard, trail of smoke floating behind.

The crow wasn't as amusing. He adjusted his belt, content to let it play with the twig in peace, when the sparkle of light flashed again from the same area. The crow eyed him when Mike took a cautious step toward the log, its black tail twitching back and forth. Fifteen feet out, Mike's foot rolled on a branch, and he lurched forward, prompting the crow to drop his prize and dart off into the trees. Mike couldn't catch his balance and tumbled to the ground short of the log. His hand came down on something soft and moist. He jerked away at the texture, rolled onto his side, and saw the crows lunch. The finger, still wearing a ring that caught the sun's rays if tilted just right, had chunks of flesh torn away near the nail.

A few days later they'd learn the name of the mutilated woman Mike had stumbled upon after he finished his business. The license identified her as Katie Davidson, but her friends called her Kat.

7

Gerard Wilcox, Jerry to most, came into this world with what some would consider two strikes. First, being born with an extra number twenty-one chromosome meant people tried not to make eye contact. Some are uncomfortable around those with Down Syndrome. If that wasn't enough, his tweaker parents named him Gerard. Nichole said her mom obsessed over a serial killer with that name. She thought he was a cop but wasn't sure and didn't care to know. The name didn't prove an issue the first six or seven years of his life. Not that first graders are especially kind to one another, but their skill in creative nicknaming is limited. By the time he hit third grade, that all changed. High school took it to a new level.

It didn't take Daniel long to figure out that Nichole, eighteen months younger than her brother, did most of the caretaking. Either their grandmother was too old or too preoccupied to pay much attention to him, or her for that matter.

Daniel found the courage to call her that Wednesday morning after breakfast and ask if she wanted to meet downtown and hang out at the park, maybe grab a burger, whatever. She agreed, but they'd have to wait until two or three, and Jerry would have to tag along. He didn't mind. He liked Jerry, and Nichole, well... He thought he might faint right there in Aunt Becky's kitchen when she suggested they could even walk to her grandmother's apartment and watch some TV if he wanted.

The afternoon started off great. An hour or so in the park watching Jerry play with the remote control car he'd brought, then a quick bite at Creek Café. Mozzarella sticks, fries, and Coke's all around, courtesy of Uncle Mike and the twenty he'd slipped him before the fishing trip with Pastor Middleton. The trouble started when they decided to try and find Jerry a birthday present. Fourteen was a big number, at least according to the boy standing on the sidewalk, toy car in one hand, a to-go cup in the other. "It's big Danny. It's big."

Daniel figured they could find a present worthy of a fourteen-year-old at one of the several mom and pop shops around Lee Square, but when they opened the door to Woodwork Gifts and Crafts, Jerry spoke up. "I gotta pee."

Nichole looked at Daniel and rolled her eyes. "He's always gotta pee."

"Nicki, I gotta go. Really." He danced in the time honored tradition of a child telling the truth about the matter.

Daniel saw a restroom sign on the door at the far end of the store, but before he could say anything, Nichole answered. "Run and use the restrooms in the park." She pointed to the small brick building across the street. "It's right there. See?"

Jerry's eye's darted to the square then back to his sister.

"It's okay. We'll be right in here. Besides, it'll be hard to buy you a present if you're in there with us won't it?"

Jerry's face lit up and for a moment the dance stopped. "That's right. It's Jerry's birthday."

"Your birthday isn't for two days, but if you're nice I might give you your present early."

Jerry grabbed his sister in a bear hug and almost dropped his remote Vette. "I will, I will."

"Okay, okay. Go and come right back. Meet us right here, outside this store. Do you understand?"

Jerry let her go and darted across the empty street to the opposite sidewalk.

She called after him. "Jerry, look at me."

He stopped and turned to her.

"Right here. If we're not out here, we're inside. We'll be out after we buy your present."

Jerry confirmed he understood with a quick dip of his head and sprinted across the grass. They waited until he disappeared into the restroom, then stepped into the shop.

"You think we ought to wait outside till he's finished?" Daniel asked.

"He'll be fine. Besides, he could be in there twenty minutes." She walked over to a table with wooden bears, horses and other local wildlife. The sign hanging from the front declared them 'Hand Carved'.

"Twenty minutes? All he had to do is pee."

Nichole picked up an intricately carved Grizzly Bear, looked at the price tag, and sat it down quickly. "I don't ask about the details, that's just how long he takes."

Minutes later, they decided Woodwork's pricing far surpassed the limited income of the Middle School crowd, or what was left of the twenty, so they walked to the square to meet Jerry. Daniel heard the wails coming from inside when he was about fifty feet away. At twenty feet, he heard the other boys laughing. "What's wrong Retard Gerard? Don't like the taste of soap?"

* * *

THE SMELL OF disinfected urine wasn't the worst thing Daniel encountered when he limped into the restroom. Even the sight of Chase yanking Jerry's underwear halfway up his back didn't compare to what he heard. Painful, pitiful sobbing, "Please...please stop it."

Jerry stretched on his tiptoes, arms across his chest clutching his car. Chase stood behind him, a fist full of red and blue briefs. In front of him, Tommy held a cupped hand up to Jerry's mouth. Pink goo slipped between his fingers. "Please...I don't want to eat it." Jerry clinched his eyes tight and shook his head vigorously back and forth.

Nichole almost ran him over when she bolted in. "What are you doing? Put him down."

Both boys looked up at the same time but held their ground. Jerry clutched his Vette even tighter. "It hurts."

"Let him go." Daniel surprised himself with the force of the words.

73

Jerry lurched forward, underwear finally freed from Chase's grasp, narrowly missing Tommy as his momentum sent him sprawling out on the floor.

"What'd you let him go for?" Tommy sounded mad at his friend. "You ain't scared of him are you?" Chase didn't reply except for a quick shrug.

Daniel couldn't see her, but he heard Nichole crying. So was Jerry, huddled by the block wall, head buried in his chest. No one said anything for what seemed like minutes, although Daniel guessed it was five seconds, maybe ten.

Jerry looked up, first at Nichole, then Daniel. "They tore my hero underwear." His voice quivered, and Tommy laughed.

Anger overwhelmed Daniel. Sweat poured down his face despite the crisp day. Afraid of the fury building within him, yet paralyzed by the sight of Jerry huddled next to a pee-stained urinal, a ripped piece of underwear hanging over his belt, Daniel closed his eyes and prayed. "Father, please do something."

Tommy moved between Jerry and Daniel. Chase, still holding a torn piece of elastic waistband, followed.

"You want to be next?" Tommy asked.

Before he could answer, Nichole rushed forward and swung at Tommy, catching him not with her fist, but the filed nail of her middle finger, opening a gash in his cheek. He screamed and pushed her across the room, sending her flailing into the garbage can, knocking it and her to the floor.

Daniel rushed to her side, but she was already on her feet by the time he reached her. "Just go," he told Tommy and Chase without looking back. "Please go."

Tommy stepped toward them, hand pressed against his bleeding face. "Who do you think you are?"

"I am Daniel," he whispered.

"What? What did you say?"

Daniel turned to the boys. "I am-" Before he could finish, an explosion of energy flashed in the room, and both Tommy and Chase fell backwards onto the concrete.

Jerry clutched his car close and watched with wide eyes.

Nichole covered her mouth with one hand as tears rolled down her cheeks.

Daniel stepped forward, bracing for a fist to the nose as Tommy scampered to his feet, but it never came. Instead, the bully stepped aside, eyes wide and face pale. Daniel walked to the sobbing boy holding the car and knelt down. Jerry's tears flowed as freely as his sisters'.

"Jerry, it's me. Danny." Daniel put an arm around him. "Hey buddy, it's okay. They're not going to hurt you anymore." He looked over his shoulder, but Tommy and Chase had fled.

"Danny?" Jerry looked up at him. His lower lip trembled, but the sobs had stopped.

Daniel heard Nichole crying somewhere behind him. "Yeah, big guy. It's me. It's safe now. You're safe."

He heard a thud as the frightened little boy with an extra chromosome dropped his precious package and wrapped both arms around Daniel's neck.

"I love you Danny."

"Love you too buddy. Let's get you home."

***

THE DARKNESS WATCHED the old woman, alone in her apartment, shuffle a deck of cards. Her name was Margie Wilcox, grandmother and legal guardian of Nichole and Jerry.

The demon had many names. The boy met him as Richard but thought of him as The Darkness. Ben Johnson nicknamed him Slick, and an ancient desert people feared him as Apep. Thousands of names bestowed upon him by hundreds of civilizations, but the boy was closest to the truth. It reflected the name given him by his creator. Before the rebellion, before The Author formed this miserable ball of dust, the first word he heard thundered from The Throne was his name. Araphel. He was darkness, devourer of light.

Margie laid the seventy-eight card deck on the table, pulled one from the top, and placed it face down to her left. She pulled the next four cards, one at a time, and laid them out, forming an arch of five. Each card hid its picture from the world, but Araphel knew their secrets, and he tingled with anticipation. He loved The Tarot.

Margie reached for a card, the one farthest to her left, then hesitated. Araphel lingered behind her, unseen and unheard, but she felt his presence. He was sure of that. He could smell the potent mixture of excitement and terror drifting up from her body, filling the room with its sour aroma. She reeked of the scent. He redirected her hand to the middle card, choosing for himself the all-important order. The first card was crucial since it revealed the overall theme of the reading.

Margie flipped the middle card and let out a gasp. *The Moon.* A wolf and dog, crouching beside a body of water, howling at the yellow disc above and the face portrayed on its surface.

"Oh dear." She knew its meanings. Hidden enemies, deception, darkness.

"Yes my child. Most certainly your situation at the moment," Araphel whispered in her ear.

He guided her hand to the far right, and she turned her second card, the one that would represent what she wanted, her desires. It revealed a knight sitting atop a horse, hand outstretched holding his symbol- a pentagram inside of a circle. *The Knight of Pentacles*. Serviceability, utility, usefulness.

"Yes, yes. I want to be useful. I want to be needed. Been such a long time since anybody but those kids needed me for anything." Her optimistic interpretation of its meaning.

Araphel bent down, inches from her neck, and drew her scent into himself. "Don't worry child, I've added you to my plans."

Margie reached for her next card, the third, and hesitated. Araphel sensed trepidation, fear of what she might uncover. He grinned because he knew her instincts were correct. The third card would foretell of an unexpected event or situation. Sometimes the event pro-ved fortunate, other times not. With trembling fingers, she turned the card. *The Tower*. Tall and narrow, fire billowing from its cap, a bolt of lightning the obvious cause. In the foreground, two figures tumbled to their death.

Margie's ample frame fell back against the kitchen chair, causing its wood to cry out against her weight.

"Calamity, ruin, catastrophe." She groaned in disbelief. "Lord have mercy."

With only two cards remaining, Araphel could hardly contain himself, but the old woman hadn't moved. Her eyes remained on *The Tower*, wide and afraid.

The demon knelt down beside her and saw goose pimples rise along her arm when their hands touched. "Almost done Margie. Almost finished."

Margie flipped the next card, the one that would reveal her immediate future. The picture showed a man hanging upside down, one leg crossed behind the other. *The Hanged Man.* Of its various meanings, Araphel knew which one came to the old woman's mind, because it came to his first. Sacrifice, a ritual as old as the earth itself.

Without hesitation she turned over her last card, uncloaking the final outcome of the reading, the culmination of the previous four images. *The Five of Cups.* A card of loss, yet something remains. In the background, a bridge crosses a stream. On the other side of the stream sits a building. However, the primary image is a figure cloaked in black. He looks down at three cups, toppled and lying on their sides. They resemble chalices, gold and elegant, and a red liquid, either blood or wine, has puddled beside them. Two other cups stand upright behind him. It is the key to the final outcome of the story. Loss- three taken, yet two remain standing.

Margie studied the card, her eyes searching for its significance. Araphel watched her attempt to solve the puzzle laid out on her kitchen table. He could feel her mind putting the pieces together. Hidden enemies and darkness. Usefulness. Unexpected calamity. A sacrifice in her immediate future. Finally, three will have been taken, leaving two.

Suddenly, she lurched forward, swiping the deck of cards from the table. Sweat poured from her face, and her color turned a waxy pale. Araphel knew it was time. He couldn't have her die; not here, not like this. What would be the joy in that? Another fat old woman whose heart decided it was time to punch out. He needed to ease her mind, put her soul at peace, momentarily at least.

With one lithe movement, he slipped into her smoother than she slipped into her worn flannel nightgown. She fell lax, back into the chair, and a single card drifted into her lap. Through the woman's eyes, Araphel glanced down. A half-goat, half-man creature with wings spread wide, stared back. Horns of a ram sprouted from his head, and in the center of those, an inverted pentagram. A man and a woman, naked and bound in chains, languished at the creature's hooved feet. *The Devil.* A toothless grin spread across the old woman's face before she rose from the chair and grabbed her cane.

***

THE THREE OF them, Daniel, Nichole, and Jerry, walked the edge of Lee square toward Alexander Street. Nichole suggested they take the longer, less scenic route along the perimeter. With a road to the left and stone wall to the right, it didn't fit the definition of tranquility to Daniel but whatever. She still seemed upset so he didn't argue. No big deal.

Their grandmother, Mrs. Wilcox, lived three blocks away in a two-bedroom apartment stacked above Second

Time Around Furniture. It made for cramped living, but it wasn't an orphanage. Jerry slept in one bedroom, grandma had the other, and Nichole got the couch. At least Mrs. Wilcox had removed the plastic cover, an argument that lasted two weeks according to Nichole.

It took several minutes, but he finally succeeded in helping Jerry get his pants and Spiderman underwear situated. He made Daniel examine his car, afraid he'd broken it when he tossed it aside. It was fine, and Daniel even took it for a test drive, letting Jerry give directions along the sidewalk.

"Do you think they'll come back?" Nichole asked.

"I'm still trying to figure out why they left." Daniel looked across the square to the swings and statue of Lee but didn't see anyone.

"They went to get Preston. That's what Tommy said."

"Come on, let's cut across. I think they're gone."

Nichole shook her head, and Daniel didn't argue.

Jerry squatted in the grass twenty feet in front of them, completely engrossed with the ground. "I love you Daniel." That's what Jerry had said. Honest words from a scared little boy, mumbled in the stink of a public bathroom.

They caught up to Jerry in silence. Nichole looked nervous, shaken. She pulled her coat close and stared down the road. Daniel wanted to grab her hand. He wanted to kiss her. He had never kissed a girl, but seeing her like this, hurting yet strong, tender but fierce, he wanted to lean in and kiss her right on the lips. Instead, he knelt down beside Jerry. "Hey buddy, we need to get going. We need to get you home."

"Ants." Jerry pointed to the little hill by the sidewalk.

"Yep. Not many though. It's not very big."

"No, lots." He pointed at the dirt. "Billions and billions. We can't see them."

Daniel got it. "You're right. They're underground." He tousled Jerry's hair. "Smart guy." He glanced up to Nichole, but she seemed lost in her own thoughts.

Jerry reached down and gently lifted a twig from the side of the small mound, seemingly unconcerned with the threat of his tormentors return. Ants poured out of the hole, eager to repair the unintentional damage.

"They felt God when you talked." He tried to scoop the dirt back onto the mound, and a good portion of the hill collapsed. More ants scrambled to the surface.

"They felt God?"

"That's right. He's The Author." He gently lifted an ant off his finger and sat its squashed corpse on the ground. When it didn't join in the rebuilding project, Jerry tried prodding it with a stick. The little boy, almost two years Daniel's senior, finally looked up, eyes filled with tears waiting to spill over. "They went to get a friend. They're coming back."

"I know. That's why we need to go."

"Okay."

Nichole knelt beside them. "I'm sorry I didn't help you." She leaned in and embraced her brother.

Daniel thought about what it might be like to have a brother, even a sister. Someone to stay up late with flashlights, comic books, and a bag of chips, talking about the Hulk and Superman. But that wasn't the plan was it? No brother. No sister. Not even a mom or dad anymore.

The feel of Nichole's hand on his knee brought him back to the moment. "I don't know what happened back there but...I think I felt something. I mean, not an angel or anything, but...I don't know, a breeze or wind. And your voice. It was..." Her words trailed off.

Daniel took her hand and their eyes met for a single breath, then both looked away. Her fingers trembled but returned his grip as Daniel spoke. "I don't know what it was. Right now, I just want to get to your grandmother's. You think she's there?"

"She was when we left."

He and Nichole helped Jerry to his feet. Thirty yards down the path, Jerry pointed to the three bikes barreling down the opposite sidewalk, but Daniel's attention was diverted by the roar of an engine and Nichole's scream. Instinctively, he grabbed Jerry by the shoulder and pulled him close.

***

MARGIE WILCOX LUMBERED into Lee square and chose a bench near the perimeter. The boards bowed as she eased back and let them absorb her full weight. Several leaves, separated from their source of life, scuttled across the walking path and came to rest at her feet. She lifted one of her orthopedic sneakers, trapped them with a thud, and thought of Pine Creek. It was the kind of place an adventurous Yankee might stumble upon on his way to Florida, then decide he'd make an afternoon of it browsing the antique stores and gift shops. Maybe even spend the night at Mrs. Wilson's B&B instead of trekking back to the interstate to overpay at one of the chain motels that dotted I-75. He might not even lock the doors to his Lincoln Town Car. For a long while she sat on the bench, strumming her fingers on the aluminum cane laid across her lap. Strumming and waiting.

She...he...it had come to the park to watch how this part of the story played out. He was powerful, but not powerful enough to wield absolute control of events. Cunning was his best weapon. Contingency layered upon contingency. His success required understanding the possible reactions of his adversary, in any of a thousand situations, and anticipating those reactions many moves in advance, adjusting his strategy when necessary. He excelled at the game. Time was a wonderful teacher, and he was already ancient when Nimrod built his great tower to the gods.

The old woman lifted her head and saw three boys racing up the sidewalk several blocks away, their bikes barely missing a pudgy blond pushing a stroller. The new mother yelled at them, but they refused to acknowledge her curses or hand jesters. They focused on the group standing across the street; the dim one, his sister, and the boy that led him to this wretched excuse for a town.

"That Darkness done come to Pine Creek," she said to the crow perched on the swing beside her. She leaned forward and chuckled. Somewhere in the distance, the roar of screeching tires sliced through the air, and her chuckle intensified, morphing into a hacking cough. "Done come to lil ole Pine Creek cause of a lil ole boy." Seconds later, a Baby Blue Nova rounded the corner in front of Patterson Hardware, two city cruisers, and one

Sherriff's deputy in pursuit. "That Billy think they after those two bags of Ice stashed under the passenger seat. Surprise, surprise Billy Boy, that warden gonna give you the cocktail for what you done to that preacher. Went and shot him in the face." Her voice softened, and the crow bounced its head in agreement. "It's alright now Billy. Mrs. Margie made sure they know it's you. Told them right where and when they could find you too, yes she did. He got plans for you. Big plans. And look, here you are, right on time."

The Nova flew by, ran the red light, and jumped the curb behind the little band of do gooders. He watched the pious boy pull the retarded one out of the way just in time. Had his reaction faltered, even by a second, the dim one's light would have gone completely dark forever. The car found asphalt again, veered hard left, and plowed through the lead bicycle. Sounds of metal, glass, and chaos echoed along Forrest Street as the Nova left the road again and slammed into one of the ornamental street lights that lined downtown. Margie smiled, and observed the carnage like she would a mildly interesting cloud.

People poured out of the shops and eateries into the madness. Some yelled for help, a few cried, but most remained silent, hand over their mouth, horror in their eyes. One cop trained his pistol on the bleeding man, dazed and moaning behind the wheel of the Nova, while three more sprinted past a pile of twisted aluminum to the bloody form lying fifty feet away. Like a macabre Rockwell painting, the other two boys stood with legs straddling their bikes, eyes transfixed on the mangled body of their friend twitching in the grass. Araphel knew the boy would live, may never walk again, but he would live. The dark aura of impending death did not hover around young Tommy. Live or die, crippled or not, he was inconsequential to Araphel's plans. Collateral damage, nothing more.

Though it wasn't one of the children he had hoped for, it would do for now. He had other ways to get what he wanted. Contingency layered upon contingency. And the pain, oh how the pain would spread. Margie closed her eyes and lifted her head. She could smell it floating from every direction, and the scent exhilarated her. It knew pain would lead to fear, and fear would lead to hate. The boy Daniel already feared. Soon the pretender, now struggling in his marriage, would feel pain.

In the distance more sirens wailed, and she shifted her gaze to the other end of the park. The sound faded, moving further down Highway 27, away from downtown, and she knew they had discovered the body at the lake. Such a waste, but it had to be done. The pretender would have enjoyed the original plan.

Margie lifted her foot off the leaves and allowed the breeze to carry them away. She followed their path, swiveling her head as they floated by the bench, past the swing, and to the statue of Robert E. Lee behind her. No one heard the snap of her neck when it broke and transected her spinal cord.

Shed of his latest vessel, Araphel strolled unseen through the chaos, stopped at the edge of the park, looked back at the dead woman on the bench, and grinned. She would have made an excellent reader of cards, but her sacrifice would indeed prove most useful. Three are fallen, yet two still stand.

8

Ben watched Jill pull into the driveway from the Great Room window. She had called him at the office before lunch and reassured him she would be home today, probably late afternoon. Said she needed time to think, and she hoped he'd done the same. They could talk today while Preston was hanging out with Tommy and Chase in the Square. She sounded like his mom. More concerned with "sharing feelings" than paying bills. No wonder dad stayed on the road.

Oh, they were going to talk. They were going to talk about why she didn't leave him a note letting him know where she'd run off to, and why she hadn't answered her phone Monday night or half the day Tuesday. Why it took her eighteen hours to send a text saying she was at Megan's, and even then she wouldn't talk to him. She'd been gone since late Monday and today was Wednesday. They had plenty to discuss.

The front door latch clicked open, and he met her in the foyer. He had to do this right, not go on the offensive until she let her missiles fly. He'd take her attack then launch one of his own, drawing her to a stalemate. It had worked before; it would work again.

But her missiles never flew. Instead, she took him by the hand. "Let's go sit in the Family Room." She led him to the sofa. "First off, I want to say you hurt me."

Ben started to counter, but she stopped him. "Let me finish. I don't know who she is, but I know you were with her at the bar so don't try and deny it, I saw you. I was worried when you didn't answer your phone, so I drove your route to make sure you hadn't wrecked or broke down or worse. I saw you outside with her." Ben's fingers quickly fell from his launch button. "I am going to ask you one question, and I want you to think about it before you answer. Who is she?"

Ben's plans crumbled, and he confessed everything. Almost everything. He avoided anything involving Eddie Stillwater. He told her about Kat and how he had hired her to help around the office. No, they were not having an affair. No, he didn't hook up with her. She drove him home, that's all, no sense in risking a DUI. No, he didn't know why he didn't mention her. He told her about his bank debt. Yes, we could lose the house. No, giving up the business and hiring on at a firm wouldn't help. No, I lost that deal Monday. Yes, that's why I flaked out.

When it was over Jill walked out without saying a word. Ben followed her through the foyer and into the dining room.

"Don't just leave. Say something."

"You don't want me to say anything right now."

He started to press, but the doorbell interrupted. Ben slid back the curtain, revealing a Pine Creek police cruiser sitting in the drive.

"Who is it?" Jill asked, void of any emotion.

"It's a cop."

Jill followed him into the foyer, and he opened the door. Two officers waited on his front porch.

"Evening sir. I'm officer Blake and this is officer Tremble, Pine Creek police department. Are you Mr. and Mrs. Ben Johnson?"

"Yes."

"Sir and ma'am, your son and his friends have been involved in an accident. I need you to come with me."

Jill slumped against the wall, nearly bringing the curtains down on top of her.

Strength faded from Ben's legs, but he managed to ask the question any parent would. "Is he okay?"

***

PRESTON, WHO WAS fine, rode with his mom on their way home from the police station. Ben didn't mind, he needed time to think. Jill acted furious. No, she acted hurt, and that was worse. Hurt because he had kept her in the dark about the money. Hurt because of the lies. Ones' of omission, he thought, but lies nonetheless. But this scare with Preston might provide a useful distraction. Enough time to come up with a way out of this mess.

He pulled into the driveway right behind them. Preston, still shaken up over the accident, couldn't sleep and wanted to go to the hospital and check on Tommy. Jill finally promised to call in the morning to check his condition. Besides, visitors probably wouldn't be allowed for several days or more. Then, after an emotional talk about death and how close he and his friends had come to it, they convinced him to go to bed. Jill walked up with Preston, presumably to tuck him in and offer comfort as only a mother can. When she didn't return after thirty minutes, Ben decided to check on them. He found Preston sound asleep. Good, maybe he and Jill could talk. Work things out. He walked down the hall to their bedroom and found it locked. Ben leaned his head against the door and groaned.

He snatched a blanket from the hall closet and settled in on the Great Room sofa. He had slept on the couch several times, but she had never locked him out. He wasn't going to end up like his parents, no matter what it took. He lay in the dark thinking about his life and the lies until he drifted off to sleep.

***

SHARP RAPPING JARRED Ben awake, and he bolted up. Ben grabbed his phone and pulled up the time, three o'clock. The sound came again but not from the door. He held his breath and heard the noise a third time. Shuffling from the back yard. Adrenalin pumped through his body as he snuck to the window and peeked outside. The full moon allowed a decent view, but nothing looked out of place. The shuffling again, this time from his right, beneath the window on the east side of the room. Ben's senses sharpened. He focused and tried to listen. A whisper, the clank of metal, anything.

Silence.

Ben crept to the middle of the room, phone in hand, heart pounding. He debated calling the police but dismissed the idea, at least for the time being. What would he tell them? He's hearing noises outside that could very well be a dog or a raccoon. That made sense didn't it? That's what it was, some animal sniffing around the house.

From his peripheral, Ben caught movement high on the front window. He jerked his head away as it imploded into the room. He dove to the floor, shards of glass ringing off the hardwoods beside his face. He rolled over and groped for his phone but came up empty. Pulling himself to his knees he spotted it, started to dial 911 then hesitated. He knew what this was. Eddie, and time was up. Calling the cops would be the worst thing he could do. He had Jill and Preston to think about.

Ben crawled to the front window, swinging around from the side and waited. Nothing.

Minutes passed until he generated enough courage to move. First the back door then the front, checking the locks. All secured. He didn't know how Jill or Preston hadn't heard the window, but they hadn't called out. He crept up to check on them anyway. Nothing had changed since he had left them. His bedroom door was still locked, and Preston lay sound asleep.

Uneasy, but confident the threat had passed, Ben eased back down to the Great Room. He needed to talk to Vince. Maybe he knew about the break-in or this. He had to know. He cursed Kat for not returning his call.

Ben pulled up his email. Nothing from her since Monday afternoon. His clock showed three twenty-one, but he called her anyway. Straight to voicemail again, and he didn't leave a message.

Ben slumped onto the sofa. What should he tell Jill? Some thug he owed money had thrown a rock through their window?

Ben paused at the thought.

Surprised by the sound of shattering glass, he had not noticed what caused it. He scoured the room looking for a rock, a brick, anything that didn't belong, but came up empty. He checked the walls for bullet holes but quickly gave up once he realized he hadn't heard a shot, and a bullet probably wouldn't have shattered the window anyway. Wide awake, he paced the floor.

Movement on the stairs drew his attention, and he swung around to Jill on the landing, eyes wide, hand over her mouth. Even sporting cotton pajamas and frazzled hair, she looked stunning. He couldn't lose her.

"Jill, we need to talk."

***

BEN CONFESSED THE whole Eddie story. "I needed the money to get up and running. We had just bought the house and were already in debt to our eyeballs. I tried another loan from the bank, but it didn't fly. What was I supposed to do? This is my dream, our dream. I went to that trade show in Marietta for a few days, remember? Anyway, I ran into Vince. He had hooked up with some security company part time and was working the floor. We got to talking and... you know how it is. We decided to grab a few drinks and catch up on old times." She didn't interrupt him.

"So we got to talking, and I told him I'd went out on my own but things weren't going so hot. The clients weren't coming. He asked if I'd ever considered taking on a partner, and I told him I hadn't, but if the right one came along it'd be worth looking into. I thought he was talking about himself, but he laughed. He told me he was living off sandwiches and ramen noodles, but he'd recently hooked up with a guy that paid well. Really well. The guy's name was Eddie Stillwater, and he owned a few bars and other adult oriented businesses. Anyway, he told me Eddie made most of his money as an investor, helping small businesses get on their feet for a cut of the action or interest on cash loans. He asked if I might be interested and how long I'd be in town. I couldn't go to Eddie directly, even Vince seemed nervous about going himself, but if I was interested, he could run the idea by him. 'Might earn me some cred with the boss,' he said. I knew it was a bad idea Jill, but I was desperate. We were going to lose it all." Ben shifted his gaze from her to the ceiling, took a deep breath, and continued.

"When Vince called the next day, he said Eddie was interested in a meeting. Said he'd call me back when he got the details. Vince gave me his number in case an emergency came up but warned me it might or might not work. He usually didn't keep the same one for more than a few days. Part of the new gig; burner phones, no details, that kind of thing. He said he'd call me and he'd drive. I almost told him to call it off. I wish I had, you have to believe me." He searched her eyes for understanding, even empathy, but saw neither.

"Vince called me that night and told me to meet him in the lobby at eleven. We drove to some dive a few blocks off Peachtree. The place was a dump, but the parking lot was full. It didn't feel real, me being in a place like that. Vince took me to a room in the back, and a couple of biker types let us in and shut the door behind us. Vince introduced me to Eddie and told me to have a seat. I was scared Jill, but I was more afraid of what might happen if we couldn't come up with some money."

"We talked for a few minutes and the next thing I knew, he laid a paper sack on the table and asked me if we had a deal. Fifty thousand cash now, and I pay him thirty-five hundred a month for two years. I should have walked away, but it was right there. Our future was in that bag."

"It went fine for a few months, but it got out of hand. My clients started getting behind on paying, so I used what cash we had to keep us afloat at home and maxed out the cards to keep the business going. Two months ago I missed the payment to Eddie. I just wanted to make it through Monday with Murphy. Once they signed the contract we'd be set. I could pay off the credit cards, pay Eddie back, and get caught up on the mortgage." He leaned close, took her hand and gave it a gentle squeeze. She didn't pull away but didn't reciprocate.

"You know how it went. What you don't know is that Monday night while you were at Megan's, and before I got home, someone broke in and went through the house messing with things. It was a message. I was going to tell you about it, I swear, but then the thing with Preston's friend. Anyway, I think this is another warning, and I don't know what to do. I'm sorry."

"Is that all of it?" Her cold tone matched the look in her eyes.

He shifted his gaze to the floor. "Yes."

Jill looked directly at him. "I'm leaving."

"What?"

"I'm taking Preston and going somewhere."

"So you're leaving me?"

"I don't know, but until you get this thing with that lunatic fixed, I'm taking our son and staying somewhere safe."

"Where? Where are you going at four o'clock in the morning? Back to Megan's?"

"That's exactly where I'm going. When Preston wakes up I'm packing some clothes and getting him out of here until you figure this out."

"The three of you in her tiny apartment? How long do you think that'll last?" A migraine began snaking its way up Ben's neck.

"Her roommate's out of town till Sunday, and if you haven't figured this out by then, we'll go somewhere else. I've got friends." She started toward the stairs without waiting for him to reply.

"All you do is run, Jill."

"All you do is lie," she said, without looking back.

9

Mike helped bury Jim Monroe on Thursday afternoon. Over two-hundred people attended his memorial service, and most cried when Mike and five other men carried the coffin down the aisle. Becky passed tissues to those sitting around her. Pastor Middleton presented the eulogy. Daniel wept.

***

FRIDAY MORNING DANIEL watched Nichole's aunt and uncle load suitcases into their car. They had driven down from Knoxville Wednesday night and identified Margie Wilcox's body. No memorial was planned, no cards of sympathy sent. No birthday party for the little boy with an unfortunate name but beautiful soul.

Both Nichole and Jerry waved out the back window as they pulled onto Forrest Street, headed to their new home three hours away. Daniel whispered goodbye to the only friends he had left, and knew his life was falling apart. Piece by piece.

10 ✛

The drive to Grace Redemption Church took less than ten minutes, but by the time they pulled into the lot, Mike had a rundown on most of the regulars.

"You have to watch out for sister Marcy. She's got a temper. I think it's because her husband left her a few years ago, but don't you dare tell anyone I told you. Now, my friend, sister Judy, she's a woman of God. I'll introduce you to her first thing. She's been at the church for years. I don't know how many, but longer than Pastor Middleton."

Mike nodded in comfortable agreement.

"And one more thing. You stay away from the little brunette that'll be sitting across the aisle from us." Becky aimed her finger at him. "She's a floozy."

Despite the cool morning, beads of perspiration rolled down Mike's forehead, stinging his eyes. Church always made him sweat. Even so, he liked this one okay. Becky could count on him joining her every Christmas, Easter, and Homecoming, though admittedly the prospect of eight different styles of fried chicken influenced his attendance for the latter. You can't ask for much more.

Grace Redemption wasn't flashy, but it wasn't run-down either. Plain landscaping and a gravel parking lot, but both well cared for. The white plank siding, single row of windows down the side, and tall steeple reminded him of one of those churches you'd find gracing the cover of a gift store nostalgic calendar. It did have that going for it.

The preacher met them at the door. "Good morning Mike, good to see you here." Mike offered his hand, but the preacher threw his arms around him and delivered a pair of swift, brotherly pats to his back. One afternoon on the lake and personal space gone.

When he finally let him go, he spoke to Becky. "Good morning Becky." The preacher extended his hand to Daniel. "Daniel, it's good to see you this morning. How are you doing?"

Daniel greeted the preacher with a weak smile. "Okay. Been praying a lot."

By the look on the preacher's face and glance he shot Becky, he seemed impressed.

"That's good young man, that's good." He turned back to Becky. "Is your friend, the one you mentioned on the phone, is she coming this morning?"

"Jill," Becky said. "I invited her and she said she'd think about it, but I didn't hear back from her."

Several more faithful, awaiting their turn with the preacher, pressed them forward, and Becky led them several rows down the middle aisle, ushering her little flock to the lightly padded pew on the left. Two women scooted down the bench to accommodate the extras, with Mike bringing up the rear.

Becky introduced them to her friends, Susan and Judy.

The taller one, Judy, spoke first. "It's so good to see you again Mike. We're glad you're here."

"Always are." Susan chimed in with a polite nod.

The sanctuary filled, leaving no completely empty pews. Mike noticed barren spots here and there, but if a family bigger than four walked in late, they'd have to split up. He didn't know if this was the norm, but it didn't surprise him. People tended to dig out their Sunday best in times of tragedy, and three dead bodies in two days seemed to have put the fear of God into his little town.

The variety of people crammed into the church intrigued him. He envisioned a whole room full of senior citizens, complete with blue suits and flowered dresses. Instead he heard several babies crying, a couple of young parents scolded their kids for arguing over crayons, and a teenage boy flirted with the girl sitting next to him. Sure, he saw plenty of the suits and dresses, but blue jeans, flannel shirts, and overalls were well represented.

A perky voice startled him out of his people watching. "Hi, I'm Missy. You must be Mike." He swung to the sound and saw a pretty brunette standing by his pew. "I've heard so much about you."

It took him a moment to respond, so Becky helped. "Yes Missy, this is my husband Mike." Her tone wasn't harsh but lacked the politeness he knew most church people used when talking to one another.

"It's nice to meet you Mike. I'm on the Visitor Committee, so if you need anything or have any questions let me know." She motioned to the seat across the aisle, "I'm your neighbor."

Becky patted Mike's knee and rested her hand there. "Thank you Missy, but he'll be fine."

"Of course. Anyway, it's nice to meet you."

Missy didn't greet the rest of the pew as enthusiastically.

Throughout most of the welcome and choir singing, Mike tried to pay attention, but the distractions proved too enticing. Three rows up and to the left, a well-dressed, red headed guy kept running his finger along the base of his nose. Mike could tell he was trying to be discreet, but his wife or girlfriend kept tugging his arm down. The show didn't last long because the third attempt apparently proved successful. An older man on the front row bobbed his head up and down at regular intervals. At first Mike thought he was trying to keep rhythm with the singing, but after closer inspection, he realized the man was trying to stay awake. That entertained him slightly longer than nose picker.

Mike listened to most of the sermon, following along as best he could, because the preacher seemed to believe what he said. Then a song, a prayer, one more bear hug, and they were walking back down the steps to the car.

The short ride home lacked meaningful conversation. Becky mentioned the brunette a few times and kept cutting her eyes at him, but he pretended not to notice. Eventually the words of Steve Earle, singing about his daddy running moonshine, filled his head, and she gave up. Daniel rested against the window and didn't speak.

They pulled into the gravel driveway before Mr. Earle finished bragging about his own plans.

Mike saw a woman pacing on the porch. A young boy, about Daniel's age, sat in one of his rockers, face buried in his phone.

"Jill," Becky said, biting her lip. "Give me a minute, this doesn't look good."

The woman got up from the rocker and greeted Becky at the top of the stairs. The boy, eyes still glued to his phone, didn't move from his chair. Mike couldn't hear the conversation, but Becky kept switching back and forth between shaking and nodding her head. Finally, they hugged, and Becky walked back to the car. Mike and Daniel met her at the edge of the driveway. "Looks like we got guests for a few nights," she said to Mike.

"What's up?"

"Megan's roommate is back," she signaled to Jill, "and she's not ready to go home. I didn't think you'd mind. Like I said, it's only for a few nights."

"It's fine honey."

"Thanks." Then, so only he could hear. "You did good with Missy and her Jezebel ways. That floozy has got a way with most men. Not mine though. Not mine." She kissed him on the cheek, patted his butt, and turned to the house.

***

DANIEL RECOGNIZED THE boy before he stepped out of the car.

"Everyone, this is my son Preston," Jill said. "You two look about the same age, do you know each other from school?"

"Yes ma'am," Preston replied. Daniel echoed the answer.

"Ain't that something," Mike said. "You see there Danny, maybe Preston here can show you around, introduce you to some other kids."

Preston buried his face back into his phone.

"Hey," Daniel said. "Sorry about Tommy."

"Thanks." A mumble more than a statement.

"Mike," Becky said, "you go grab their bags, I'm going to put lunch on the table. Preston can bunk with Daniel for a few nights." Then to Daniel, "You good with that?"

He wasn't, but what could he say. "Sure."

Jill beckoned her son. "Preston, go help Mr. Hill."

"I'll help too," Daniel said. They didn't need him to manage the two small suitcases and shoulder bag, but it felt right going with the guys. Just to make it look respectable, they each carried a piece.

The house smelled of smoked ham and charred wood. The kind of smell that made you want to kick back on the couch and rest your eyes for a couple of hours. The rattle of silverware rang from the kitchen as the guys dropped off their loads by the front door.

"Danny, you want to show Preston your room? We'll figure out these bags after we eat."

Danny glanced at Preston, hoping to ease the obvious tension. "I've got a PS3 hooked up." It came out more a question than a statement.

"Maybe later." More than a mumble, but still not overly enthusiastic.

Becky called them before Daniel could respond, so the two trudged into the kitchen and found Mike already at the table loading his plate. Jill sat with her hands in her lap, her plate empty. Lunch was delicious, but the atmosphere distinctly awkward. Lots of small talk about Pastor Middleton's sermon, how good the ham and beans tasted, everything but why Jill and Preston had joined them, and the chaos that had swept into Pine Creek.

"May I be excused?" Daniel asked, already standing from his chair.

Preston looked at his mom. "Me too."

"No you may not," Jill said to her son.

"You either." Becky summoned Daniel back to the table. "I know it's been hard but that don't excuse bad manners."

"Nichole hasn't called has she?"

"No, I'm sorry sweetie." Becky reached over, patted Daniel's hand, then looked to Preston. "I'm sorry about your friend. Your mom said he's out of Intensive Care. I've been praying for him."

Daniel pushed away from the table again. "I'm finished eating. Can I please be excused now?"

Becky grabbed the back of the chair, bringing it to an abrupt stop. "Not yet. Your uncle's got something to ask you."

Mike didn't let the mouthful of cake hinder him. "I'm going camping this weekend, Friday and Saturday night, up at Gordon's Bluff. Maybe last time till Spring. Anyway, I thought you might like to come along."

Daniel hesitated before answering. He'd never tried camping, but the idea of getting away for a couple of days appealed to him.

"Yeah, I guess so."

"Good boy. We'll pack up Thursday night, then I'll pick you up from school Friday. Only takes about an hour up the mountain, but we'll have a little hike to the camp site. It's not hard, pretty flat trail, but I can't get the truck all the way back. I figure if we're on the road by three or so, we can get there with plenty of daylight left to get set up." He sat his fork down, reached for a napkin, and shot Becky a wink.

"Preston, me and your mom were talking and she thinks it would be good for you to go with them."

"What?"

"I think it's a good idea," Jill said. "After everything that's happened the past few days, I feel like you need it."

"But-"

"No buts. You're going and that's final."

"But I don't know them!" Preston seemed not to care about the normal politeness expected at southern dinner tables.

"I do," Jill said. "They're good people, and you need the influence of good people right now." It amazed Daniel that Jill didn't raise her voice to the level of her son's.

Preston sat back in his chair, arms crossed, and glared at his mother. "Dad's good people." By the look on everyone's face, his sarcastic tone didn't go unnoticed.

Jill let out a long sigh and leaned closer. "Yes, he is a good person, but right now he has some things to figure out. Don't make this harder than it already is."

Preston straightened in his chair. "If dad's got some things to figure out, maybe he needs to get away too. Maybe he should come with us."

11

Ben double checked the front door lock and closed the blinds. He didn't entertain many walk-ins but no sense taking chances. He had to get a handle on this.

The office phone rang, but he ignored it. He paced the front room, stopping every so often to peek through the windows. Even though he'd only slept three hours, he'd come in at eight, a few minutes before the detective arrived. Kat was dead, murdered. Detective Hodge made that clear. Foul play, no question about it. Even cut off a few fingers and her pinky toes. Sicko. Hodge didn't mention him as a suspect, but who knows what's going on in the minds of Pine Creek's finest when they played their games.

Ben replayed the night in his mind. Did he miss anything? Something she said? Someone she talked to? He told Hodge about Mr. Gray Toupee, and the detective jotted a few lines in his notebook, but didn't seem concerned. Nothing odd during the ride home either. Then she dropped him off, he watched her pull out of the driveway, and he went inside. Hadn't seen or heard from her since. Still, Hodge pointed out, he was the last

known person to see her alive, and the Medical
Examiner believed she died between midnight and three
Tuesday morning. Just his luck.

Hodge didn't mention the phone calls, but he knew.
Ben could see it in his eyes. What did it prove though?
Nothing. Nothing at all. Finally, the cop had left. Before
he walked out, the guy actually pointed his little blue
pen at him and told him to stick around town in case
they needed him to answer more questions. What a jerk.

Then there was Jill. He hadn't talked to her since
right after she and Preston set up camp at her friend's
house yesterday afternoon. It wasn't much of a conversation though, long enough to let him know where they
were and that she loved him. At least she still loved
him. He hated himself for getting them into this mess.

Tired of pacing, he opted for the comfort of the
lobby sofa. The cool leather eased the vise tightening
around his neck muscles. He'd have to down something
soon, aspirin or alcohol, didn't matter. Both numbed
the pain.

A deep brown stain on one of the tiles above his
head caught his eyes, and he made a mental note to call
the landlord. Can't have a couple gallons of water rain
down on a client because Sheldon and Sheldon Properties
didn't include roof repairs in this year's budget. He
scanned the rest of the ceiling and saw no more
offending squares, just a security camera that needed
adjusting. Ben chuckled to himself. Security cameras,
the age of Big Brother. He had installed them in every
room, and now he wished he'd done the same at his
house.

The thought sprouted an idea. Maybe the camera caught a clue about Kat's conversation with Vince, but a quick evaluation proved futile. Kat took three calls during his meeting without writing a single note. Obviously she wasn't as competent as he thought.

Maybe he should call Hodge back and tell him about Eddie, the money, Vince's call to the office Monday afternoon, the intruder, the whole story. Lay it all out and let them do their job.

What would they find though? His involvement with a career criminal who kept his hands clean by paying other career criminals to do the legwork? Not a chance. The evidence would rule him out as Kat's murderer in a couple days, so why take the risk of getting himself more entangled. Besides, he had to remind himself, if Eddie wanted him dead he would already be dead.

It all boiled down to one clue. He needed to know about that call from Vince. He needed to talk to him and find out Eddie's end game. Getting in touch would be tricky though. He rummaged through Kat's desk again to make sure she hadn't written anything down but came up empty.

Ben poured another cup of coffee, considered adding a splash of bourbon, but opted for the aspirin instead. Kat's desk sat across the room, files stacked on one side, and a picture of her and some random woman on the other. A short, fat chick about Kat's age, proudly displaying a row and a half of teeth in serious need of a dentist. They always ran like that; you were either the hot one or the hot one's friend. Ben had never asked about the woman, and frankly, he didn't care. The extent of his caring involved getting his wife and son

106

back home. To do that he needed to fix the problem with Eddie. He had no idea what that would entail, but maybe it was time to start thinking about a trip south to Atlanta.

***

BEN PEEKED OUT the Great Room window for the third time in ten minutes. Jill had called a couple of hours earlier, and he begged her to come home so they could talk. She agreed, saying she needed to grab some things anyway. He had no idea what those things were and didn't care. It was a start.

Several minutes later he heard the front door open. Jill called to him from the foyer, but he resisted the urge to run to her.

"I'm in here." He hoped she'd be carrying her bags, but she walked through the door with empty arms.

"I see you boarded up the window."

"Yeah. Contractor is supposed to be here tomorrow with the new one."

Jill pointed to the stack of boxes by the far wall. "What's all that?"

"Security equipment I had in inventory. Thought it might come in handy. It'll only take a few hours to set up. Jill, I'm so sorry for all of this. I'm going to fix it."

"The police came to Becky's this morning asking questions about you and Katie Davidson. They found her dead Ben. They said you were the last person to see her."

Her words...Jill speaking Kat's name, punched him in the gut. "I know. They came to the office this morning. What did they say?"

She didn't answer.

"Jill, what did they say?" Ben knew if he didn't control himself he'd say something he would regret. "Baby, please. We've been over this. I didn't have an affair."

Jill walked to the sofa and sat down. "I know. Or at least I think I know."

Ben didn't believe her, but sat down and reached for her hand. She snatched it away.

"Then what's the problem?"

Jill brought her fist down on the armrest. "You know the problem Ben. You lied to me and now we have some lunatic breaking out our windows."

Ben withdrew, startled by her outburst. "I told you I'll fix it. I've got it under control."

"Yeah? How? How do you have it under control?" Jill spoke at a decibel level Ben had never heard, and he didn't know how to respond. Truth was, he didn't have it under control. He didn't have a plan. The closest he had was a vague notion he needed to get to Atlanta and find Vince.

"Answer me!"

"I don't know, okay. I don't know." Ben let his head rest on the back of the sofa.

"We need to get the police involved Ben." Her tone was calmer; yelling sometimes helps.

"You know we can't do that. These type of people don't take kindly to snitches. Calling the police would be the worst thing we could do." Ben wasn't putting on a show. He'd heard stories about the precautions Eddie took to stay out of jail.

"What are you going to do?"

"I don't know."

"I'm scared Ben. I'm scared of this madman, I'm scared for you, I'm scared for us. I need you to fix this. I need you to fix our family before it's too late."

"I'm going to Atlanta to find Vince," Ben said before he could stop himself. "He's been trying to get in touch with me. Maybe he can help."

"What? No you're not."

"Tell me Jill, what should I do? Tell me that."

"You should get away."

"You mean run and hide? Uproot our family, give up everything we've worked for and go where? He'd track us down."

"No, not run and hide. Not uproot the family. You need to get away for a couple of days and think. Clear your head. I know you better than anyone, and I know you'll figure this out, but you can't do it here. Not with everything that's happened over the past few days."

"What do you suggest? I head to Pigeon Forge and hole up in a cabin; maybe take in a show at Dollywood?" Harsh, but lately the words came faster than his internal filter censored them.

"See what I mean? This isn't you." She was right, and he hated when she was right. "Preston's going camping with Becky's husband Mike and his nephew in a couple of days, and they've invited you. They don't know anything about what's going on, only that we had a fight. This is exactly what you need. What we all need."

"What about you? I'm not going to leave you at the mercy of some monster like Eddie."

"I'll be fine. No one knows I'm at Becky's, and even if they did, she knows how to use a gun. And believe me, they've got plenty."

"What does Preston think about it?"

"It was his idea. This whole mess is killing him," she paused, "He needs his father."

The words hit home. He'd lost his own father almost thirteen years ago. Of course, Ben didn't have any intentions of following in his footsteps and leaving this world by way of a .45 to the tonsils. Besides, even though Ben wasn't the outdoor type, what Jill said made sense. He needed to clear his head and come up with a plan. He could figure his way out of any tight spot if he had a plan. Another thing he learned from his dad, for what it's worth.

"When would we leave?"

"Friday afternoon after Mike gets off work and be back Sunday afternoon." Her eyes burned into his, "Ben, this is it. Last chance to make things right with us. Understand?"

"Tell them I'm in."

By the way Jill's face relaxed, he knew he'd made the right decision, and she confirmed it by wrapping her arms around his neck and pulling him close. "You'll figure it out. At least you better."

Ben wished that hug would never end, but eventually she stood from the sofa and walked toward the foyer.

"Does this mean you're coming home?"

"No. It means I want you to figure out a way so it's safe for us to come home. I'm going to grab a couple of things and head back to Becky's. You look like you've got a lot of work ahead of you," she said, nodding to the boxes along the wall.

He watched her until she disappeared up the stairs. She had a way of making him understand the big picture, of grounding him. He still had a few days to work on gathering the money, maybe call a couple of prospects that showed some interest recently. Maybe even call Murphy, see if he could have another chance.

A light knock on the front door startled him back to reality. Ben edged to the narrow window in the foyer and looked onto the front porch. A kid he didn't recognize, wearing blue jeans, a light jacket, and a baseball cap sporting the logo of Pine Creek's tee ball team, shuffled his feet on the welcome mat. He held a small package and kept looking over his shoulder. Elementary school age, definitely younger than Preston but old enough to ride a bike through the neighborhood, Ben guessed nine or ten years old. He answered the door prepared to tell the kid he'd already bought raffle tickets for their new uniforms or bats. Thanks anyway.

"Are you Ben Johnson?"

"Yep, that's me. What are you selling?"

"Here," the kid said, and handed him the package. It fit easily into his hand and didn't have much weight.

"What's this?" But the kid was halfway down the stairs.

"Hey get back here. What's this?"

Junior jumped on his bike and peddled hard down the street without looking back.

Ben heard shuffling from the upstairs bathroom and debated on whether or not to call for Jill. He had made progress with her, and part of him knew moving forward his policy should be full disclosure. He was tired of the lies, even if they were lies of omission.

The other part of him won this battle. Ben tore the brown packing paper that covered a small box. He eased the lid off, and as he did, a folded piece of paper slipped to the floor. Ben picked it up and read a note scribbled with red ink. It consisted of one ugly word, MURDERER. Ben dropped both the note and box, and when it hit the floor, a shiny chain spilled over the side. He reached down, pushed the top half of the box away, and saw the silver necklace and its white trimmed dove charm.

12

Daniel answered the phone on the third ring but didn't recognize the woman's voice.

"May I speak to Mike please?"

"He's not here right now. Can I take a message or do you want to talk to his wife?"

"Just tell him Missy called."

"Missy? Is that all?"

"Yes. I wanted to tell him it was nice to meet him at church and let him know I hope to see him again soon."

"No problem," Daniel said and hung up the phone.

He turned and saw Becky standing in the door. "Who was that?"

"That lady Missy from church."

Becky folded her arms across her chest. "Really?"

Daniel nodded.

"She not want to talk to me?"

Daniel shook his head no.

"Don't stand there gyrating your neck. What did she want?"

"Um...She wanted to talk to Uncle Mike. I told her he wasn't here but you were. She didn't want to talk to you, but wanted me to tell him it was nice to meet him and um...she hoped to see him again soon."

"That's all?"

"I think so."

Becky took the phone from its cradle.

"Are you mad?" Daniel asked.

"I don't know yet. I'll tell you after I have a little talk with her."

She dialed the number and waited. After a moment, she hung up and marched to the sink. Daniel wasn't sure if he should say anything, so he kept quiet.

"I know she's there, she just called for goodness sake." Dishes clanked together as she scrubbed a lunch plate under the running water. "I told him that woman's trouble."

"Yes ma'am." Daniel couldn't think of anything else to say, and experience had taught him that when a woman like his Aunt Becky was mad, "Yes ma'am" was the safest option.

"I don't want you lying, especially to your uncle, but don't you tell him she called. I'll tell him about it when he gets home."

"Yes ma'am."

"I'm going to have a talk with Pastor Middleton too. She's going to stir up more trouble in the church than a fox in the hen house. Already has if you ask me." More dishes rattled as she moved on to a large pan. "Listen to me go on. This ain't nothing you need to worry about. Your Uncle Mike's a good man, but that woman...that woman is the very definition of floozy."

"Yes ma'am"

"And another thing, I found this on the porch." She pulled his student ID from her apron and tossed it on the counter. "When your uncle gets paid we're buying you a wallet."

Daniel grabbed the card and shoved it into his pocket. "Yes ma'am."

***

DANIEL ROLLED OVER on his back, pulled the covers to his chin, closed his eyes, and counted to twenty. Sleep wouldn't come no matter how many times he repeated the process. Mike and Becky had argued most of the night about the call from Missy, and although two rooms away, he heard their hushed voices. He hadn't eavesdropped, but Becky's voice seemed to carry, even at a whisper. She was mad because Mike wasn't mad.

Jill had made a quick trip home to pack a few extra woman things, then stayed in Emily's old room most of the night, venturing out only twice that he saw. One time he heard the toilet flush, the other time she peeked into his room and told Preston goodnight. Daniel wondered if she also heard the quiet commotion from down the hall.

He and Preston had managed a tense, but cordial, co-existence over the past twenty-four hours. Video games and general angst had penciled a tenuous bond.

"I didn't know they were going to do it," Preston said, from his mattress on the other side of the room.

"Didn't know what? Your mom and dad?" Daniel rolled over on his side.

"You know, the thing with Nichole's brother. What Tommy and Chase did. I didn't know they planned on messing with him. I was hanging at the sub shop, talking to Kaitlee. You know, flirting...whatever. Her friend Jenna told me she liked me." He paused and Daniel could tell he was struggling to find the right words. "Anyway, I was going to catch up with them in the park, then they came back, yelling about you. We jumped on our bikes and...well you know the rest."

"Yeah."

"Anyway, it wasn't right."

"Thanks."

For several minutes the only sounds were the hum of the refrigerator from the kitchen and Mike's muffled snoring through the door. Daniel, now decidedly awake, tried not to think of Nichole or Jim. Not because of what he'd lost, but how and why he had lost them. Every memory traveled a path that led to the man he met on the library steps.

Eventually the silence turned awkward, and propping himself up on his elbow, Daniel blurted out, "Sorry about your mom and dad. I'm sure whatever it is will blow over."

Preston didn't respond, so Daniel laid back down. Within minutes, he heard soft, rhythmic breathing from Preston's side of the room and decided to let him drift off to sleep. It hadn't been an apology Preston had offered him, but it was enough for now.

Five minutes passed, then ten. Sleep would not come. Restless, Daniel crept from his bed and out into the hall. A nightlight, plugged conveniently beside the bathroom door, lit the way to the living room. Daniel wasn't sure what shows ran this time of night, but tossing and turning in his bed had grown old.

He found the remote and hit the power, careful to turn the volume down as the TV came to life. Scrolling through several tired sitcoms and an old movie, he settled on a documentary about honey bees. The narrator seemed awfully concerned about them and what would happen if they went extinct. Daniel stretched out and made himself comfortable, confident this show would skirt that fine line between boring enough to put him to sleep and interesting enough to hold his attention until he drifted off.

He had hardly taken a step into the shifty world of sleep when a sharp clap stirred him. At first he dismissed it as part of a dream, one not yet completely formed, but beginning to take shape. But that didn't feel right. Dreams are rarely audible. Could be the TV, he thought, but his mind immediately rejected the idea. The volume was too low and the clap too sharp. He sat up and forced his eyes open wide. On the television, a man with no hair and a long gray beard sat in front of a fireplace, jar of honey in his hand. Several models of bees and beehives displayed proudly on the mantel behind him. Daniel glanced at Mike and Becky's fireplace and noticed the picture frame immediately. It had fallen over on its side. Had it fallen forward, it would have toppled off the mantel and onto the hearth.

Wide awake once again, Daniel navigated past the coffee table and recliner. The TV offered enough light to see the picture was of Mike and Becky's wedding. He must have passed it a thousand times without noticing it.

Afraid to touch it, he inched closer. The glass cover remained intact, but the picture was wrong. He cocked his head, hoping his eyes would fully adjust to the light and the frame's new position. Then he saw it. The picture was torn down the middle, separating his aunt and uncle.

Almost immediately after the discovery, the soft voice of the man holding a honey jar was abruptly replaced by the distinct sound of static. Daniel swung to the TV, where a blanket of white nothingness filled the screen. He watched, transfixed by the sight, the sound, the absurdity of it all. Then it went black. No bald man sitting in front of a fireplace, no static or white noise. Only black and the steady hum of Aunt Becky's old Frigidaire.

Slowly, almost imperceptibly, a soft, yellow glow rose to life from the TV. One letter, then a word, appeared. More letters, and another word followed, conjured to the screen by an invisible hand carefully sketching the message. TALK SOON.

Daniel stumbled back, tripping over the table, and falling into the couch. Too terrified to cry out, too exhausted to care, he surrendered and waited for darkness to overtake him. Eventually, the yellow glow faded from the room, and sleep mercifully came.

***

MELISSA MOSBY CURLED up under her leopard print throw and sipped a mug of chocolate cocoa, unware he lounged right beside her. She held a well-used tissue in the other hand and watched the love story on her second hand TV reach its climax. The little apartment, clean in a stale sort of way, stank of cheap incense and burnt popcorn. Slivered bits of pictures littered the coffee table, her project for the evening almost finished.

She glanced down at the last remaining intact photo, her and a man at a Halloween party, laughing and raising their bottles to the camera. With a grunt, she tossed her half-empty cup to the floor where it landed with a dull thud. Araphel smiled. Melissa Mosby, Missy to her friends, would do fine. In fact, she had already laid the ground-work on her own.

Missy shed the throw and hunched over the table, eyeing the last picture. Araphel knew the man partying with her. Knew him well in fact. The lanky blond with a crew cut, usually covered by a crimson cap with Roll Tide across the front, had served him in the past, quite recently even. The young man would be an asset in the prison system.

She snatched the scissors from the edge of the table, slid the memory between the blades, and in one quick motion, excised the latest love from her life. Missy laid the scissors down and eased back on the sofa. Her crying drowned out the drivel coming from the television across the room.

Araphel leaned over and stroked her cheek. "The pain is good child, but you know you can't handle it. Dull it for now, tomorrow we'll find you a real man. One that can take care of you like you deserve."

Missy reached down and opened the small drawer on the end table. After fumbling around several spent batteries and two broken remotes, her hand returned with a small brass pipe. She lit the end, inhaled and waited. Finally, a stream of white smoke escaped her lungs. The last few hits of Billy's personal stash. When her eyes closed half an hour later, the love story had ended, and the pipe held nothing but black tar and ash.

Araphel relaxed beside Missy as she slipped off to sleep. After all these years, thousands of them, he still delighted in the power to watch undetected. Humans called it voyeurism, but watching is so much more. He learned by watching. In his short time with Melissa he had learned, among hundreds of other things, she sleeps with the light on, has no close family, and hates men. Boyfriends came and went, but at her core she hated them even more than she hated herself.

He laid beside her, stroking her hair, whispering in her ear, and invading her dreams. By the look of contentment she wore most of the night, he knew she heard. Humans like her almost always did. He had planted the boy's uncle firmly in her mind, and Araphel knew he wouldn't have to lead her to the next move. They were becoming one in their thoughts.

13

Becky came up with the idea to treat the preacher to a nice dinner, Mike chose the restaurant. He spotted a table near the buffet and led his foursome through the crowd. Pastor Middleton followed close behind, then Daniel, with Becky bringing up the rear. Jill had opted out of the invitation to join them, instead treating Preston to a movie. No great loss in Mike's humble opinion.

Ronnie's was the place to eat Tuesday nights in Pine Creek, and it wasn't the trendiness or even the laid back atmosphere Mike enjoyed; he hated the crowds and the new country music they constantly blared through the speakers. Give him Hank or Willie, but Tuesday was seafood night, so he let it slide. He led his group through the maze of wooden tables and crying kids.

"This work for y'all?" Mike pulled out a chair and sat down.

"It'll do fine," Becky said.

Daniel took the seat beside Mike, and Becky sat beside the preacher. The waitress hadn't even taken their drink orders, and his palms were already damp. He didn't know why, he liked the preacher, but every time he ended up around him, he broke out in a cold sweat.

Becky hung her purse on the back of her chair. "Honey, tell the waitress I want sweet tea. Come on Daniel, let's go grab a plate."

Mike watched the two walk to the buffet, creating an atmosphere where his sweat beads could flourish.

"So Mike, how'd you like the service Sunday?"

And here we go. "It was fine."

"Good. I don't want to pressure you, but I sure hope to see you back. We do it every week you know." The preacher let out a soft chuckle.

"Yeah, Becky told me." Mike joined in with nervous laughter.

"Daniel's a good kid isn't he?"

"Yeah, he's great. Smart, polite, got a good head on his shoulders. It's been a rough few months for him."

Pastor Middleton's sad, understanding eyes spoke for him.

Mike continued, "He's had some trouble fitting in at school, but all kids go through that I think."

"He'll come around. It's tough for kids like him. Seen it all my life. He's got a love for the Lord most kids his age don't understand."

Mike looked past the preacher toward the food bar, uncomfortable with the direction of the conversation. Becky hadn't even made it halfway down the line.

"When a kid loves the Lord..." The preacher continued speaking, but Mike's attention wandered to the front door. A woman, beautiful and familiar, loitered by the counter, her eyes searching the room. Shoulder length brunette hair, firm yet petite figure, he knew her.

It came to him the moment their eyes met. Missy. A slow smile settled on her lips, seductive, yet somehow innocent. Her hand went to her hair as she glanced to the floor, then back up to him with upturned eyes. Missy turned and took an empty table near the front while Pastor Middleton droned on in the background.

"Mike. Mike, you okay?"

The preacher's voice jolted him out of the trance. "Yeah, sorry. Just remembered a project I forgot to finish at work," he lied.

Before Pastor Middleton could continue, Becky and Daniel returned from the buffet, plates stacked high with shrimp and catfish. Thankfully, Becky's chair faced away from Missy. He couldn't imagine the scene his wife would cause if she saw her. Mike and the preacher each filled a plate, then after giving thanks, they all put their forks to work.

Little conversation passed between them as they ate. Becky and the preacher made small talk about the church. Sunday School attendance and choir robes didn't interest him. Daniel kept to himself, picking at his food on occasion. Mike tried not to look past his wife to the corner table but struggled. Missy called out to him, drew him in a way he didn't understand. He thought of a book assignment from high school. He couldn't remember the name, but in it women sang a song so irresistible, sailors lost their lives chasing it. Sirens, they were called. Two days ago, Missy's song meant nothing to him. Tonight, he wondered if he had the strength to resist.

He shifted his attention to the woman sitting in front of him, the woman he had vowed to love through good times and bad. She was talking to the preacher about

123

an out of tune piano. An issue that threatened to divide the congregation if something wasn't done right away- at least according to Becky. He loved her. Always had. He reached across the table, and without looking she did the same. It was as if her hand knew the intention of his, and they made the blind connection without effort. She smiled, and so did he.

Ten minutes later the group prepared to leave. Mike and the preacher briefly debated who would pick up the check, before Becky snatched it from Middleton's hand. "No way my pastor's buying his own supper."

The group pushed away from the table, and Mike stole a look at the corner while Becky fidgeted with her purse. Missy was leaving, already walking to the door. Her short skirt flitted back and forth, keeping rhythm with her swaying gait. Like she knew he was watching, she looked back over her shoulder, shot him a wink, and left into the night. The Siren Song reached out again.

***

ARAPHEL RELAXED ON the sofa, waiting for the sniveling bootlicker Middleton to return home. He had hoped to shadow him all night, but a hoard of Guardians accompanied the group on their outing. Instead, he decided to prepare a surprise for him. The Guardian inside the door didn't offer resistance, rightfully stepping aside when Araphel demanded entrance.

He watched the old man hang his coat in the foyer closet and wander to the kitchen. Araphel followed. The house repulsed him. It reeked of communion with The Author.

He slipped beside the pastor and gently brushed his face as the Bootlicker poured a glass of milk. Such a waste, spending his whole life as a servant. He'd never know the joy of hatred, of lasciviousness. Wonderful states.

Pastor Middleton finished the milk in three gulps then retired to his study. Again, Araphel followed. For this, he didn't need or want a vessel to conceal his identity.

The old man screamed when the demon slammed the door behind him. Araphel spread his wings and bared a mouth full of jackal teeth. Making himself visible drained his energy, but this would be worth it, assuming he didn't spend himself before he finished the introductions. Pastor Middleton reeled back and groped the corner of his desk, knocking off several books and a stack of papers. The demon sprang like a lion, covering the length of the room in less time than it took for the last paper to float to the floor. The impact sent the pastor sprawling over the desk. Not even an inch separated their faces.

"Do you know who I am?" The words came out as an angry whisper.

The pastor, eyes and mouth wide, didn't respond.

"I said, do you know who I am?" Louder this time.

"Jesus." The word barely audible.

The laugh that escaped Araphel caused the pastor to recoil. "No, I'm afraid not. Guess again."

"Jesus." Stronger this time.

"Enough." A crack echoed off the plank paneling when Araphel backhanded him. The blow bent the frame of the preacher's glasses.

A surge of strength rushed through the demon as a tear found a wrinkle and followed its path down the pastor's face. The joy of fear. "I may let you live tonight servant, but you are going to make me a promise. You will stay away from the boy. Do you understand? I've given him one message. Don't force me to deliver more."

Pastor Middleton clenched his chest and clamped his eyes shut, squeezing out another trickle of salty tears.

"I said, do you understand?" Araphel gripped the man's throat harder than he intended.

The word came out as a gasp. "Jesus."

The bookshelf across the room crashed to the floor, toppled by the power of Araphel's roar. He lifted the man above his head and pinned him to the ceiling. The pastor's bible, one of the books knocked from the desk, was directly below them. Draining the blood of a servant onto the servant's book. A fitting end. Araphel snatched the back of Pastor Middleton's head and exposed his neck. The joy of evil. Talons extended, he lifted his hand and brought it down in a flash. A hand caught his swipe inches before it penetrated flesh.

"Enough." A Guardian, the one who had submitted to his entry.

Araphel struggled, but The Guardian held firm. He summoned his sword, letting the pastor fall, and prompting The Guardian to release his grip in order to save the old man from breaking his neck on the wood below. It was all the distraction he needed. He brought his sword across the front of the Guardian but sliced only air. This one moved quick. Quicker than most. Araphel positioned himself for the counterstrike, but it never came. He looked down. The Guardian knelt eight feet below him, sword by his side, head bowed toward The One kneeling beside the moaning pastor.

Intense horror swept through Araphel when The Author looked up. The fury from His eyes burned his skin like fire.

"Leave us." It was the first time since the war He had spoken directly to him.

His voice shattered Araphel's strength, and he crumbled to the floor at the power of The Author's words.

14

Cars and people filled the downtown streets, odd for a weekday morning but not unheard of. Neither retirees nor unemployment are ever in short supply in small town America. Becky parked her van in one of the only available spots in Value Food's small lot and hurried into the store. She needed flour and butter for supper, and although Daniel had convinced Becky to let him skip school, he needed out of the house.

He grabbed a buggy from the corral and caught up. She was already half way down the first aisle, inspecting a head of lettuce or cabbage, Daniel wasn't sure which one.

"Grab me one of those plastic bags." She pointed to the stand beside him.

Daniel handed her the bag, and she stuffed the ball inside and tossed it in the cart.

She rounded the corner at the end of the aisle, and the front end of another cart barreled into the side of hers. The loud clank of metal buggies colliding caused several shoppers to whip their heads toward the sound.

"I'm sorry," a familiar voice from behind the endcap said.

"Missy?"

"Oh, Becky. I didn't see you."

The other patrons returned to their shopping, unconcerned with the two women facing off beside a display of Hamburger Helper. Missy backed her cart up and checked the eggs, which had flipped on their side. "Shoot. Cracked a couple of them."

"Maybe you should watch where you're going."

Missy's mouth dropped open. Daniel knew his aunt could be blunt, but the words came out sharp, even for her.

"Maybe you shouldn't be sprinting down the vegetable aisle like you were trying to win a race." Missy's words took an equally sharp tone.

Becky took a deep breath. "Look, let's not make any more of a scene than we already have. The only thing hurt was those eggs, so let's go about our day like nothing happened."

"Fine with me." Missy flashed a wide, plastic smile. "How's Mike?"

"Mike is none of your business." Becky hesitated, then returned an equally toothy grin. "But since you brought it up, we might as well talk about why you're calling him."

Missy's smile relaxed into a thinly veiled smirk. "I'm on the committee remember? We do a follow up with all visitors." She laid the carton of broken eggs on the stack of Hamburger Helper.

Daniel could almost feel the heat coming off Becky's face, but her voice remained calm. "I don't know what you think you're trying to do, but it needs to stop now."

"I'm not trying to do anything, so if you want to get smart with somebody, go talk to your husband."

"What's that supposed to mean?" Becky's grip on the handle tightened.

Missy grabbed a bag of salad and tossed it into her cart. "All I'm saying is you need to keep an eye on him. I got a funny feeling when he looked at me the other day."

"You stay away from him. You hear me?" Becky didn't give her time to answer before turning and storming back up the vegetable aisle, leaving her cart behind. "Daniel, let's go. Food World is cheaper anyway," she said without looking back.

She slammed the van door hard enough to stir up the dust on the dash. "That woman. Lord help me not to..." She turned to Daniel, face splotched red, "Sorry, I just don't know what to do with her, but you don't need to be hearing all this."

"It's okay."

Becky pulled out of the parking lot, and they drove in silence for several minutes. She still looked mad, but at least her face had returned to a healthier shade of pink.

"What did Pastor Middleton say?" Daniel asked.

"About what?"

"About her? When you talked to him."

"I haven't had a chance and last night at dinner didn't seem right. Mike wasn't himself, you hardly ate," she gave the steering wheel an affirming pat; "It'll be fine sweetie. It will all work out."

Daniel could see the Food World sign up ahead as he fiddled with his seatbelt. He missed Jim. He missed Nichole and she'd only been gone a few days. He missed his mom and dad.

Becky's phone rang from somewhere inside her purse.

"Grab that and tell them to hang on a second."

Daniel fished the phone out while Becky pulled into a parking spot.

"It's your friend from church, Mrs. Wilma." He handed the phone to her.

"Hey Wilma."

Daniel only heard one end of the conversation, but it was enough to tell him something was very wrong.

15

Mike pushed the button to the fourth floor, the Cardiac Care Unit, while Daniel held the door for an elderly couple getting off. Pastor Middleton's heart attack nearly did him in according to Becky.

"You think we ought to cancel our camping trip?" Mike asked when the doors closed.

"I don't know. What do you think?"

Mike wasn't sure what to think. Becky had called him at work hysterical. He finally managed to calm her down enough to get the story. Neighbors heard a ruckus late last night and called the cops. They found him sprawled out on his study floor, books and papers scattered around the room. Even a bookcase had tipped over. Their first thought was home invasion, but in the end the report simply read *medical emergency*. When Becky got the call from Wilma, she rushed home and dropped Daniel off with Jill. He protested, but Becky didn't want him there if it was as bad as Wilma let on.

"Your aunt thinks we should go."

"Then we should go."

132

The elevator stopped and opened to a young woman standing behind a little girl in a wheel chair. Mike pointed up, and the woman offered a polite smile, gave a quick shake of her head, and pointed down.

"What do you think happened?" Daniel asked when the doors closed.

"What do you mean what happened? He had a heart attack."

"No, not that. I mean, well, what do you think caused it?"

Mike shrugged and stared at the digital numbers above the door. "Things happen, he's old." What could he say? The story the preacher told Becky seemed ridiculous, and he told her so. He told her the preacher might have suffered more than a heart attack if he's talking about monsters or demons. She got so mad he'd be on the couch tonight for sure.

The doors opened again, this time to a deserted hall, except for several nurses sitting behind the station in front of them. Only one looked up. Becky had told them to take a right off of the elevator and his was the third door on the left, room 413.

The preacher turned to them when they opened the door.

"Come in. Come in." He seemed pretty spry for someone whose ticker nearly fouled a valve. "I need a bit of good company."

Balloons, flowers, and cards, littered the room. Not bad for less than twenty-four hours in the hospital.

"How you feeling preacher?"

"I've been better, but The Lord is good." Then to Daniel, "Ain't that right young man?"

"Yes sir." Daniel shoved his hands into his pockets.

"I didn't think we'd get to see you this soon. You know, with heart surgery and all." Mike eased into the worn recliner across the room, and Daniel took a seat in the chair beside the bed. What do you say to a man you barely knew, much less one that might be a little off?

The preacher gave a hearty chuckle. "Oh, it wasn't as bad as some made it out to be. Doctor says I could have gone home today, but they're making me stay an extra night because of the bruises and cuts."

They talked about his prognosis, it looked good. The surgeons didn't have to crack him open. Ran a wire into his leg and opened the artery right up. They talked about the weather, cold and rainy, typical southern November. They talked about hospital food and Georgia football. All safe subjects.

After twenty minutes of chit chat, Mike glanced at his watch. It wasn't that he hated Preacher Middleton, in fact, he liked the man a great deal. He didn't like hospitals, and he most certainly didn't care for the lecture he knew was coming. Preacher types, at least the hard core ones, always ended up in the same place.

"Well preacher-"

Pastor Middleton cut him off mid-sentence. "Mike, have you thought any more about our conversation at the lake?"

Mike gathered his jacket, wanting to escape. "No, not really. I mean, I've been busy you know, with everything that's happened."

The preacher nodded and took a sip of water.

"Alright then," Mike said, "it's been good talking to you. I'll let Becky know you're doing better. I'm sure she'll be back up in the morning if they haven't let you go."

"I was attacked."

Mike stopped short of the door.

"I heard." Mike looked back and gestured for Daniel to get up. Apparently, the boy wasn't in a hurry. "Becky told me about it."

Preacher Middleton waved him back to the recliner, straining his IV. "I didn't tell her everything. Come, sit back down, there are a couple of things you need to hear."

Daniel leaned forward, making it obvious he had no intention of leaving yet. "What happened?"

Mike made his way back to the chair and settled in. "He doesn't know. He wasn't there when Becky told me."

The preacher seemed to think about how to proceed. "What do you think?"

"I think it's up to you. You're the expert."

"I don't know what?" Daniel leaned closer, his backside barely clinging to the edge of the chair.

The preacher reached for Daniel's hand and sighed. "Okay, here goes."

He spent the next ten minutes recounting his attack. Mike hoped he would leave out some of the more intense parts, but he didn't. Daniel hung on every word, nodding occasionally but not interrupting.

When he finished his story, the preacher looked at them in turn. "So, there it is. I've only told a couple of people. Not sure why The Lord wanted me to tell y'all, but He did."

An uncomfortable silence settled over the room. Why do they always say that? "The Lord wanted me to do this, The Lord told me to say that." Mike thought it was nothing more than a way to justify what they wanted to do in the first place; the drugged out mom who drowned her screaming baby in the tub because The Lord told her to do it, or the man who offed his fiancé because she wore black and howled at the moon. But the preacher believed it. Mike shifted in his seat, jacket still folded across his arm.

"What about the part you didn't tell Aunt Becky?"

The preacher closed his eyes and lifted his head toward the ceiling. Mike didn't know if he was praying or falling asleep. He hoped for the latter, but wasn't that lucky. Never was.

"At Monroe's, when Jim died, was there anything you didn't tell the police?"

"No," Daniel spoke up first. "We told them everything didn't we?" Mike thought he heard a twinge of panic in his nephew's voice.

Mike wiped the sweat from his face with the sleeve of his jacket. "Why do you ask?"

The preacher reached for the bible that sat on his bedside table, but didn't open it. Instead he clutched it close to his chest.

"What aren't you telling me preacher?" Mike said louder than he intended.

"What's wrong uncle Mike? What's going on?"

The preacher seemed reluctant, looking first to the bible, then at Daniel. "He said he told you it was a message."

Mike gripped the arms of the chair to keep from falling forward.

"When he had me...up," he waved toward the ceiling, "he told me that before killing Jim, he gave you a message. Just like he gave me."

Daniel asked the question Mike couldn't.

"What message?"

The preacher looked at Daniel with a tenderness that gripped Mike's heart. "To stay away from you son."

Daniel slumped forward in his chair. "I'm sorry. I'm so sorry."

Middleton leaned close to Daniel. "Son, you don't have anything to be sorry about. This isn't your fault." Daniel opened his mouth to speak but the preacher cut him off. "God has this. I saw His power last night. I can't explain it, but I have a feeling you know what I'm talking about. There's a reason for all of this. I don't know what it is, and you don't know what it is, but The Author does. It's His story."

Pastor Middleton leaned back onto his bed, visibly emotional, and no one spoke. Mike's level of discomfort finally reached its breaking point so he rose, determined to reach the hallway this time. "Daniel, we need to go. The pastor needs to rest."

Daniel wiped his cheek with a sleeve. "Thank you."

The preacher waved him off. "No need, but you're welcome. I do have a favor to ask though." He motioned Mike to him. "Please take some of these plants and balloons with you. I'll stop by your place and pick them up when they let me go." A weak laugh escaped him. "When they release me, I don't want to spend an hour moving out."

"Sure," Mike said, already gathering two potted plants into his arms. Anything to escape this room. "Daniel, grab a handful of those balloons." He pointed to a cluster, huddled against the ceiling by the far wall.

Daniel grabbed the dangling strings, and they waved goodbye, promising to check up on him tomorrow and reminding him to call if he needed anything.

Neither spoke on the elevator ride back to the first floor, or through the maze of halls that led to the front lobby. Nor did they speak as the automatic doors slid open, granting access to the parking lot and a cool autumn day. Mike wanted to say something when Daniel stopped, took a single balloon, held it up and released it into the sky. He wanted to ask why but didn't. Instead, they watched it float into the heavens in silence.

***

THE SIX-PACK Mike picked up after dropping Daniel off at the house was still cold. Three years without a drink, but the draw returned in earnest a week ago, about the time bits of poor Jim's brain smacked him on the arm. Three days ago it grew into a constant buzz. Three hours ago, when the preacher finished his story, the draw won.

He looked out over the lake, purposefully avoiding the tree line, and wondered what kind of God would deal him such a crappy hand. Crummy job, bum knee, and an overdrawn checking account barely scratched the surface of his lovely life. Want to get serious God? How about a dead daughter or the extra mouth to feed because he had to take in his dead sister's little boy? Now Becky wants another one after what they went through with Emily? That all you got?

Mike slid the can from the plastic ring and sat the rest of the pack on the tailgate. The first couple would be tough, he never was a beer man, but the convenience store on Route 29 didn't carry whisky. At least the last few should go down easy. Come to think of it, he should have sprung for the case. He knew the difference between buzzed and drunk, and tonight he wasn't going for either. He wanted can't walk, no memory, country messed up, and a six pack wouldn't do that for him, even after three years sober.

People say the moment you take your last drink your life starts getting better. That's crap. It may not have gotten worse, how could it after Emily died, but it certainly hadn't gotten better. Mike popped the tab and lifted the can. Three years.

He thought about Emily as cool aluminum touched his lip. This was the same spot he'd ended up the day they'd buried her. He got so blitzed he'd passed out in the mud. At least he avoided the onslaught of casserole toting well-wishers that descended on their house after the funeral. Fine with him, though Becky didn't talk to him for a week. But Emily, they'd come not only for them but for her, to honor her life. The short, beautiful life of his daughter.

He let the can linger against his lips a moment longer, then launched it into the lake. Three years, it wouldn't end tonight.

***

BECKY MET MIKE on the porch, clutching her robe with one hand, a bible in the other. When she spoke, Mike knew she was scared.

"Thank God. I don't know what's wrong with him."

Mike bolted up the steps, grabbing her arm and rushing through the door. "Where is he? What happened?" He didn't give her a chance to answer.

Daniel's door hung open, and what he saw stopped him cold, causing Becky to slam into him from behind. Through the dim light offered by the moon, Mike saw Daniel sitting upright in his bed, eyes open, hair matted with sweat, lips forming silent words. He didn't turn to them when Mike flipped on the light.

"Danny. Hey buddy, wake up." Mike didn't know what else to say.

"I've tried everything," Becky said through fresh tears.

"How long has he been like this?"

"Twenty or thirty minutes, but he was talking before. Scared Preston so bad Jill took him to the late movie."

"Talking? What'd he say?" Mike grabbed Daniel's shoulder and gave him a light shake. "Wake up son. It's okay."

"Should I call 911?"

"And tell them what?" Mike didn't mean to sound hateful but Becky flinched at his tone. "Sorry. It's just...what's happening to him?"

"I don't know."

She pulled the bible to her chest and began praying out loud.

"Becky, listen to me. What did he say?"

Her prayers continued without pause.

"Becky!" He grabbed her and spun her toward him. "What did he say?"

She looked up to him. "I don't know. It didn't make sense. Something about a woman, over and over."

"What woman?"

"I don't know. It sounded like 'this woman."

Mike let her go, walked around the bed, and ran his hand over the Superman sheets. He thought Daniel was a little old for them, even if the first signs of manhood hadn't sprouted from his body. Without warning, Daniel laid back down, still fast asleep.

"What? You know what woman he's talking about?"

He did. He'd never forget that phrase or the man that uttered it. "Yeah, his mom."

16

By the time Friday morning rolled around, Ben had made up his mind. He needed to talk to Vince, and it had to be tonight- tomorrow afternoon at the latest. He sat at his desk and thumbed through the stack of receivables he spent all week chasing. He thought collecting the debt owed him would be the quickest way to come up with the money. New clients took time to cultivate, and even if he landed a contract it'd be at least a month before he saw the money. He didn't have a month. If Vince's call had been a warning about Eddie, he had a week tops. Probably less based on the reminders he'd gotten over the past few days.

His collection efforts hadn't worked though. He netted about two-thousand dollars, not nearly enough to appease the punk ruining his life. To make matters worse, he was pretty sure he'd pushed some of his clients too far and lost any future business, but he'd worry about that another day. Maybe he should adopt some of Eddie's collection techniques. The thought made Ben laugh.

Preston would be devastated when he didn't show up to meet them after school, and Jill would be furious, but he couldn't think of any other way. If she knew about the unexpected package maybe she'd understand, but telling her would be a mistake. He'd have to explain why he bought his assistant jewelry. Not a conversation he wanted to have. She might go to the cops, or she might pack her things, grab Preston and disappear. He wasn't risking either. He got them into this mess, he'd get them out.

Ben decided against calling Jill and letting her know about his change of plans, no point in starting another fight. Instead, he wrote her a letter explaining that a new development came up concerning Eddie, and there might be a chance to work it out with him. He didn't get into details; those have a tendency to come back on you when you deal in deception. No, he kept it simple. He had to go to Atlanta this weekend at Eddie's request. Another one of his business partners needed some discreet computer help, and they would pay handsomely for it. Eddie had proposed Ben work off a portion of the debt. It was a lie of course, but it might keep Jill from worrying...or leaving him. He left the envelope in the Hill's mailbox then headed for I-75.

***

THE RIDE TO Gordon's Bluff was quiet except for three phone calls from Becky checking up on them. Mike had argued for an hour about taking her phone. Didn't need it, might lose it, might accidently call India and run up the bill. Eventually he ran out of reasons, and she won. She usually did.

His uncle tried to lighten the mood by telling stories about his teenage camping adventures, but Daniel's stomach churned from the obvious tension. Preston didn't want to be there, especially after his dad ditched them at the last minute. He had called his mom and begged her to let him come home, but it didn't work, and he hadn't said a word in the hour since they'd left the library. They turned off the main road onto the dirt path that led to the bluff, and Mike tried again to break the ice.

"You know boys, there's a legend up in these woods I really need to tell you about."

Daniel caught a glimpse of Preston rolling his eyes and decided to play along. "Really, what's it about?"

"You really want to know? I mean I couldn't tell the women about it or they might not have let you come."

"Sure," Daniel said.

"What about you Preston? You think you can handle it?" Mike asked.

"Whatever." It wasn't much, but it was the first time Preston had opened his mouth since they'd left.

Mike's eyes narrowed in the rearview mirror. Daniel heard him take a deep breath but continue despite his obvious frustration.

"Legend goes, a couple of hundred years ago an old man by the name of Curve Gordon put a curse on the mountain. You see, he'd lived in these hills alone for many years. He never owned the land, but he built a cabin and made a simple life for himself. Grew a garden, hunted squirrel, rabbit, the occasional deer. You get the picture."

The truck rolled over a small log, sloshing Mike's sweet tea all over the center console. Daniel thought it wouldn't be too much further until they'd have to finish up on foot. He hoped they wouldn't have to hike far.

"A logging company, Georgia Timber I think it was, owned the land back then. They owned most of the land around here. One day, a couple of men in suits showed up at Curve's cabin and told him he was going to have to move. They had papers from the court and threatened to bring the police into it if he gave them any grief."

Daniel tried to get a read on Preston without being obvious. He hadn't spoken, but at least he seemed to be paying attention.

"Tale is, Curve didn't give them a chance to finish their business. Shot them both and threw the bodies over the bluff."

Daniel cut another glance at Preston and noticed his eyes had widened.

"A few days later, a search party found the bodies and a whole team of them swooped in and took the mountain man in for murder. The trial was quick and turned out poorly for Curve. Guilty. Now, back in those days they didn't wait through years of appeals and letters to the Governor. No sir. They took you out back to the gallows."

Daniel wasn't sure how much of this to believe, but his uncle knew how to tell a story.

"They got him to the platform, hands tied behind his back, noose around his neck, and right before the hangman put the sack over his head, he asked old Curve if he had any last words."

The truck stopped, and Mike turned the headlights off. No one said a word. Mike, making no move to open the door, relaxed his hands in his lap. He had the boys' full attention, and after several seconds, Preston spoke up.

"What happened? What'd he say?"

"Boys, he looked out over that crowd, narrowed his eyes and told them 'y'all just small town players, but so help me, if you hang the Curve, you'll never make it to the big leagues.'"

The boys didn't say a word. He wasn't sure about Preston, but Daniel had been so taken in by the story the punch line soared right over his head. When it hit, he looked to his right toward Preston and the two burst out laughing.

"That was bad uncle Mike. Really bad."

"Yeah Mr. Hill, no offense, but that was the cheesiest joke I've ever heard."

The two were still trying to stifle their laughs when Mike turned off the truck and opened his door.

"Boys, we walk from here. Let's grab the gear and head out. Got a bit to go and we're already behind in the count."

Daniel watched Mike gather his gear and camp supplies, then help Preston slide his backpack on.

Maybe this weekend would be alright after all. Curse or no curse.

***

DANIEL WOKE WITH a start, his thermal shirt soaked with sweat. It took several seconds for him to get his bearings and figure out he was in the woods on a camping trip, but once he did, his breathing began to

146

slow. He heard Mike snoring, and Preston looked fast asleep. He hit the backlight on his watch, three-fifteen.

The hike to the campsite hadn't been bad after all. Mike found three fallen branches and handed them out as walking sticks. Grateful, Daniel wondered if he did that for his benefit. They didn't talk much, but at least the heavy tension from the ride vanished. By the time they set camp it was full dark. They spent an hour sitting around the fire, eating beans from a can and talking. Even Preston joined in occasionally. Daniel sensed he didn't want to be there, but it seemed like he tried to make the best of it.

Now, at three in the morning, Daniel felt alone. The dream, and this was just a dream he kept telling himself, had stirred him awake. It wasn't terrifying, at least not as bad as some of the others, but he sensed this one had weight. A dream with a purpose.

In it, he walked along a muddy creek bank. The clear water looked about twenty feet across and deep. A massive snake stood on the other side. It stood. Not on legs, but its size gave the illusion as it watched him. He sensed the snake wanted to cross but couldn't. An unknown, powerful force forbade it. The water? He wasn't sure but thought so. When he walked, the serpent mirrored his movements on the opposite bank. He limped ten feet upriver, and the serpent slithered ten feet. His head told him he couldn't outrun the serpent, but fear won the day. He ran until his foot gave out and left him sprawled in the mud. Minutes or hours passed, time is slippery when the subconscious pilots the ship. When he dared look across the creek, the serpent glared back. He cried out for his mom, but instead the serpent answered. Three simple words, "I took her." Was it a lie? He didn't know. Before Daniel could respond, the water at his feet pulled away, slowly at first, then the creek began to vanish as the earth swallowed it in large gulps. He tried to run, but his foot gave out and sent him sliding down the bank. Frantic clawing didn't slow his descent. A few more feet and the serpent would have a way across, a clear path to him. The water slowed to a trickle.

That's when he saw the girl. She looked about his age, maybe a little younger, and he had the feeling he should know her. Her eyes captivated him, and for a moment all thoughts of the serpent vanished. They were identical to his mom's.

"What's your name?" he heard himself ask.

"Hannah," she answered, then stepped into the quickly drying creek bed. Daniel yelled for her to stop, it wasn't safe, but when she stepped forward the serpent recoiled. She took another step and drove the serpent back even further. It opened its jaws wide, exposing two fangs, and hissed. Hannah didn't flinch, and when she stepped forward again, the serpent fled. She glanced over her shoulder at Daniel. "You don't have to be afraid Daniel."

Then he woke up.

Daniel tried to doze off by analyzing the dream. Most people would call that crazy. Try to think of something else, something pleasant after a nightmare, they'd say. But for Daniel it usually helped. Going over every detail, at least the details he could remember, put his mind on autopilot and helped reassure him it was only a dream. It didn't work this time. The image of the serpent, waiting patiently for the last trickle of water to disappear, wouldn't leave him.

But neither would the girl with his mom's eyes. Hannah.

After twenty minutes he decided fresh air might help. Fresh air and prayer. Daniel slipped from the tent and walked to the edge of their campsite. Cool air sliced through his damp thermals, sending a chill from his scalp all the way to his toes. The woods, once alive with a chorus of crickets and frogs, lay silent. The stillness troubled him. Daniel sat on the cooler and tried to maintain his composure. Dying embers of the fire provided barely enough light to illuminate the camp. It wasn't much.

Darkness. Not enough light. The serpent across the creek.

A shiver radiated from the center of his body. He tried to convince himself it was the mountain air and wet shirt but failed. He knew better. The serpent was biding its time. Waiting and watching.

***

RICHARD EMERGED FROM the shadows without warning. Daniel wasn't startled, the presence of evil had weighed heavy in the air since he had woken from the dream.

"Beautiful night, is it not?" Richard knelt in front of the cooler, head tilted to the stars. "I love the mountain air this time of year."

"Why are you here?" But he already knew didn't he? He had come to hear his answer. TO TALK.

Lost in the night sky, Richard didn't acknowledge the question. "I wasn't in favor of the rebellion, at least not

149

initially. I couldn't imagine turning my back on my creator, warring against my brothers, but Heylel convinced me."

Again, Daniel found himself snared in a conversation with evil. Richard's words reached into his mind and fed a primitive hunger he had attempted to starve since meeting The Author. "Who is Heylel?"

Richard glanced at him, then back to the sky. "The Author's book calls him by his Latin name, Lucifer. Heylel is from a much older tongue."

"The devil?"

Richard chuckled. "The Devil, Satan, the Serpent, all of those and more. He is a being of many faces, but to me he will always be Heylel, the bright morning star." He paused and closed his eyes, the look of someone lost in a memory. "I followed him, not out of love, but for independence. A chance to taste freedom, to control my own destiny. That is what he offered, and why I joined- why I fight." He looked at Daniel. "You and I, our...conflict, is merely a minor skirmish on a much larger battlefield. We are nothing more than two soldiers fighting over a tiny plot of land in a war that transcends both time and the boundaries of the universe as you know them." Richard rose and clasped his hands at his waist. "But it is a tiny plot we both value, so this is our fight. And it is a fight I intend to win."

Daniel still hadn't spoken. He wanted to hurl himself at the man, tell him he would never forsake The Author, even though part of him longed to savor Richard's words till dawn.

"You've lost much already Daniel, and you will lose much more before this is over."

Daniel tried to keep his face from showing the fear building inside. He shut his eyes and thought of the balloon, trying to imagine it leaving his hand and ascending to heaven. To The Father.

Richard continued, "I know you will not abandon The Author. I've known since the day you were born. Part of me hoped I was wrong, that I had somehow misread the signs, but it wasn't meant to be, you and I."

"Then why?" Daniel asked.

"The same question you asked your former mentor before his unfortunate death." He paused, reminiscing, a slight smirk on his face. "If you are my adversary, then your family, your friends, your enemies, they are nothing more than tools I wield at my leisure. He was right in what he told you though." Richard drew a deep breath, holding for several seconds before exhaling a visible puff of vapor into the chilly night air. "The simplest answer to why, is that I hate."

Then he was gone.

17

The drive to Atlanta proved uneventful. He had left late enough to avoid the worst of the morning traffic, early enough to miss afternoon rush hour, and paid cash for a room five miles from downtown. He planned on heading out around ten that evening, his first stop Vince's favorite hangout, a dive called The Moonlight Bar. Allowing time for a shower gave him seven hours to grab a burger then a long nap. He needed sleep to pull this off without getting himself killed. The nap refreshed him, and with a new sense of purpose he drove down Cleveland Avenue.

If Ben remembered correctly, he needed to take the next right. After that, he had about a mile of government housing and hooker lined streets to get through. He'd only been there once, over a year ago, but that time Vince drove, and it wasn't raining. Without thinking, he checked the fuel gauge and door locks.

Several minutes later he pulled into the gravel lot, found a spot near the edge and backed in. He watched the building for several minutes, trying to burn the layout into his mind in case his adventure turned ugly.

The steady rain and lack of outdoor lighting hindered visibility, except for when the occasional burst of lightning lit up the sky. He counted a dozen cars in the front lot and at least three stashed in the alley that ran along the side of the building. He didn't know how many more sat in the employee lot out back. The place looked even sketchier than he remembered. Graffiti and a half-lit neon sign showcased the front. Eddie certainly wasn't spending his money on upkeep.

A big guy wearing jeans and a light jacket camped out beneath the front awning. A steady stream of smoke rolled up from his right hand. In a place like this, it could be anything.

Ben didn't notice anyone else outside until lightning arched across the sky and illuminated a lone figure creeping amongst the cars in the alley. Looking for an unlocked door, maybe a purse left in someone's passenger seat, but the darkness returned within a second, and the figure vanished into a sea of black. He should have bought a gun. Too late now.

Ben returned his focus to the front door and rehearsed his plan. Find Vince without drawing attention. Feel him out about Eddie's intentions and willingness to bargain. Offer the stolen Murphy data as payment. Eddie could make a bundle with the information stored on the thumb drive in his left pocket. If fate had an ounce of mercy, he would spot Vince right away. If not, he would leave the bartender word an old friend asked about him, one he had called a few days ago, and to meet him tomorrow at noon. No names, and he would know where. If they worked for Eddie they'd know how to get in touch with Vince, and the vagueness wouldn't bother them in the least. Of course, they could just as easily pass the message straight to the boss, and he could end up dead within the hour. It was a chance he had to take. He hoped his instincts would be enough to save him.

The night sky exploded, this time a series of silent flashbulbs revealed the city outline. Instinctively, Ben peered into the alley. The figure had disappeared. No surprise though, this wasn't the kind of neighborhood you wanted to get caught messing with a stranger's ride. They certainly wouldn't call the cops. Cops weren't welcome in this kind of hood.

Ben turned his attention back to the front door. The big guy, now finished with his smoke, leaned against the wall, arms folded, hard stare on his face. Probably a bouncer. Ben knew if he stayed in the car much longer he might arouse the guy's curiosity enough for him to investigate, which would complicate his plan of discreetly locating Vince. Enough stalling, time to suck it up. Ben stepped into the rain and closed the door. He turned to the building, and a blunt object jabbed him in his lower back.

"We gonna do this nice and easy boy."

Ben froze. Thick fingers reached into his back pocket and lifted his wallet.

"Don't you go turnin around when you do it, but I want you to ease your hand into your front pocket there, and get me those keys."

Cold drops slid down his forehead and across his eyes. Mr. Bouncer leaned against the wall and lit another smoke. For a moment, Ben wondered why he hadn't rushed inside to call the cops about one of the locals giving some suburbanite a real inner city welcome, but the thought left almost as fast as it had come. Mr. Bouncer had seen it all before, and as long as it stayed outside it wasn't any of his business right? Might even know the guy and expect part of the haul. That's the way the world worked, I watch out for mine, and you watch out for yours.

"I said give me the keys boy. You drunk or stupid?"

Rage overcome Ben. He hadn't come this far, risked everything, all to be jacked by some two-bit street thug. His hands balled into fists, refusing to obey his head. He exhaled, and from deep inside he answered. "No."

Hard rain smacked the roof of his car, and Ben wondered...no, he expected the next sound to be the crack of the pistol. Several seconds passed, until finally the voice spoke. "What did you say?"

He turned around slowly. "I said no. You can't have my keys." Ben recognized confusion on the man's face immediately. "You can't have my keys, and you can't have my wallet you low life piece of-"

The click of the pistol's hammer cut Ben's words short, as cold wet steel pressed against his forehead. "You going to die tonight boy." But the man, not much older than Ben, froze, pistol cocked, hesitant to deliver on his promise.

"No I'm not." The calm in his voice surprised him because the rage hadn't subsided.

The sky lit up once again, offering a clear look into the man's eyes. What he saw was unmistakable. Fear. The muzzle of the pistol trembled against his skin, sending tiny droplets of water across his field of vision and onto his nose. The man was afraid, possibly stoned. Likely both.

Slowly, deliberately, Ben reached up and wrapped his fingers around the wet barrel. Part of him expected to die, but the more intuitive part knew he wouldn't. The fear in the thug's eyes wasn't the kind that prodded cowards to bravery, or drove a cornered animal to attack. It was a paralyzing fear. The kind of terror induced when, in an instant, the brain has processed a thousand scenarios, and conceded that neither fight nor flight is an option.

Ben took the pistol, turned it around, lifted it six inches, and centered it on the punk's left eye.

Thoughts of Vince, Eddie, Jill, this whole mess, faded into the deep recess of his mind. All that mattered was this thief who dared to threaten his plan. The plan would make it all okay again.

"Listen, I was just trying to get some money for rent." The man's cold tone gave way to a pitiful plea. "I wasn't gonna do nothing, I swear. Man I got kids."

"On your knees."

"What? Hey man, no don't do this. Please man, I got a baby girl."

"Get on your knees." Ben thought he saw a tear slide down the man's cheek but he couldn't be sure. Maybe it was rain. Gravel crunched when the man dropped. His eyes begged for mercy.

Ben heard someone call out from behind but couldn't make out what they said. He didn't care about the words or who shouted them. He held another man's life in his hand's, and he cared for the power. Adrenaline surged through his body as he lifted the pistol and hammered the butt down across the man's forehead. The low life toppled over.

Vaguely aware of footsteps running up behind him, Ben reached down and picked up his wallet, then slid the pistol into his pocket.

"What'd you do? He dead?"

Ben turned to the man. Mr. Bouncer.

"I saw the whole thing. I was going to call the cops for you."

Ben knew the idiot was lying.

"Is he dead? I mean did you kill him?" The bouncer talked fast.

"No, but when I leave you should call an ambulance." The man was alive for now, but even in the dark Ben noticed a wide gash below his hairline.

"Sure man." The bouncer looked back over his shoulder. "What am I supposed to tell the police?"

"I don't care what you tell them. All I want is to get a message to a friend of mine. You might know him; he works for Eddie."

That got the bouncer's attention.

"Sure, whatever you need."

"You know Vince?"

"Tall, slender guy? Tattoo of Ace of Spades on his neck?" The bouncer eyed him cautiously.

"That's him."

"Yeah, I've worked with him a couple of times."

"Tell him an old friend is in town and needs to talk. If he doesn't know who you're talking about, tell him it's the one he called last week. Tell him to meet me at noon tomorrow. He'll know where."

Ben stepped around the crumpled body and opened his car door. "Oh, and one more thing, unless you want Eddie to know you let a thief roam his parking lot looking for ways to steal from his customers, you'll keep this between you, me, and Vince. Eddie might think it would be bad for business, and we both know how he feels about things that are bad for business."

***

SLEEP DIDN'T COME easy for Ben that night. The rush hadn't died but a few Benzos and a cold beer helped him along. He dreamed of the man in the parking lot. His name was Alfred Brown, and he had told the truth about needing money for rent. He also needed food for his kids, three-year-old Alice and five-year-old Kennan. They hadn't eaten in two days. The most vivid part of his dream however was Alfred's eyes when he turned to face him. Eyes wide and afraid. The paralyzing kind of fear. Not anger or even surprise. Terror. Then lightening flashed, and in a split second of illumination, Ben glimpsed an image, a reflection. In the mirror of Alfred's eyes, he saw the image of a monster, lips snarled into a hideous grin. A grin full of jackal teeth.

18

Ben recognized his old friend immediately upon entering Wilson's Tavern. Only he wasn't sure if the term *friend* still applied. He spotted him lounging in a corner booth near the back, by the restrooms. Ben hated the booths by the restrooms. The stench always found its way out, no matter how strong the air freshener.

Most patrons sat scattered at random tables eating burgers, fried chicken, or one of the other dozen dead animals on the menu. No salads here, not even for the lunch crowd. The smell of grease and blue collar living hung heavy in the air. A few men, dressed in work coveralls, loitered at the bar laughing. No one took special notice of him.

Vince looked up and saw him about the time he'd made it past the first table and waved him back. He hadn't changed much in a year, though the ponytail was new.

"Long time no see, Ben my man." His calm tone didn't help Ben's nerves.

Ben slid into the booth "Yeah, what's it been, a year?"

"At least. It was good hooking back up with you at the show in Marietta. Man, I saw you, all tricked out in a suit and tie and thought, my boy did good."

"You look like you're doing okay," Ben lied.

"Yeah, I've got some things going down," Vince said, mindlessly fingering the sugar packets crammed into the little container by the napkin dispenser. "So why didn't you call me back?"

"I didn't get the message." Ben didn't know how much information he wanted to offer; not yet anyway. He certainly wasn't going to lead with Kat's murder. Not even with an old friend like Vince.

"I called about a week ago and left a message with your secretary. Hot sounding little thing. You and her got something going on?"

"Vince, I need your help figuring out what to do about Eddie. I came across some information he may be interested in. I'm hoping we can work a deal, but I wanted to lay it out to you first. I'm in deep."

"What are you talking about?" The look on Vince's face told Ben all he needed to know about his involvement with Eddie's recent collection practices. He was clueless.

"Someone's been harassing me for the past week. They broke into my house, busted out a window a couple of nights later, and then, a few days ago, they got a neighborhood kid to drop this off at my door." He pulled the necklace out of his jacket and slid it to Vince.

"What's this?"

"You tell me. It belonged to Kat, the girl from my office you talked to the other day." Ben laid the folded note on the table. "They found her dead."

"Dude, what have you gotten into?" Vince picked it up and spoke the word scrawled across the page. "Murderer. Look Ben, I don't know who sent this to you, but I promise it wasn't Eddie."

"What do you mean 'it wasn't Eddie'? I'm in to him for fifty grand, I missed my last two payments and have been dodging him ever since. It's Eddie, and if you can't see that you're..." He stopped before he said something he'd regret. Snapping at his only connection to the boss wasn't in his best interest. Not to mention Vince was a friend...Maybe a friend, he reminded himself.

"I'm what?" Vince leaned forward, hand's folded on the table.

"Nothing. It's been a rough couple of weeks, that's all." How could he make Vince understand the urgency? He didn't have skin in the game. His business wasn't in jeopardy. His home wasn't at stake. He didn't have a wife who had abandoned him and a kid that hated him. A lunatic wasn't busting out his windows or sending kids to his front door with gifts from the grave. "I need to know about Eddie. That's all. Anything you can tell me."

"Eddie's dead," Vince said, and slid the note back across the table.

"He's what?"

"He's dead. That's what I called you about. Keeled over a couple of weeks ago. Massive heart attack. Died in the john. I told your girl on the phone. She was supposed to tell you." The look on Vince's face might have passed for amusement. "I guess she never got around to it."

"No, that can't be right. All this started a little over a week ago. I even mentioned Eddie to the bouncer last night. He didn't say anything about him dying."

Vince cut him off. "It's the truth. His son Eddie Jr. took over the operation, guess he thought you meant him. Good kid but not as bright as his dad. Better in some ways, worse in others. His dad was ruthless. Eddie junior is...let's just say he ain't the brightest bulb in the pack." Vince leaned toward him. "Anyway, you're my boy so I pulled you from the books. Looks like you and Eddie Stillwater never had any dealings what so ever."

Ben's mind whirled, trying to validate the timeline. "But how? I mean how can you make that kind of cash disappear. What about bank records or his accountant's books? What about-"

"Bank records?" Vince laughed loud enough to turn the heads of several of the men seated a few booths away. "You kidding me? Eddie kept the kind of business he did with you in one place, his personal notebook. You really think he reported that as income on his taxes? He didn't even keep those files in his computer.

"How'd you get it?"

"Easy. Eddie Jr. asked me to go through it with him and give him a run down. He didn't have a clue who owed his dad what. At least the one's he dealt with in cash. Took most of the night, and Junior kept telling me to slow down so he could take his own notes. About halfway through he got a call and took it outside. I thumbed through it until I found the page with your

162

name. Actually you had several pages, but I got them all and stuffed them in my pocket. When I got home, I flushed them."

"Eddie Jr. got you to help him with the books?" Ben tried to grasp the implications of Vince's story. "Why? I mean, no offense, but..." Ben tried to think of how to say it. "I didn't know you were that high up the ladder."

Vince laughed even harder this time, initiating more curious looks. "Hey man, right place, right time." He pulled a pack of smokes from his pocket, coaxed one out, and slid it behind his ear. "Trying to quit."

Ben gave an understanding nod even though he'd never picked up the habit, and Vince continued without prompting. "Anyway, it's no big deal. I knew daddy wouldn't be running the show forever. A man that fat has got to have some health problems, so I covered for junior a couple of times when he screwed up, kept him out of hot water with his old man. What can I say? He likes me."

Ben heard a faint rustling sound and realized his hands were shaking, rubbing the cuff of his jacket.

"So it's done? I'm free and clear with Eddie?"

"Senior and Junior. You never existed buddy." Vince reclined and stretched his arms across the back of the booth.

"Thank you Vince. Thank you, thank you. You don't know what this means to me."

"No problem dude. Like I said, you're my boy. But what about this?" Vince slid the necklace back across the table. "You obviously owe somebody. Who else are you into it with?"

The weight, momentarily lifted by Vince's revelation, crashed down on him like a boulder. Cool sweat materialized on his forehead, and the room shifted. He stumbled out of the booth as saliva filled his mouth, glad the toilet was only a few feet away.

***

BEN WASTED THE afternoon in his motel room. He ordered pizza and finished the whole thing in one sitting. Jill definitely wouldn't approve. Nor would she approve of the fifth of whiskey he'd put a good dent in over the past several hours. He didn't care. Here in this thirty dollar a night dump, complete with transvestite lobby clerk running the front desk, he didn't need the mask. He was tired of the mask.

He paced the stained strip of carpet at the foot of the bed. Though he had closed the blinds, dirty rays of the setting sun seeped through several busted panels. It didn't make sense. Kat's murder, the pictures, the window, and most of all this. He stroked the dove charm mindlessly.

Outside, a shout broke his trance. He walked to the door, double checked the lock, then over to the nightstand and opened the drawer. He pulled the small revolver out and turned it over in his hands. The spots of blood on the butt fascinated him. He didn't know why. Blood had never bothered him or intrigued him either way, but now, holding the .38, stained with the blood of a stranger, he was enthralled. He could have killed the man, but he didn't. He'd shown mercy. He'd held life in his hands and chose to allow life to continue. He wasn't a murderer.

From the breezeway another shout, louder this time, and the sound of crashing glass. Probably some pimp setting one of his girls straight. He needed a plan but couldn't begin to formulate one until he knew what he was up against. The half-empty fifth caught his eye, but he couldn't lose it now. Got to stay straight, have all of his faculties if he had any chance of figuring this out. How much time had passed since his lunch meeting with Vince? Five hours? Six?

Get it together. Think.

The more pieces of the puzzle he tried to assemble, the more distorted the image appeared. He found a complimentary notepad in the nightstand, sat on the edge of the bed and jotted possible enemies.

He scanned the short list. He'd kept his nose clean and avoided bad company, with Eddie the obvious exception. No one on the list hated him enough to want him or his family dead. At least he didn't think so.

Sounds from the street grew louder as he fought to piece together a scenario that made sense. Obscenities flew from outside his window and he drew the revolver close to his side. A siren screamed past, followed by more shouting.

He had to get home, but first he had to call Jill. Make sure she stayed away from the house. She needed to be as far away as possible until he could figure this out. He dialed her number, and it went straight to voice-mail. He slammed the phone on the bed without leaving a message, reached for the whisky, but pulled back.

Got to stay straight. Think clear.

He redialed the number but this time spoke. "On my way home. Stay away from the house until I see you. I'll explain everything then. It's all going to work out."

Twenty minutes and a cold shower later, he pulled out of the motel parking lot. The shower proved an ineffective remedy for a half bottle of whisky, but what choice did he have? He'd give anything for a cup of black coffee, even Jill's, but the last thing he needed was an over-zealous clerk to call the cops and tip them off to a potential drunk roaming the streets. He hated clerks.

19

Araphel followed the two boys up the trail and onto the bluff. He would give anything for the opportunity to jerk the little one up by his hair and toss him over the cliff. If it weren't for the two Guardians by his side he would do it, Rules or no Rules. He wasn't sure how he'd managed to get so close before without a fight. He hated the boy, but he had to maintain control, had to operate within The Rules. He hated The Rules even more than he hated the boy, and today the cripple would live. This afternoon he wanted the other, the one without a Guardian, the fruit of the pretender. He would live too, he'd have to make sure, but the pain would come.

Araphel had followed the boys most of the day. The cripple grew stronger by the week and somehow had managed to bond with the unprotected one. It didn't surprise him. He had always marveled at the way they forgave. Forgiveness wasn't a sentiment he understood.

He almost intervened during their lunch when Daniel began talking about his father, but decided the time wasn't right. He had spent thirteen years planning, cultivating, warring with Guardians, and he had no intention of throwing it away now by being stupid. He jumped onto the bluff, still twenty feet from the boys, prompting one of the Guardians to step toward him.

"No further."

Araphel didn't recognize him. "I do not wish to fight," he said. "I have no interest in your charge today."

The Guardian towered over Araphel, much bigger than Daniel's standard protector, but he had defeated bigger. What were even two of The Author's warriors against him, a Prince. Even the great Michael had called in reinforcements against him once.

"Leave now." The second Guardian stepped into position beside the first.

"Why would I listen to a servant? If I remember correctly, it was you who left your charge not too long ago and allowed me free access."

"The ways of The Author aren't for you to understand demon."

"Demon? Such a nasty term don't you think? So spiteful. We were brothers once, remember? I simply chose to free myself from bondage."

The two Guardians drew their swords, and on reflex Araphel summoned his own. The hint of a smile played on his lips. "You don't want this today my friends. You can't win this fight." Araphel sheathed his sword and spread his hands out to his side. "Besides, I say again, I am not here for your charge."

***

DANIEL HEARD THE warning before he saw it. It sounded like someone had dumped a thousand BB's into a plastic drum. A bone chilling sound. He froze, scanned the ground, and spotted the rattlesnake coiled on a rock six feet away. "Don't move," he said, without taking his eyes off of the serpent. The hair on his arms tingled to life, and he felt Preston stop behind him.

"Where is it?" Preston asked.

Daniel pointed to the flat rock, about the size of his sleeping bag. The sound intensified as Preston stepped up beside him. "Man, I've never seen one in real life. A rattlesnake I mean. Have you?"

"Yeah," Daniel whispered. "Take a slow step back and it'll crawl away."

Daniel eased back, but instead of following, Preston bent over and picked up a good size stick.

"What are you doing?" Adrenaline raced through Daniel's body and he had to force himself not to run.

Preston circled around Daniel, eyes focused on the serpent, stick held close to his chest. "I just want to mess with it a little. Don't worry, I've done it before with a Corn Snake. I know what I'm doing." He inched further past Daniel and stopped a quarter way around the rock, in between the snake and the bluff. A black, forked tongue flicked in and out as it lifted its body from a tightly coiled position to one ready to strike. Its head wavered back and forth between the two boys before finally stilling on Preston.

"Don't!" Daniel barely got the word out when Preston poked the stick forward.

The strike came fast and long. Daniel tried to call out a warning, but it was over before he could shout the first syllable. Lunging forward, the snake flew past the end of the stick, landed inches away from Preston's shoe, then retreated under a small log next to the rock.

Daniel jumped at the sound of skidding gravel and scoured the ground around his feet, sure another snake had crawled into the mix.

He jumped again when Preston screamed.

It happened so fast that for a brief second he thought the Rattlesnake had found its mark. Then he saw. Preston clawed at loose dirt and rock, desperately trying to keep himself from sliding off the bluff.

Daniel ran to him, careful not to trip and go flying over the edge himself. "Give me your hand."

Preston tried to reach, lost considerable ground in the process, and grabbed again for a hold. Daniel threw himself on his stomach and reached over. He caught a hand, struggled to pull him back to safety but didn't have the strength. Preston's scream echoed through the valley below. He thought he could save him but his fingers brushed the top of his shirt, and he grabbed air. He was gone. The scream ended abruptly with a faint thud.

"Preston!" Daniel peered over the edge, rocks scraping against his chest. "Preston!"

The figure, forty feet below, didn't answer.

Daniel scooted backward, away from the edge, and rose to his feet. Uncle Mike. He had to get to his uncle. Working his way through the underbrush, he made it to the main trail. He hoped his foot would hold out for the half mile back to camp.

It did, and he started calling for Mike a hundred yards from the tents.

"Help! Uncle Mike, Help! He fell!"

Mike emerged from a tent and ran to meet him. "Slow down. What happened?"

Daniel rested his hands on his knees and struggled for air. "He fell. Over the edge. Preston fell."

Mike grabbed him by the shoulders and pulled him upright. "Preston went over the cliff?"

Daniel could only nod.

Mike fished Becky's phone from his front pocket and held it up for a better look. "No signal. Come on."

He took off toward the path that led to the truck, and Daniel followed.

They ran hard. Daniel could have sworn someone had plunged a spear into his side. The mile run to the truck took fifteen minutes, but once Mike shifted into gear, the tires threw dirt and pebbles as they fishtailed down the old logging trail.

"Here." Mike handed Daniel the phone. "You know how to use this better than me. Let me know when you've got a signal."

The status remained 'No Service' for several minutes. He kept a tight grip as the truck rolled up and over shallow trenches, the bottom scraping along the crests.

Five minutes later the 'No Service' status disappeared, replaced by a single bar. Then it was gone.

"Anything yet?" A Styrofoam cooler flew from the bed when Mike gunned the engine, and the truck bounced through a mud hole.

"Almost."

A moment later the truck broke through the cover and onto smooth asphalt.

"We got a signal. Two bars."

"Call 911," Mike said, and slammed the brakes.

20

Ben made good time north of Kennesaw. Light traffic and the effect of southbound headlights numbed his mind. Maybe it was the whisky, he didn't care, another hour and he'd be pulling in his driveway. The sound of crunching gravel jarred Ben from his daze, and he pulled the wheel to the left, bringing his car back into his lane. Have to focus.

Twenty minutes later he exited the interstate, turned left off the ramp, and headed toward Highway 27. The next twenty miles would be nothing but forest and the occasional mailbox. He rolled down the driver side window despite the cold night. Anything to help him stay awake and focus.

Ten minutes and halfway through this leg of his journey, oncoming headlights pierced the darkness ahead of him. He redoubled his concentration efforts and checked his speed. A DUI would be disastrous, but within seconds the headlights passed without incident, and Ben relaxed.

From beside him, his phone rang. Ben reached into the passenger seat, grabbed it, and checked the number.

Not one he recognized. Given his already impaired condition he decided not to answer. They could leave a message.

Ben tossed the phone into the seat, glancing away for only a moment, but a moment was all it took. Seemingly from nowhere, his headlights illuminated a figure standing fifty yards ahead, straddling the double-yellow line. Ben slammed his brakes, but the thing didn't flinch. Without thinking, Ben jerked the wheel to the right, skidded through the shoulder, and off the road. The car slid toward the tree line and took out a rail fence. Ben braced for the blow, as his Volvo sheared a small pine and fishtailed into a much larger oak. The airbag snapped Ben's head back into the headrest, and an instant later the impact of the tree threw him sideways into the doorframe.

He didn't know how long he was out, seconds, maybe minutes. Maybe not at all, simply lingering on the edge of consciousness, never crossing the threshold into nothingness. What he did know was that his head throbbed, and from the sticky warmth by his ear, he figured he'd sustained a pretty bad gash. He reached up and drew back bloody fingers. "Not bad," he mumbled, but he thought he might need stiches.

A voice from outside the window startled him. "Quite a show. We'll need to patch up your head, but other than that you'll be fine."

The voice sounded familiar, but he couldn't place it. The figure blended into the night.

"What happened?" Ben asked, purely out of custom.

"It seems you've had quite the accident." The figure made no move to help Ben out of his car. Ben thought he sounded eerily calm.

"You were in the road. I swerved to keep from hitting you." Ben's memory gained momentum. "Listen, I've got to go. I've got to get home now. Got to warn my wife."

"That might be a problem. You've lost your ride."

His voice.

Ben struggled with his seatbelt, punched the release, and shoved it to the side. He was angry. No, he was livid. He had to get home. Ben shoved against the door with his shoulder, and it popped open, spilling him to the ground. In an instant he was up, revolver in hand.

"I said I've got to get home now!" The choler in his voice surprised even him. He'd often wondered if he had the guts to die for his family, but at this moment he knew he'd kill for them.

Ben whirled around to face the stranger, gun leveled shoulder high. The instant their eyes met, the revolver fell to his side.

"Actually Ben, you're right on time. Come, we have a lot to chat about."

***

BEN'S HEAD SWAM as he sat in his Great Room. He thinks he slept while Slick drove the rest of the way to his house. Maybe he'd passed out from the alcohol still in his system or the blow to his head, he wasn't sure. Come to think of it, he wasn't sure about much. None of it made sense, and Slick, or whatever his name was, hadn't spoken a word the entire ride.

The man pulled a Queen Anne to in front of the sofa and eased into the chair. "I assume you have questions."

At first Ben didn't acknowledge the statement. The whole scene felt surreal, and the man didn't press. He seemed content with the silence. After a few moments, Ben was not.

"Who are you? And what do you want?"

"Ah, my friend, the two most relevant questions. One, so complex you could never comprehend its depth; the other so simple even a child could answer." He considered Ben then continued. "We'll start with the complex and I'll try to simplify it so your pitiful mind can grasp enough to move us to the next question."

Ben leaned forward, sure he was going to vomit all over his Persian rug, but his stomach held its peace.

The man continued. "You may call me anything you wish, but my given name is Araphel, and I've walked this earth since its creation."

The words didn't register with Ben. He searched for the revolver on his right hip.

"It wouldn't do you any good. Here, see for yourself." Araphel pulled the gun from his jacket and handed it to him. "Take it. Shoot me in the heart. Or the head for that matter. You would certainly kill this body, his name is Richard by the way, but I wouldn't be harmed. It's simply a matter of slipping out. Like taking off a jacket," he said and removed his. "But I should warn you, if you do force me out of this body, we're still going to have our chat, only then it won't be with the handsome young executive type sitting across from you. I promise, you don't want that."

The gun grew heavy, and he lowered it to his lap. The man's words didn't process in Ben's mind. Walked this earth since its creation. Like taking off a jacket. None of it made sense. It had to be the wreck. The impact had sent his head into the door causing a concussion. Might even be a fractured skull. Surely those caused hallucinations. Or, if he was lucky, it was the whisky, still hitching a ride through his blood, showering his brain with nonsense. If so, this was the worst buzz he had ever caught.

Ben scanned the room for something real, something his mind could cling to and ground him in reality. His eyes landed on the picture of Jill and Preston. It hung on the wall over the man's shoulder. A tidal wave of rage washed over him again, and he screamed. "NO!" He centered the revolver on the man for only an instant before it flew from his grip, knocked away by an unseen hand. Ben felt a sharp yank on the top of his head, followed by the sudden sensation of flying. Pain shot through his back when he slammed into the wall behind the sofa. First his right, then his left arm snapped back against the sheetrock, perpendicular to his body. The only thing that reassured him his scalp remained intact was the feel of a hand gripping his hair and slowly twisting his head back and forth.

The man in the chair rose to his feet, retrieved the gun, then looked up at him.

"I told you. You don't want to have this conversation that way. When I must engage your wretched species in business, it is necessary I play the part so to speak. I find it helps put simple minds at ease. And Richard here fits the business type very well don't you think?"

Ben struggled to free his arms from the vice pinning him to the wall, but they wouldn't budge.

"Now for your second question, 'what do I want'?" A smirk spread across Richard's face. "I want blood Ben. A payment for what you owe."

Ben lost control of his bladder, and the demon laughed.

The grip on his hair released, and he dropped two feet to the floor, and crumpled into a fetal position.

"You see, fourteen years ago you failed the one simple task I required of you, leaving you in debt to me. Now the time has come to collect on that debt." Richard said, his tone all business, his demeanor relaxed; arms hanging in front, hands clasped.

Ben tried to speak, but a parched mouth left his tongue virtually useless. Task? Fourteen years ago?

Richard continued, "You allowed a life to continue which began a chain of events that has hindered much of my work. Now a price must be paid. Blood must be shed. A sacrifice must be made." Richard chuckled. "You get the idea."

Ben attempted to stand but his knees buckled. He plopped back against the wall. "Do I have a choice?" His words barely audible.

"Of course you have a choice. In fact, you have three."

***

BEN LEANED FORWARD on the edge of the sofa, head hung, eyes closed, contemplating how he had allowed this thing into the lives of his wife and son.

Finally, he raised his head and forced himself to look at the man he preferred to think of as Richard. "Before we go on, can I ask one more question?"

"By all means."

"It was you wasn't it? The pictures, smashing my window, Kat's necklace." Ben paused. "Kat. You killed her didn't you? You followed us from the bar, and then you killed her."

Richard sat without speaking or breaking his stare. Ben tried willing himself to do the same but failed. "Are you going to answer me?"

"The whys are much more complicated than the whats, but as for Kat, a most unfortunate casualty. I wanted you in Atlanta, so I couldn't let her pass along the news of Eddie's demise could I? I need you in a certain mindset for what you are about to face. If it's any consolation, I had other plans in mind for you and her, plans I believe you would have enjoyed, but it wasn't meant to be. Unfortunately, Mr. Stillwater's heart gave out sooner than I expected, forcing me to alter my approach. Honestly, I was looking forward to seeing how you would handle a face to face with the man." Richard smiled, relaxed in the chair, and cocked his head. "It was a lesson Ben. A lesson in self-discovery. A lesson in choices. You chose yourself over your family. You should have seen little Preston's face when you didn't show."

"Leave my family out of this! Everything I did, I did for them!" Ben wanted to attack the man, wrap his hands around his throat and squeeze until no breath remained. But this wasn't a man was it? Whatever this thing was, he couldn't kill it any more than he could take back time. He closed his eyes, trying to calm himself, to clear his mind so he could sort illusion from reality. Monsters aren't real. Strangers don't appear in the middle of the road and drive you home, then pin you to the wall with only a look.

But this one had, and more.

The anger slowly abated, allowing fear to reclaim its spot at the forefront of his emotions. "How did you know what I'd do?"

"More than one question, but I'll indulge you." He paused and studied Ben. "Instinct."

"What?"

"Instinct Ben. That's how I knew, how I know. Does a spider need someone to teach it the art of spinning a web?"

Ben wiped his forehead, and found he couldn't hold the man's gaze. His eyes settled again on the picture of Jill and Preston. A glimmer of courage welled up and threatened to spill over. An echo of the man he used to be.

"If you're going to kill me do it now. Just please, don't hurt my wife or son."

"Ah, the good man is starting to raise his head. But you're not a good man Ben, you never were. I've been with you since that fat doctor ripped you from your dear mother's womb."

Richard leaned closer. So close Ben smelled the odor of rotting meat on his breath.

"I was with you the first time you snuck out and spied on little Elizabeth Ridley. Do you remember her? Of course you do, because twenty years later you still dream about her. Dreams you would never share with

Jill. The kind of dreams society frowns upon. How about the time you choked the life out of Mrs. West's cat? You wanted to see how it felt to kill with your bare hands didn't you? I tried to convince you Elizabeth would be more satisfying, but you were too much of a coward. Much like that night fourteen years ago. The night that has brought us to this moment."

The monster leaned back in his seat, closed his eyes and continued with a flick of his wrist. "Enough. I am giving you a choice Ben. A courtesy I rarely afford, but circumstances dictate I must."

Richard opened his eyes. The smell of death lingered.

"Your transgressions against me require a sacrifice. A sacrifice to me. Your death will fulfill that obligation, but The Rules dictate I cannot be the one to take it. You must do it by your own hand. That is your first option."

Ben's guts turned over, and he swallowed hard.

"You may give me your son, and I will take his life in return for yours. That is your second option. The simplest I think. He may never wake up anyway. Nasty fall he took today. Lots of internal damage. Your wife tried to call you from the hospital, but you chose not to answer. You should have heard him scream before he hit the ground. But not to fear, he's alive. At least for now. Pity you weren't there for him." Richard smiled revealing a row of unnaturally white teeth.

"What did you do to my son you-" Ben lunged at the man, but before he cleared the edge of the sofa his head snapped back. The sensation of being scalped returned, then a slight prick on his throat and claw tracing a line across his skin.

Richard looked at him with what might pass for amusement.

"Don't worry, it's not deep enough to kill. Against The Rules remember? Can we continue our business?"

Ben managed a slight nod, and the pull on his hair released.

"Your third option is to offer the one that would have never been born if you obeyed me on that night. A boy named Daniel. Since he is not your flesh, you have no power to give him to me so that I can handle the deed myself. You must make the sacrifice. Again, The Rules." Richard leaned back in the chair and folded his arms.

"You want me to kill a boy? What kind of monster are you? If you want him dead do it yourself. You don't seem to be the kind of person who cares about rules and I'm not a murderer."

"Yes you are Benjamin. You are a murderer. I know all of the dusty skeletons tucked away in the back of your closet. And concerning The Rules, there is no discussion."

"Give me the gun. Give it to me."

"So you've chosen?"

"Give it to me!"

Richard held the revolver out to him, and without hesitation, Ben took it and closed his mouth over the barrel. He forced himself not to circle his tongue around the muzzle. He straightened his head, searched for the picture of his family, found it, then closed his eyes. The last thing he saw on this earth wouldn't be this monster. Cold steel rattled against his teeth.

Not like this. Not the way his dad did it.

He pulled the pistol from his mouth and pressed it against his right temple. It settled into the soft spot behind his eye.

Just do it. Do it now and end this nightmare. Ben slid his finger to the trigger, touched the curvature, and applied slight pressure. Squeeze and end the pain. Do it and save your son.

Ben screamed and let his hand fall to the sofa. He couldn't do it. He wouldn't let Preston suffer like he did when his dad killed himself.

He began to sob.

"I see you are not choosing the first option." Richard flicked a moth from his wrist. "Coward."

Ben stared at the blurry figure sitting across from him but didn't answer…couldn't answer.

"So, we're down to two. Your son or the woman's son."

"What woman? What boy?" Ben slumped forward, still hoping he would wake up and find Jill snoring softly beside him. "I think you've got the wrong guy."

Richard didn't speak. He didn't flinch, or smile, or blink. He waited.

A flash of inspiration offered Ben a glimpse of hope, a possible loophole to squirm through before the noose tightened around his neck. "What if I refuse? You said you can't kill, and I have to willingly give you my son. What if I refuse to make a choice?"

The monster immediately tightened the knot. "You misheard what I said, so listen carefully." The color in Richard's eyes melted from dark brown to white, and Ben recoiled in terror. Maybe it was his imagination, a trick the mind sometimes plays when the veil between reality and make-believe is razor thin. A cheap parlor trick of the psyche. He bit his tongue, hoping the pain would thrust him out of this nightmare, but it didn't help as Richard continued. "Make no mistake, I am dangerously adept at killing. It is the ritual of sacrifice that is the point. If you refuse to choose, I will kill your son while you and your wife watch. Then I will kill her. You, I will let live and go to prison for their murders. I will do everything in my power to keep you alive. I will visit you each night when you close your eyes, and you will dream of what I did to them and why."

"The third." The words sounded far off even though they came from Ben's own mouth.

"Good Ben, that's good."

"Who is he? I mean who is this boy?"

Richard stood from the chair. "Like I said, his name is Daniel and you'll know him when you see him. Please don't make me keep repeating myself."

"Know him? What do you mean 'know him'?"

"His eyes my friend, you'll know it's him when you see his eyes." He signaled for Ben to stand. "Now let me take you to your wife and son. It's the least I could do."

21

The cool glass refreshed Ben as he rested his head on the window and let the blur of passing streetlights numb his mind. The wipers ticked a slow, steady beat, clearing the windshield of the light mist that hung in the air. He wondered if it was real. It couldn't be. He reached up, gently touched his throat and brought back a finger lightly smeared with blood. Richard was right, it wasn't deep but he'd need to change the bandage soon. It was real.

"What happened fourteen years ago?" Ben didn't break his gaze from the passing lights. "What'd I do?"

"Open the glove compartment," Richard said in a cold, calm voice.

Ben opened it and retrieved a slender wooden box. Someone had carved a hand and crude eye into its top. It looked old, ancient.

"Open it," Richard said without taking his eyes off the road.

Ben lifted the top and pulled out a large, slightly curved, knife. The eight-inch blade, polished to a mirror finish, came to an impossibly sharp point. It's cutting edge resembled a razor as it caught the glare of the streetlights. Ben turned the handle over in his hand and thought it might be ivory, but it was too light, too rough. He noted two rows of strange marks, lines and dots, etched into the sides.

"A friend gave it to me over twelve-hundred years ago." Richard brought the car to a slow stop at a red light and turned to Ben. "His name was Tynan, human yes, but a friend nonetheless. His relationship with my kind is…rare." Richard turned back to the road, and for a moment Ben thought he might not continue, but he did. "The time of the Druids was drawing to a close, he saw it coming, they all did, and we couldn't stop it. But Tynan, he knew things, saw things. Other cultures might call him a seer or prophet. Do you understand?"

Ben nodded and the light turned green.

"The night he died he told me of a vision. I won't go into details, you wouldn't understand, but I'll allow you the condensed version. I would build my empire and rise through the ranks. Friends and enemies alike would tremble at the mention of my name."

Richard pulled up to a stop sign, and Ben noticed a young man standing on the corner. The man flicked his cigarette onto the sidewalk, looked up and down the street, then stepped toward the car. He could see the butt of a pistol hanging out of the man's jacket. Ben fumbled for the controls and found the button to lock his door. The stranger bent down, knocked on the window, and reached into his pocket. Ben started to yell for Richard to floor it, but instead watched in shock as the passenger window eased down. The man, gun now in hand, leaned into the car, started to speak, froze, bowed his head, and backed away. The passenger window eased up.

Richard chuckled. "I command more soldiers than Nero and Napoleon combined."

They continued, and Ben glanced in the side mirror at the punk on the corner. His head was still bowed in a posture of reverence. "Was he one?"

"Yes, the soldier that controls him is. I don't know his name, but he knows mine." Richard glanced into the rearview mirror. "All of this Ben, everything I've built is in danger. In his vision Tynan saw it destroyed by a child. I've spent over a thousand years searching for that child."

"You found him?"

"I believe so. My search led me to your father, and by association you once you were born. I knew I was close, but I didn't know the identity until the night of your father's last tent revival. Do you remember that night? Do you remember the woman you picked out of the crowd, the one who so desperately wanted a child but was barren?"

Ben did but wished he didn't.

Richard grinned. "Of course you do. You dream about it."

"Her? The woman my father was prophesying over when he collapsed?"

"Her son, the one she miraculously brought to term. I perceived it the moment your father began to speak. I believe this is the child Tynan warned me of."

Ben fought to push the memory from his mind. "Why me? What do I have to do with any of this?"

"Our stories, yours and mine, have been interwoven since long before that night, long before you were even born." He paused, as if savoring a distant, but fond memory. "Do you remember the night you turned sixteen? Do you remember the name of the homeless man you ran down, and left to die in the middle of the street?"

Ben snapped to him, his face hot. "He was drunk. He ran out into the road!"

"Maybe," Richard nodded casually, "but do you remember what you and your friends did after?"

Ben did. They hadn't stopped, hadn't even called for help anonymously. Instead, they stole a bottle of liquor from his dad's cabinet, got drunk and gathered around his Ouija board. Nothing but a game, harmless entertainment to take their minds off the man pushing a shopping cart across 3rd Avenue. He even came up with the absurd idea of asking the board to make the whole thing go away.

It did.

Richard pulled into the hospital's parking lot. "I was the one who made the incident disappear. Ask and it shall be given, seek and ye shall find, knock and it shall be opened unto you. I believe that's how The Book says it. I had waited sixteen years for you to ask, and when you did, you indentured yourself to me. Now I have come to collect the debt."

"I still don't understand. What debt, and why now?"

"Two years after the incident concerning the homeless man, you chose the woman for healing at the tent revival. Then, after she did indeed become pregnant, I encouraged you to kill her before she delivered the

187

baby, but you resisted. You refused to heed to my voice. Once he was born, my options were limited for a time, but now he's old enough to fall under The Rules. However, I am bound by those same Rules, which requires me to think creatively. The arrangement I have made with you falls within the guidelines." He slowed, allowing an older couple to pass in front of the car, scuttling across the lot to the lobby. The gentleman's small umbrella not nearly enough to cover the both of them. "Know this Ben, I regard the child, and any damage he might bring to my kingdom, your responsibility."

"How? I just met you."

The rain fell harder now, and Richard found a spot near the entrance. He closed his eyes, exhaled slowly, and turned to Ben. "No, you need to learn to listen. I'm growing weary of repeating myself. I've known you your entire life. How do you think you and the boy ended up here together, halfway across the country from where we all first met?"

"You mean he's here? From Pine Creek?"

Richard struck a match, lit a smoke, and then tossed the flame out the window. "You have no idea of the planning, of the effort, involved. You see, The Author has his prophecies, we have ours." He took a long drag, savored the flavor and released it into the night air. "Ben, you come from a long line of humans sympathetic to our cause. I've been waiting for you for over a thousand years."

Ben started to speak, but Richard cut him off.

"Now, tell me, how did you spend your nights after that tent meeting?"

Ben fought the urge to flee the car. "What do you mean?"

Richard's eyes narrowed into dark slits. "You know perfectly well what I mean." He reached across and placed a cold hand over Ben's eyes.

The memories rushed through his mind like a decade of home movies edited down to a few seconds. He had become obsessed with the woman and learned all he could about her. Rachael Palmer, wife of Pastor Mark Palmer from Walker, Texas. They lived in a trailer park outside of town and across the street from Super Suds Laundry. No kids, but she got pregnant shortly after the night of the revival. Her brother Michael stayed in trouble with the police. Nothing major, stupid kid stuff really, but eventually ran off to Georgia with his girlfriend.

As the story unfolded in his mind, a single thought echoed beneath the surface. He had wanted to kill the woman. Every night for nearly a year he dreamed of it. Not the same dream, his method varied. Sometimes he used a knife, other times a gun or even his bare hands. Once he used an old Buick and ran her down in the driveway. The urge didn't stop once her stomach rounded over with child. It only grew. Ben had never used crack, but he could imagine how an addict must feel when they needed a bump. During that time, one thought consumed him. Kill the woman. But he didn't. He wasn't a murderer, and he told himself that over and over.

Then his dad shot himself and the urge disappeared. He never went back to the trailer park, and the dreams vanished. Weeks later, Ben left for college in Atlanta, where he would meet Jill, get her pregnant, drop out of school, and move in with her parents- all within four or five months.

Richard removed his hand and the memories faded. "Do you remember the day your father killed himself?"

"Yeah, December 21st. Four days before Christmas."

"Would it surprise you to know that was the same day the woman gave birth?"

It wouldn't, but he didn't respond.

"It shouldn't," Richard said with little inflection in his voice. "Your father was one of my most profitable servants until The Author silenced his tongue. The day Daniel was born, I decided your dad's part in my story had run its course, and the time had come for yours to begin. You failed me when you were young. Now I am giving you an opportunity to redeem yourself."

Richard motioned to the knife and Ben held it up.

"Tynan had it crafted for this one purpose. No other blood has ever wet its blade."

Ben rubbed the handle between his fingers. A warm energy passed through his hand. "What is it made of, the handle I mean? And the marks, what are they?"

Richard leaned in close, his hot breath rolled over Ben's face. "The marks are Ogham, alphabet of the Druids, and they depict two names." He pointed to one line, "Daniel," then to the other, "Benjamin."

Ben couldn't speak.

Richard leaned back and continued. "Beautiful isn't it? A Master Craftsman designed it; the best Tynan could find. I was disappointed my friend couldn't see the finished work, but at least one of his bloodline can."

Ben ran his finger across his etched name "You mean me don't you?" Ben asked the question, but he knew. The connection flowed from the marks.

"Yes, you. And as for the handle, Tynan donated his femur."

22

The surgery lasted six hours, but his boy pulled through. According to the rescue team and the doctors, it was a miracle he had survived. Trees and soft dirt had saved his life, but thirty-seven feet was still a long fall. Fourteen broken bones, collapsed lung, and lacerated liver. They took his spleen, but managed to get the swelling around his brain under control. He couldn't remember the rest. Didn't want to remember the rest, only that his son was holding his own.

The ICU, nearly deserted with the exception of a middle age woman a couple of doors down and an older man in the room beside her, smelled of antiseptic and lilac. Ben sat in the small room's only chair and listened to the whir of machines doctors insisted were keeping his son alive. He had convinced Jill to grab a bite to eat in the cafeteria, and she reluctantly agreed, but only after the surgeon assured them all went well. Now they wait.

He would give anything to do it all over. The missed ballgames and school plays. He skipped Preston's Junior High Academic Honors Banquet because a client asked him out for drinks. Jill thought it might be the only time until his wedding she'd get to see Preston dressed up. She drug him shopping to pick out the perfect ensemble, a light grey three piece with navy tie. Ben remembered because an identical suit hung in his own closet. Jill told him later nothing else would do after Preston saw it. He wanted to look like his dad, and from the pictures he did look handsome.

Ben eased to the bed and stroked his son's hand. He barely recognized him. Bandages hid most of his bruised and swollen face, allowing only a peek at the pale yellow and dark purple skin beneath. Wraps, stained with blood and antiseptic, completely covered his head. Ben thought of the man in Atlanta, Alfred Brown with two kids, three-year-old Alice and Keenan who was five. He wondered if Alfred ended up in an ICU, tethered to his own tubes and wires.

"Mr. Johnson," one of the nurses appeared at the door with a cart of supplies, "we need to change his dressings and check the catheter. You're welcome to stay, but I'll need you to step outside the door."

"No, that's okay. Do what you need to do to make him better."

The nurse, an overweight, middle age woman with tired eyes, pushed the cart to the other side of the bed. "We will. He's a fighter."

"He is." Ben leaned down and kissed his son on the forehead, the only place not bloody, bandaged or swollen. "I'll go find his mom and give her an update."

"Give us about thirty minutes, and we'll be finished," the nurse said, and began unloading rolls of clean gauze from the cart.

Ben rode the elevator to the first floor and navigated a maze of halls to the hospital's main cafeteria. The aroma of baked chicken and vegetable soup hit his senses the moment he walked through the swinging doors, a definite contrast to the sterile smell of Preston's room. He scanned the thin crowd and spotted Jill sitting with a man and woman, neither of whom he recognized.

"How is he?" Jill asked.

"The same. The nurses are changing his bandages, but they said it would only take thirty minutes or so. I think they're pretty optimistic now that the surgery is behind him."

Jill offered a tired smile. "Ben this is Mike Hill and his wife Becky."

Mike stuck out his hand. "I'm so sorry about what happened Mr. Johnson. I can't help but blame myself-" He stopped mid-sentence and gave Ben a curious look. "Have we met before?"

"I don't think so, maybe at the school?"

Jill interrupted them, "Mike, this isn't your fault, and you know it. We've went over this. It was an accident that's all. If we start playing the blame game, I could join in by saying I made him go on the trip, or Ben's to blame because..." She closed her eyes and rested her head in her hands, "Never mind. It was an accident, and the surgeons seem to think the worst is over." Jill glanced at Ben, but he couldn't read her eyes. She looked exhausted.

Mike reached across the table and took her hand. "I know. And thank you for not blaming me. He's going to be alright."

Becky patted Jill's other hand and seconded her husband's encouragement.

Jill reached to the table behind her and grabbed an extra chair for Ben.

Becky slid a napkin across the table to her. "We wanted to come and be with y'all. We'll stick around for a while to make sure you're all set."

The group chatted about everything but Preston. Mike talked about his new boss, and Becky spent five minutes giving a complete rundown on the new teller at the bank. "Sent me away with a handful of wrappers she did. Told me I had to roll all that change myself. I don't know where that floozy learned customer service, but the bank ain't been the same since Mr. Kemp sold out last year."

Finally, bored with small talk, Ben slid his chair back from the table. "They should be about finished by now." Then to Jill, "You want to go up with me?"

Jill's friends seemed okay, a little backward, but he could fake interest long enough to carry on polite conversation.

"It's okay honey, you go be with your boy," Becky said. "When Daniel gets back from the restroom we've got to get home."

Ben hesitated. "Daniel?"

"Daniel. Their nephew," Jill said, motioning to Becky and Mike. "His mom and dad died in a car wreck a couple of months ago and they took him in."

"Speak of the devil."

A boy that looked about Preston's age, but much smaller, walked up to them.

"Daniel, this is Mr. Johnson, Preston's dad. Ben, this is our nephew Daniel. He's one of Preston's friends from school."

Ben sank back into the chair. The boy had his mom's eyes. Richard was right; he'd never forget those eyes.

23

Even at eighteen years old, Ben Johnson knew his father was a fraud, not that it mattered. He had helped him with the traveling tent meetings since the summer of his freshman year of high school. After he got his license, Reverend Johnson let him drive if they didn't have to travel the interstate. By the time he turned seventeen, chauffeuring his dad from town to town became a full time summer gig. He drove and listened to whatever oldies station he could find, while his dad slept off the previous night's abuse to his liver. Good times, until the meeting in Walker, Texas.

They had left a meeting in Oklahoma the day before and stopped for the night three hours outside Walker, thirty minutes from home, and site of what turned out to be his dad's last revival. The advance team had arrived a week earlier to "prepare the soil," as his father often quipped. By the time they rolled into town, the faithful already filled the tent, cooling themselves with paper fans stapled to popsicle sticks. At least fifty more loitered around the entrance, stirring up the dirt and talking amongst themselves.

Ben usually handled sound, but that night the Reverend let him pick one of the marks, suckers his dad would bring onto the stage for *healing*. "Thought it might be a good time to start teaching you some of the subtle points of the business," he told his son. No other words of encouragement other than to point out his scar looked bright pink. "Try not to be so stressed," his father scolded. Ben reached up and traced it with his finger, a permanent reminder his dad was a mean drunk.

Ben chose the young woman before the show began. He wasn't as much drawn to her as guided. Guided, no better word. Ben watched her wait outside in the hot sun with a boy about his age, maybe a year or two older. The resemblance made Ben think little brother. Shouts echoed from inside the tent, and he knew he had to hurry. He edged closer, careful not to draw attention, hoping to overhear a nugget his dad could capitalize on. Everybody needs healing. Five minutes later, sure he had picked a winner, Ben pointed her out to his father hoping the Reverend would agree, and he did.

The Reverend's team offered to let several local choirs and solo acts provide the worship music. Standard practice for the meetings. In exchange for the opportunity to highlight their talents, most churches provided men to help his advance team set up. This way he didn't have to pay a full crew to provide the worship. It also served the added benefit of drawing a larger crowd. The Reverend Lonnie Johnson was not merely a man of God; he was a businessman.

Thirty minutes into the meeting, the Reverend took the platform. "Blessed be the Lord, brothers and sisters. Blessed be the Lord."

The crowd went wild, stirred to a frenzy by the gospel sounds of their cousins and next door neighbors.

He dressed more like a modest rancher than an evangelist, but his father had explained it well. These people worked farms, ranches, and in factories. Working class folk with a handful of immigrants scattered in for good measure. This meant they were shrewd, wise to the flashy preachers on television that used the Lord's money to buy vacation homes. It also meant they gifted in cash.

After his father recited several well-rehearsed scriptures and gave a brief but fiery homily, the real show began.

"Who believes God wants to heal them tonight?"

A few hands shot up, mostly plants from the advance team. People always needed encouragement from those with a greater measure of faith.

"I said who believes God wants to heal them tonight?" The Reverend pumped his fists in the air, playing the part of a true cheerleader for the Almighty. "Lift your praises to God. Raise your hand to heaven, and an usher will help you into line."

Ben's mark waited fifth in line that night, right behind a wheelchair, two cancers, and a heart problem. The wheelchair was a plant, one of three for this meeting. The Reverend believed in going big early. It made it easier on the ushers when basket time started four or five people into the healings, depending on the crowd's enthusiasm.

The wheelchair plant put on a marvelous show, struggling at first before flopping back into the seat. The Reverend placed his hand on her forehead and raised his face to heaven. "You gotta believe God wants to heal you sister. Ask Him to help your unbelief. Now, in the name of Jesus, rise up and walk." Plant number one, actually a woman named Linda from Oklahoma, did as commanded, slowly at first then finding her legs like a newborn colt. The crowd erupted into a symphony of praise Jesus' and Hallelujahs. And the baskets came out early.

The next three healings went as expected. Nothing flashy, but it's hard to make a show out of cancer and heart disease. The traveling evangelist and his crew would be long gone before lab tests and doctors broke the bad news. Even then, some held out hope until the end, insisting God and the Great Reverend Johnson had healed them. Idiots.

The second plant of the night, Cory, waited behind his mark on crutches. While not as dramatic as a paraplegic in a wheelchair, his healing would keep the rhythm, and the cash, flowing. Most evangelists equate oil with the Holy Spirit. Not Reverend Johnson though. When he spoke of oil, it was in the context of his show, a machine that ran because of proper lubrication. And it did, at least until that night.

Ben's mark, the woman who wanted a baby, shuffled across the platform without making eye contact with the Reverend or the crowd.

"What's your name young lady?"

"Rachael. Rachael Palmer." She said without looking up.

"Rachael, the Lord spoke to me and told me you and your husband are without child. Is this true?"

She nodded.

"And you wish to have a child, but the doctors told you it was impossible?"

The woman lifted her head and replied, and though Ben couldn't hear from across the stage, her slight nod confirmed his earlier reconnaissance.

The Reverend shot a knowing look in Ben's direction. "Sister, be of good cheer. God has spoken and informed me that you will have a child. Tonight we are going to heal your womb and introduce those doctors to the Great Physician."

A few amens sprang from around the room, and Ben noticed several of the women pulling Kleenex from their purses. Momentum had slowed, but with the second plant up next, he relaxed knowing the cheers would resume the instant Cory tossed his crutches aside. His father didn't show a hint of concern.

The Reverend laid his hand on her forehead and began the routine. "God, heal-" His words ceased mid-sentence, hand on her head, mouth gaping open. This wasn't part of the show. His father's lips moved, but it wasn't his voice that boomed through the tent.

"God has numbered your kingdom and finished it. You have been weighed in the balances and found wanting. I have divided your kingdom and given it to two servants that I will raise up in My time. In My Name."

The Reverend swept his arms across the crowd. "And it shall come to pass afterward, that I will pour out my spirit upon all flesh; and your sons and your daughters shall prophesy, your old men shall dream dreams, your young men shall see visions." He turned his head to Rachael. "Daughter, I have given you and your husband the son you desire. Evil will pursue him because your child will see through The Veil as he follows The Author. His life will spark the parched land, lighting up the night sky, and overcoming The Darkness."

Not one of the three-hundred or so people made a sound. No amens. Not a single praise God. Utter silence.

Then the Reverend screamed.

Ben watched in horror as his father fell to the stage. Not a soul moved for a few seconds. Finally, two men from the front row rushed the platform and knelt beside him. They tried to talk to him, but Ben couldn't hear what they said over the horrible sound coming from his father.

The yell of a woman near the rear snapped Ben out of his daze. "Call 911!"

Ben ran toward the kneeling men and recognized them as Ted and Marty, two of the advance team. By the time he reached them, the scream had morphed into a primal wail, his father's face twisted into a montage of emotional expressions. Ben sensed the confusion behind him, and prayed someone had a phone.

"Dad, what's wrong? Tell me what's wrong?"

The Reverend didn't respond, though the wail died to a pitiful moan.

"Dad talk to me!"

"This woman." The Reverend's lips hardly moved when he spoke.

Ben turned to his mark and their eyes met. She had the most beautiful eyes. Flecks of blue dotted her amber irises. The look on her face wasn't one of concern or fear as a young man ran to her. She gently pushed him away. For all she knew his dad was dying, and she just stood there with that peaceful look on her face...except the fire in her eyes. They told a different story as the blue and amber colors danced like flames.

She knows what's happening, Ben thought. She knows and she's happy. Without warning, he hated the woman. He didn't know her, but he hated her more than he had ever hated anything in his life. The thought of following her home and strangling the life out of her flashed through his mind. The urge came on so fast and so strong that his dad's moans faded into the background noise.

"Dad? Please say something."

The last words the Reverend spoke until his suicide eleven months later came out like a man gasping his last breath. "Son, this woman."

24

The Hill family, Mike, Becky and Daniel, walked in their front door a little after one o'clock Sunday afternoon. Brother Wendell, a fill-in for Middleton from some church over in Longview, had preached on loving thy neighbor, a topic Mike found ironic, since there didn't seem to be much love floating around Pine Creek these days. Daniel had requested prayer for Preston, whose condition was still touch and go when they left the hospital last night. Daniel's voice cracked when he told them how he tried to hold on. How he grabbed Preston's hand, then let him slip away. Nearly everyone ended up down front, kneeling by those little wooden benches, passing out tissues like they were gospel tracts. Becky, of course, made note of Missy's absence. "Probably a good thing she wasn't there. She's already got that spreading the love thing down pat," she said, as they drove home from the service.

Mike tossed a stack of mail, four days' worth, onto the coffee table, and kicked off his shoes. He hadn't wanted to go this morning, but Daniel talked him into it. Two weeks in a row, a feat he hadn't pulled off in twenty years or better, though admittedly, part of his willingness stemmed from hoping to see Missy. He hated himself for that.

"Y'all sit there and relax while I get lunch on the table." Becky leaned over and kissed Daniel on the head on her way to the kitchen.

"You need some help honey?" Mike asked, more out of guilt than anything.

"Nope," Becky said, and walked past him without looking down.

Daniel picked up a book and thumbed through the pages, while Mike fumbled in the recliner's side pocket for the remote, found it, and turned on the news.

Almost at once, the soothing voice of Ron Cole, Channel 3 weekend anchor, drowned out the silence coming from the kitchen. He wasn't sure what he had said to put her in a mood, but a good bet would be when he commented on Becky's snip about Missy spreading the love. All he'd said was "wonder where she was?" Women.

Mike picked up the pile of mail and sifted through it, tossing the first two pieces back onto the table. Junk.

"Danny, you want to help me weed this out?" Mike asked when the local news went to commercial break. "Most is junk, but pull out the bills. I'll look at them this evening."

Daniel tossed a couple of envelopes into the trash pile. "What do you want me to do with the keepers?"

"Make a separate stack," Mike said, without taking his eyes off of the new weather girl on screen. Cute, but butchering the forecast of a storm front expected to roll through in a couple of nights.

"Uncle Mike, what about this one?"

Mike glanced in Daniel's direction, but his attention remained on the newscast. "What about it?" Now the sports reporter was teasing an interview with Coach Smart about Georgia's chances of getting to the SEC title game.

"Here, look at it." Daniel held the envelope up.

"Yeah, I see it, who's it from?"

"It doesn't say. All it has is your name."

"Well, open it up and see."

After a few seconds, "Um, uncle Mike, you need to see this." Daniel forced the picture into Mike's field of vision.

He started to push Daniel's hand away, then stopped. "Where did you get that?"

"Here." Daniel held up the envelope. "There's more."

Mike snatched it from his hand, sifted through the remaining pictures, and jammed them back into the package. Images of Missy, less clothing, lingered in his mind.

"You gonna tell Aunt Becky?"

"I don't know. I mean I will, just not right now." He couldn't spring a surprise like this on Becky without preparation. "I need to figure out how to go about it."

"What do you want me to do?" Daniel asked.

"Nothing. I'll talk to her later tonight. Go tell her I'm going to wash up, and I'll be there in a minute." Mike stuffed the envelope into his back pocket, and made his way down the hall and out the side door. He didn't know how he was going to bring this up to Becky, or even if he should, but until he figured it out, the glovebox in his truck should keep them safe. With Becky's obsession with laundry, no way he was stashing them in his sock drawer. Out of the house, tucked safely away in his glovebox was the best bet.

After another quiet supper, as the last dish sounded in the sink, Mike started into the mud room off the kitchen when Becky called to him. "She called again yesterday morning. Twice, and hung up both times. She didn't say anything when I answered, but I know it was her." Mike stopped and turned, but she was already walking away.

He called after her, "I don't see why you're in a mood with me." If he ever figured out how a woman's mind worked, he'd go on a speaking tour for a month, then retire to Florida.

Storming off in the other direction, Mike gathered his tools to fix the busted latch on the screen door. A storm was coming, and the last thing he needed was for it to blow into the house.

25

Pinnacle Parts and Machine would have to make do without one of its shop foremen for the next week because Mike Hill needed a break. They would manage, but of course this time next Monday he'd be working a double to get caught up.

Becky didn't seem to care either way. She managed a lackluster "fine," when he told her he was going out for a while. He tried to lean in and kiss her bye, just like every other day for the last dozen years, but she turned her head at the last moment, and he ended up catching her on the cheek. Worse, his hasty "I love you," was countered with a flat "ditto," her standard response during the rough times after Emily's death. Times he wasn't sure he wanted to go through again.

He had two stops this morning, both in town. The first, Pine Creek Florist, didn't have the most unique name, but from what he heard, carried the prettiest flowers; much fresher than the Floral Department at Food World. His second stop, if he didn't change his mind, was only a couple of blocks from the florist.

The ten-minute drive seemed much longer this morning. His mind and eyes kept wandering to the glovebox and the secret stashed under his insurance paperwork. He even pulled into the parking lot of an abandoned car wash and opened the envelope, the whole time telling himself it was wrong. Knowing it was wrong, but the promises those images held cried out to him like a screaming itch nestled safely out of reach; the kind that commandeers your every thought until you find relief. Only this itch was buried in his mind, and the harder he tried to ignore it, the louder it yelled.

This time he managed to push it away, and he tossed the envelope back into the glove compartment with nothing more than a courtesy glance. Just enough to abate the hunger. But it would return, because hidden or not, the images called to him, sang their sweet song through the dash, begged him to give up the fight, to surrender.

Mike found a parking space in front of the store, and for the first time in his life, he patronized a florist. The store smelled good, it had that going for it, but he didn't have a clue about how to go about ordering a bunch of flowers. Thankfully, the little fellow behind the counter knew exactly what he needed, and within five minutes he was back in his truck thinking about his next stop. Before he could change his mind and head back home to Becky, he pulled onto Forrest Street and turned right onto Alexander. Two minutes later, he was there.

***

THE CEMETERY COVERED roughly six acres, most of it occupied. Emily's grave was near the center, across from the fountain and only a few rows over from the walking path that meandered past headstones spanning five generations. Over the last two years, he'd stop by a couple of times a month, usually alone. Most of the time he talked to her, filling her in on everything she'd missed, and how much he missed her. Sometimes he sat on the bench by the fountain and watched people visit their own loved ones, telling the same type stories he supposed. However, the one thing he had never mustered up the courage to do, up until this day, was bring flowers. No particular reason. It's just not the kind of thing a man thinks of. Flowers for the wife's birthday, or after a fight maybe. But bouquets and arrangements usually fell squarely in the mental checklist for women. Women like Becky. She must have spent a thousand dollars on flowers the first year after Emily died. The bad year. The year he drank and she shut him out. She still visited, fussing over any withered stems or the random weed sprouting up from beside the headstone, but her trips had slowed since Daniel came.

The flowers Mike brought, mums and sunflowers, with a touch of fall leaves, all held together with a burlap bow, fit nicely in the concrete vase beside the headstone. She would love it.

Walking back to his truck, he made a decision. No matter what it took, he was going to break the spell Missy had cast over him. If that fellow from the book he had read in high school could make it past the Sirens, so could he.

Halfway down the path, Mike stopped and looked up into a grey sky. "God, I still don't know if you can hear me, don't even know if you're real, but if you are,

210

you've got to do something. Get rid of all these thoughts about...well you know who she is." Then, feeling foolish, he scanned the cemetery and added, "Amen."

***

ARAPHEL SPEACIALIZED IN an intimate knowledge of human behavior, which is what made Mike's trip to the cemetery so frustrating. Not because he didn't have an alternate plan, in fact he had many, but because his instinct was wrong.

He had witnessed the lover's spat, and left the Hill house with Mike that morning. He sat in the passenger seat, not out of necessity, but because real watching requires closeness. What can be learned from following at a distance? What valuable knowledge can be reaped from lurking in the shadows? Not enough. He had spent countless hours studying everyone involved in this battle. Body language was useful because the face rarely lied. Like a jeweler examining a diamond, he had appraised every line, every hair, every involuntary movement. Sometimes he studied them while they went about their miserable, mundane chores, but his favorite time was while they slept. He couldn't pry open their minds and see their thoughts, but crafting their dreams was a skill he learned long ago. Crafting, watching, learning- his methods worked.

Take for instance the way Mike averted his eyes when he passed a liquor store, or how his left eye twitched whenever The Author came up in conversation. How Ben displayed a slight smirk, one that pulled his chin up with it, whenever someone complimented his house, his business, or Jill's good looks. Or how Becky cut her eyes whenever a thin woman passed her on the street. Subtle idiosyncrasies a lessor warrior might overlook.

Araphel's excitement rose when Mike pulled off the road and opened the glove compartment. It waned slightly when he shoved the pictures back inside, but the anticipation became almost unbearable when he pulled into the florist. He knew the next stop. Or at least he thought he did. That's why watching is so important, why contingency plans are so important. Unfortunately, the often reliable combination of predictable humans and close observation doesn't always play out the way you think...or hoped. The game is rigged in favor of The Author.

Araphel didn't make the trip home with Mike. No need. Everything was in place, stacked nicely on top of the insurance papers in the glove compartment. All he needed was Richard's voice and a phone.

***

DANIEL HOPED THINGS would improve when Uncle Mike returned home. That the three of them would sit down to supper and carry on like nothing had happened. Mike would crack a marginally off color joke, Becky would reprimand him, and Daniel would laugh. He hoped they could be a family again. A family that laughed together. There had been so little laughter the past couple of weeks.

Aunt Becky hadn't spoken a word all morning. Daniel tried to stay out of her way while she went from room to room, dusting, wiping, vacuuming, then dusting again. By the time Mike walked in the door, almost two hours after leaving, she was cleaning the oven.

Daniel looked up from his bowl of cereal, praying they would stop and talk, but that's not what happened, though Mike tried. He told her he was sorry about not understanding why she was mad, but that seemed to make things worse. His second try worked out a little better.

"Honey, I know you're upset I would be too," Mike said, walking around the table, but stopping short of her by several feet. "You know you're the only one, always have been, always will be."

"I know." Becky stopped scrubbing mid-stroke and turned to him. "We'll be okay, just let me finish taking it out on the house."

An unmistakable look of relief showed on Mike's face, and he took the last couple of steps toward her and planted a soft kiss on the top of her head. "I'll be in the shop."

The phone rang minutes after Mike closed the door behind him.

Becky answered. "Hello."

Daniel only heard her side of the conversation.

"This is Becky Hill, who's this?"

"Yes, that's our truck. What's this about?"

"Lapsed? I think you've made a mistake. I've never let our insurance lapse."

"You bet I can verify the policy number. Hang on and let me grab the card."

Becky laid the phone on the counter and walked to the truck. When she cried out a couple of minutes later, Daniel rushed to check on her.

***

MIKE SAW BECKY open the passenger door of his truck, but remembered the pictures several seconds too late. The roar of his table saw rendered his shout useless as he watched her lean in, half of her body out of sight, then back out. She was staring at the thing in her hand. A single piece of paper about the size of a postcard. Mike didn't know which picture, only that a naked Missy would be staring back at her. She held it in her hand, considering it, tilting it left and right, and Mike saw recognition register on her face. Her head disappeared into the cab once more, this time emerging with the envelope and more pictures. One slipped from her fingers, but she didn't notice, or if she did, she didn't care. She flipped through them, taking only a moment for each. Mike watched as her knees unhinged and she plopped to the ground.

He stumbled over a pile of scrap lumber in his haste to get to her. Though only thirty feet separated them, it felt like a mile. Each step took greater and greater effort; his boots grew heavier the closer he came to facing her. At some point during those thirty feet, the drone of the table saw faded, replaced by Becky's hard, labored breathing.

"Why?" She managed the question between breaths. "Why?"

He didn't know what to say. He had planned on burning the pictures when he got back from the cemetery, but for reasons he couldn't explain, didn't.

Mike knelt in front of her, trying to think of what he should say, how he could explain.

"Becky," he reached out to her, but she shoved his hand away. "Becky, it's not what it looks like."

"Shut up! Just shut up and leave me alone!" Becky threw the envelope and pictures in his face. "Here, you want her, then here you go!"

Out of the corner of his eye, Mike saw Daniel turn the corner and skid to a stop. He didn't focus on his nephew long, because though he loved the boy, his marriage was in the process of going terribly wrong.

"I don't want her! And if you'll shut up and listen to me for a minute I'll explain."

Becky's breathing had slowed, but she was still crying and still sitting on the ground. "How can you explain this?" She picked up a picture and flung it at him, though it fell considerably short. "Or this, or this." She hurled the pictures one by one. "Is that where you were this morning? Why you were so secretive about your plans for the day?"

Mike wanted to remind her of how she wouldn't hardly look at him before he left. That the most conversation she had been able to muster were two words, "fine" and "ditto," not exactly pillow talk. But he didn't. He had been wrong also. After all of these years of marriage he knew Becky's insecurities, especially when it came to attractive women with single digit dress sizes. And what had he done? Played it off like it didn't matter, like her feelings didn't matter.

"I went to put flowers on Emily's grave this morning." Mike sat down in the dirt beside her. "I stopped at the florist downtown and went to see Emily."

Becky looked up at him, her face flush, and eyes pink and swollen.

"I bought her a bouquet of sunflowers and moms. The guy that works there called it the 'Flowers of Fall'. It came with a burlap bow and everything. He sounded smart, the flower guy, I mean."

"Mums," Becky said, not exactly under her breath, but close.

"What?"

"The flowers are called mums, not moms."

"Yeah, mums. Anyway, let me explain about the-" Before Mike could finish, Daniel darted around the corner of the house, this time carrying something in his hand.

"Please don't fight. Please, it's my fault." He was beside them now, also red eyed and holding a picture frame.

"What are you talking about Danny?" Mike asked, then looked to Becky hoping she knew.

Becky took the picture from Daniel. "What happened to it? It's ripped down the middle." Her face caught midway between shock and anger. Then to Mike, "Did you do this?"

Mike shook his head, wondering the same thing about her.

"Then who did?"

Daniel told them the story, starting with his first night at their house and ending with him showing them the ripped picture. Both Mike and Becky listened without much interruption. Mike asked the occasional question, especially about the man who called himself Richard, and Becky protested several times that they should call the police immediately. By the time Daniel had finished, the sun was halfway down the western sky, and all three were exhausted. Mike couldn't tell if Becky believed all of it, he wasn't sure what he believed, but both could see Daniel believed it.

Becky stood first. "Here's what we're going to do. First, we're calling the police and telling them about this man. What did you say his name was?"

"Richard."

"That's right, Richard." Daniel opened his mouth, but Becky threw her hand up. "We're calling. We won't say anything about what you think he is, but they need to know about him. Next, we're going to pray. As a family."

This time Mike wanted to protest, but he knew better. This was his Becky; the Becky he knew and loved.

"After that, I'll put us on some supper."

She bent down and gathered the pictures of Missy. "I don't ever want to see these things again," she said, handing them to Mike.

"You won't."

"And you're going to talk to her. Tell her to stay away from you and our family. Do you hear me?"

Mike nodded.

"I'm afraid of what I might do if I ever lay eyes on her again, so you've got to put an end to this." She grabbed his arm. "I mean it Mike. If you don't, I will."

He knew she meant it. "I will. I'll talk to her." Even as he said the words, a knot formed in his stomach, and he hoped he could resist one more time.

26

Jill stayed at Preston's bedside though his condition had not changed. She frosted over quickly after the first night, and now, three days into the ordeal, Ben wondered if he had lost her. If she would lash out or shed a few tears, he could hope one day their marriage might resume unscathed, but her silence and dead eyes told a story he wasn't ready to accept.

The doctors hadn't abandoned the prospect of a full recovery but didn't offer many words of encouragement. They endured a cold, methodical process. Medicine, vitals, chart. Medicine, vitals, chart.

Ben put his time in, but the preparations took precedence, even over his son. He obsessed over the instructions and plan. Richard made it clear that the offering, that's what Ben preferred to call it, was to take place in Walker, Texas, the same hick town as the Reverend's last performance.

Since he had trashed the Volvo, his insurance offered to provide a rental, and he requested a van, but Richard caught his mistake. The less of a paper trail the better. Instead, he scraped together cash, scoured the

Pine Creek Trader and found what he needed. A retired plumber clipped him for two grand, but the white 1981 Chevy Sportvan Beauville with Two Brothers Plumbing printed on the doors would get the job done.

He intended to grab Daniel after school, outside Pine Creek Library. Risky, but less so than taking him from the Hill house. They would drive straight through, stopping for gas only once. Ben also decided against taking I-20 through the heart of Alabama, Mississippi, and Louisiana. It was the quickest route, but if someone saw the abduction and an Amber Alert went out, the digital signs across the region would mark his van to thousands of fellow travelers. State and county roads would be safer. He mapped out a route that took him north into Tennessee, then west across the state before dropping into Mississippi. From there he'd skirt the Tennessee line through Louisiana and into Texas from the east. This route offered the benefit of long stretches of isolated country roads that would prove handy for inconspicuous bathroom breaks and gas stations without video surveillance. The less Big Brother saw, the better.

Barring unforeseen complications, he could leave this whole business behind him sometime Thursday night.

He double checked the supplies. Knife, towels, rope, several days' worth of food and water, napkins, duct tape, the list was substantial. He wasn't sure if he would need the hammer and nails, but he packed them anyway. Exhausted, he stumbled into the dining room, poured himself a drink and spread his notes across the table. Plan the work and work the plan. Three glasses later, Ben trashed the papers, stumbled to bed, and dreamed about a boy standing by a river.

27

Mike weaved his way through the maze of branches that littered Dry Valley road, a one-lane along the base of Black Bow Mountain, which wasn't really a mountain but a glorified ridge. The storm blew in hard, leaving he and Becky without power sometime after midnight. The church's emergency phone chain started in earnest by eight, and by nine all but three of the flock were accounted for. His trip down Dry Valley confirmed Marcy Henry and Inez Lamb had both weathered the storm with nothing more than a few scattered branches. Barring an emergency on the return trip, he would make it back in plenty of time to pick Daniel up from the library.

Things improved when he turned onto Holiday Street, nothing but leaves and small limbs, no match for his truck. His last stop, Mrs. White, had lost her husband to cancer three years ago. Becky absolutely adored the woman. She lived on a hobby farm two miles outside of town but had donated or sold most of the animals. Becky made it a point to stop by at least once a week and catch her up on church gossip. Mike turned onto Highway 27 and found it wet but clear. He reached back and patted for his chainsaw just in case.

He saw the car sitting on the shoulder about a mile from Mrs. White's driveway and almost didn't stop. Instead, he pulled off the road and eased up behind it.

Missy peeked out from behind the hood and waved.

"Hey Mike. I broke down." She sounded concerned but not distressed, wiping her wrist across her forehead and leaving a dark streak of dirt and grime.

Mike eased toward her car, unsure of how he wanted to handle the situation. He had decided Becky meant what she said about it ending. No woman gets that tore up unless she means business. He also agreed it should be him that talked to Missy, less chance of someone ending up in jail or the hospital. His dilemma was more a question of how than who.

"I see that. What happened?" Mike asked, wanting to ease into the messy business ahead.

"I don't know. I was driving along, then bam. I heard a noise and it quit."

Mike leaned under the hood and surveyed the engine. "Say you heard a noise?"

Missy moved closer to his side. "Yeah, like a pop."

"I'm not a mechanic. Your best bet is to get her towed to Dunford's Garage over by the BBQ place on Bragg Street."

"Please, can you give it a good once over? I don't have the money for a tow, much less a repair bill."

"I told you, I'm not a mechanic."

Despite the mild day, sweat trickled down her cheek, dragging a speck of make-up with it. "Please. I don't have any money, and I really need to get home."

"Tell you what, I don't have long, but I'll call Dunford and get him to send someone out. He owes me a favor. If it's gotta be towed, it'll be fifty or sixty bucks, but he'll work with you."

"Will he take me home?"

"I don't see why not. Might be an hour or so, depending on how busy he is."

"Do you think you could drive me?"

"Can't. I'm on my way to pick up my nephew from the library."

Missy looked up at him, her eyes peeking from underneath a tease of brown hair. "I'm on the way. What do you say?"

Mike hesitated. All the circuitry in his brain that directed how he should proceed suddenly went on the fritz. Instead of green for go, red for stop, or yellow for caution, his lights blinked all at once. What are you supposed to do? Stop? Leave her on the side of the road? Go? Take a trip to the Siren's home?

"Hop in the truck. We need to talk anyway."

"You'd do that for me?" She touched his hand and moved in closer. "Thank you Mike, you don't know what this means to me."

Mike backed away and ordered her to the passenger side. "Just get in."

Neither spoke on the ten-minute ride to her apartment, except for her telling him the name of the complex. He knew it, so no need for directions. No small talk either. Mike had decided it might be better to have their talk at her place. Doing it driving down the road seemed too casual, too callous. After all, she was a person, and even crazy people have feelings. He would wait until he got

222

her home, then they could talk in the parking lot. He'd be quick about it. Say his peace, make sure she understood, then shoot down Forrest Street to the library. No sweat.

But that didn't happen.

Mike pulled up in front of her building and found a spot beside an older Buick Regal. His first ride had been a Regal, and his first date with Becky had been in that car. Funny, the things your mind points out when you're stressed. A car leads to a memory, and the memory leads to his wife.

"You want to come up for a minute? I can put on some coffee, and you can call your friend with the wrecker."

His gut told him to stay outside, his heart told him not to go into her apartment, but his head found a way to justify ignoring both. No need to take a chance on Missy causing a scene in public, which Mike thought a likely scenario. People would see, rumors would spread. It wasn't him or his reputation he was worried about, but Becky's. Even if she knew the truth, that he was here to tell the woman to get lost, people would talk. And if there was one thing he'd learned from his occasional attendance at Grace Redemption, it was that gossip spread through some churches faster germs in a daycare.

"Sure." He glanced at his watch. Daniel usually wasn't ready to go anyway. Besides, the police assured them they would be on the lookout for someone matching Richard's description, but they didn't seem overly concerned. Of course Becky left out the more peculiar details of Danny's encounter on the library steps, and, much to his nephew's relief, didn't mention anything about glowing TVs or surprise campsite visits. What's a few more minutes?

Missy's apartment was small and clean. Not frilly like he had imagined, but nice. A couple of prints hung on the wall, one of the Eiffel Tower, another of a big clock Mike recognized but couldn't remember its name. The TV was an older model and the sofa worn. No pictures of her or anyone else.

She disappeared into the kitchen, and Mike spotted the phone on the table by the recliner. He made the call to Dunford and soon heard the gurgling of a coffee maker doing its job. Missy bounced back into the living room as he hung up.

"He said he'd get it and take it to his shop. Said it'll be tomorrow before he-"

She closed on him before he could say more. The smell of Jasmine and the feel of her body overwhelmed him as she slid her fingers behind his head and kissed him. A deep kiss that threatened to sweep Mike away in its passion. He pulled her close, for a moment not caring about anything other than her body against his. Her petite, yet firm build felt exotic and unfamiliar. Nothing at all like Becky.

Becky.

He pushed away, knocking her to the floor. The taste of cherry lipstick lingered on his lips.

"What are you doing?" Mike said, and wiped his mouth with his shirtsleeve.

"I thought..."

"What's wrong with you woman? You send dirty pictures to my house, you call five times a day, you attack my wife in the grocery store, now this." Mike started to help her up but pointed at her instead. "I'm married, and this stops now Missy. It stops now. No more calls. No more following me or Becky. Got it?"

For several heartbeats, her face matched the reaction he expected. Stunned silence. The look of a hurt woman on the verge of either an emotional meltdown or homicide. Maybe both.

Then her countenance changed. Her eyes darted past him, over his shoulder, and she managed a single blink before her mouth dropped open, frozen in a soundless scream. A force slammed into him from behind and sent him to the floor. A chill wrapped around his throat and pulled him backwards. Missy was lying against the door, not moving. He wondered if she was dead, prompting a strange sadness to pop up through the fear. Pain shoved the thought away when the vise around his neck tightened, threatening to separate his head from the rest of his body. He reached back, determined to grab hold of an arm or hair, anything to pry himself from his attacker, but there was nothing to grasp, and like Missy, his tongue failed to perform when he tried to cry out.

Without warning, a flash of white lit the room, followed by a strong but quick gust of wind, and the attack stopped. Mike's head hit the floor, and his world began to fade. As his grip on consciousness weakened, he heard voices. At least he thinks he did. They were fighting, arguing about something or someone. Him? He couldn't tell, but he thought so and found it odd. Then nothing but darkness.

28

A surge adrenaline hit his heart when Ben spotted Daniel meandering across the school's courtyard. Other than several kids loitering on the sidewalk, he was alone. Not a surprise since most headed toward Lee Square or around back to the athletic fields after the last bell. Not Daniel though. Daniel was predictable.

He parked near the north end of the library, away from Forrest Street which was crowded with over-worked mom's and dad's rushing to pick up their precious little ones before mischief found them. A trio of pine trees at the edge of the lot provided cover from the south. If he kept to his pattern, Daniel would walk between his van and the pines on his way to the entrance. That's where he would take him.

Ben reached for the small wooden bat lying in the passenger seat. Only twelve inches long, nothing more than a ballgame souvenir, he had bought it several summers ago on one of his precious few outings with Preston. Solid wood and small enough to slide up the sleeve of his jacket, Daniel would never see it coming.

He hated Richard for putting him in this position, but others deserved to share the blame. Jill allowed Preston to go on the blasted trip, and Mike certainly didn't live up to his role of Master Woodsman. Both were at fault. Then there was the boy, a loser not strong enough to save his son. For all he knew Daniel snuck up from behind and shoved Preston off the cliff, jealous over some girl no doubt. Stupid kid probably deserves to die. Ben closed his eyes and took a slow, deep breath. He couldn't kill the boy yet, not for another couple of days. Calmer, he watched Daniel cross the road, taking care to position the bat up his sleeve so it remained hidden. The polished surface kept sliding around in his fingers, but he finally managed to secure it against his forearm.

Ben finished adjusting his jacket as the boy jumped the curb and entered the parking lot. Maybe this will work. It has to work. Ben thought of the look on Richard's face when he had made his promise, took another calming breath, opened the door, and met Daniel in front of the van.

"Excuse me son, aren't you Daniel? Daniel Palmer?"

The boy jerked his head up with a gasp, almost dropping the backpack dangling in his left hand.

"Sorry, I didn't mean to scare you. I'm Benjamin Johnson, Ben. Preston's dad. We met at the hospital a few days ago."

Daniel relaxed but remained silent. He hadn't moved either. This is good.

"You're friends with him aren't you?"

Daniel shrugged. "He's in my class. I don't know if I'd say we are friends." The boy paused, waiting for Ben to reply, but he forced himself not to. Finally, the boy continued. "I'm sorry about what happened. I tried to help him, I really did. How's he doing?"

Ben cupped his hand to keep the bat from spilling onto the asphalt. "Not good. He's still in a coma, and the doctors aren't sure if he going to pull through." Ben didn't have to fake the emotion in his voice.

"I'm sorry. I requested prayer for him at church."

"Thank you." Ben struggled to stay calm, stick with the plan. "Hey, I'm glad I ran into you. We're giving t-shirts to all of Preston's friends, kind of a rally thing. When he wakes up he'll have a long recovery ahead of him, and we're hoping seeing everyone wearing these will give him a boost." Ben rested his free hand on Daniels shoulder and guided him to the side of the van. "It would mean a lot to his mom and me if you'd take one, maybe a few to give out to some of the other kids." The boy looked sympathetic so Ben went for the close. "What size are you?" Ben pointed inside the van.

"Small," Daniel said, and moved close beside him.

Ben stepped back and let Daniel have free access to the open door. "Dig in and take what you need."

He let the bat fall into his hand as Daniel reached for the box. Ben shot a quick glance around the lot, and after confirming they were alone, brought the piece of wood down on the back of Daniel's head. The kid plopped into the door with a thud. Ben tossed the bat inside and lifted Daniel's legs over the edge. Less than a minute after sliding the door closed, the pair pulled out of the parking lot and headed north on Forrest street. Several miles out of town Ben glanced back when he heard the kid moan. The boy was alive which was good.

Richard made it clear, he wouldn't accept a deceased sacrifice. It was against The Rules.

***

MIKE OPENED HIS eyes to a water stained popcorn ceiling. The discolored patch reminded him of a brown eyeball looking down on him, daring him to move. He was cold, and the squawk of a crow outside the window slammed invisible boards against his skull. He tried to turn his head to the sound, but the slightest movement of his neck brought nothing but agony.

He started with his toes and worked his way up, making sure the equipment still functioned. His right leg hurt, almost as bad as his neck, but he'd live. He struggled to his feet and limped around the apartment searching for Missy. She was gone, and other than a picture frame that had abandoned its post on the wall, everything looked in order. No overturned furniture. No clothes strewn across the bedroom. And other than a few drops where he had hit his head on the floor, no blood...thank God, no blood.

It took him at least ten minutes to work his way down the stairs and back to his truck. He turned the ignition and the engine stalled, sputtered, then caught. The clock on the dashboard lit up 5:25. Mike stared at it for a few seconds, sure he had forgotten something.

"Daniel!" He smacked the steering wheel and shifted into drive.

Five minutes later he pulled into the parking lot, empty except for a station wagon in one of the employee spaces. Daniel wasn't on the steps but that didn't mean anything. It was cold out and he was over an hour late.

Mike burst through the front door and spotted a woman behind the desk. He expected Mrs. Walsh but instead the assistant, Tiffney something, greeted him with a gasp. He'd only met her once, when she'd been waiting on the steps with Daniel.

"Have you seen Danny?"

"Excuse me?" She grabbed at her blouse like a woman about to be assaulted.

"Danny, my nephew. Is he here? I'm late."

Faint recognition registered on her face, and she relaxed slightly.

"You're his dad right?"

"No, his uncle. He lives with us."

She released her blouse, though her hands stayed close to her chest. "No, I haven't seen him today."

"What about Mrs. Walsh? Has she seen him?" Mike scanned the first two aisles.

"I don't know." Mrs. Kendall rose gracelessly to her feet, and Mike could tell he was making her nervous. "I got here about twenty minutes ago, but she didn't say anything before she left. Is Danny okay?"

Mike didn't take time to answer. He sprinted back through the door, jumped in his truck, fish tailed out of the parking lot, and headed home.

Becky met him on the porch, a worried look on her face. "Mike Hill, where have you-"

"Is Danny here?" Mike didn't wait for her to answer and ran into the living room calling his name.

Becky followed. "What's wrong? Where's Daniel?"

He turned and one look told him all he needed to know. Daniel wasn't home.

Becky stumbled backwards, "Oh my goodness, what happened to you? Why is your hair all messed up? And is that blood on your collar? What's going on Mike?" She grabbed the edge of the sofa and sank into it. Mike covered a cut on his arm with his hand. He hadn't even thought about what he must look like. Becky fumbled around the end table and found the box of tissues. He sat down beside her.

"I was..." Mike couldn't think of the right word. "attacked."

"You were robbed? Was it him? Was it Richard?"

"No, and not robbed. Just attacked. Assaulted I guess. When I got to the library Danny wasn't there. I was hoping he came home. I think we need to call the police."

***

DANIEL AWOKE TO a steady hum. He hadn't opened his eyes, but the sound comforted him. He was sleepy and the hum drew him down. Before consciousness slipped completely away, a bolt of pain ripped through the back of his head and out his eyes, snapping him alert. He opened his mouth to speak and the pain flashed again.

He was laying on the floor of a van. Mr. Johnson's? Heavy silver tape held his feet together tight enough that both tingled. He knew before long they would be completely numb. Zip Ties, he had learned their name from Uncle Mike when he helped strap some old hose in the barn, bound his wrists in front. Hard plastic cut into his skin as he struggled to free them.

A man's voice spoke from the front of the van. "Sorry about the knock. I couldn't think of any other way."

The blinding whir of white and yellow from an occasional street light caused Daniel to wince. He closed his eyes to shield them from the onslaught. "Why..." He tried to speak, but that hurt worse than the light, and he laid his head back down on the floor.

"You're wondering why? All I can say is because I had to. Sorry kid, but this is how it's got to be."

Questions zipped through Daniel's mind. Am I being kidnapped? Why would Mr. Johnson hit me? Where are we going? He wanted to ask all of these and more, but his brain and tongue had not found their normal rhythm, so he shielded his eyes from the passing lights and listened.

"We're west of Fayetteville. You've been out for a few hours. How's your head?"

"Hurts." He didn't know if Mr. Johnson heard him, and frankly he didn't care.

They drove for another hour before Mr. Johnson spoke again. "We're going to have to stop for gas soon and here's what you're going to do. Absolutely nothing. You're going to lie still and keep quiet. You understand?"

His head still ached but the fog began to lift, unveiling the fear lurking in its protective shroud. His breaths came in short bursts as the interior of the van grew smaller. The hum of tires rolling along weathered asphalt faded, replaced by a rapid but steady thumping he soon realized was his pulse.

"I said do you understand?" Mr. Johnson's voice was loud enough to overcome the heartbeat attempting to rupture his eardrums.

"Yes."

"Good. You're going to pull that blanket in the rear seat over you. All the way over you, and you're going to lie perfectly still until we pull away. If you obey, I might consider undoing your legs."

Forcing himself to focus on Mr. Johnson's words helped ease the panic attack, and his breathing slowed. Daniel inched toward the blanket and pulled it to him. It was cold anyway, and after a few minutes he sensed the van slowing down.

"All the way over your head."

Fighting through the throbbing pain at the base of his skull, Daniel managed to pull the blanket over his head and waited. He heard the engine shut down and Mr. Johnson step out of the van. Running wasn't an option, at least not yet. He lowered the blanket enough to see they were not in the city. A single light hanging from a telephone pole lit the area around the van, but beyond that, nothing but darkness.

"Lord, please help me."

The closed blinds on the side windows offered some privacy, but he still needed to be careful. He eased the top flap of the box back and reached in. He felt around, working his hand across each item. A few bottles of water, a roll of duct tape, and some cans, which by the size Daniel guessed potted or canned meat. He patted around the bottom of the box and touched something soft. A towel, maybe several of them. He also found a hammer and a container that he quickly determined were nails.

Daniel heard the clank of the gas cap when it closed. He slipped the blanket back over his head and heard the door open. Mr. Johnson slipped behind the wheel, and within a matter of seconds, they were back on the road.

"See, that wasn't too bad was it? You did good."

Daniel didn't answer. His thoughts lingered on what he'd found in the box. The sickening sound of blood pulsating through his head made a comeback, and he tried not to think of the hammer and nails.

29

Becky loitered in front of the living room window, stopping every couple of minutes to peek through the blinds, while Mike talked with Hodge. According to the report, Mrs. Myrtle Walsh told officer Tremble, (a rookie who's only contribution to Pine Creek's crime scene thus far had been two DUI busts), that she saw Daniel crossing the street toward the library that afternoon. Not unusual, though she did notice him stop and speak to someone in the parking lot. Nothing suspicious about it. Tremble asked for a description, but she couldn't tell him much because she didn't see much. Certainly didn't match the man he asked about though. No, this one had blondish hair, not dark and slick. The phone rang after a few seconds, and she took the call at her desk. Problem with the Classification Software, huge mess. By the time Tiffney showed up to take her shift, the parking lot was empty.

Only it wasn't empty. Officer Tremble found Daniel's Student ID on the north end of the lot and called his Sergeant. Might be more to it than just another kid ducking supper with the folks.

235

"Didn't she have anything that would help?" Mike went to Becky. "I mean she had to have seen something." He took Becky's hand and tried to lead her to the sofa, but she turned back to the window.

"Tell me again about what happened to you," Hodge said, and flipped through his notepad.

"I told you. I gave someone a ride home and got jumped."

"Melissa Mosby?"

Mike knew he didn't need his little notebook to remember that. "I don't see what this has to do with Danny."

"I've spent the past two weeks filling out reports, most of which have you or your nephew's name somewhere in them." He looked up from his pad, "Coincidences give me heartburn Mr. Hill," then jotted a quick note. "Why didn't you call the police when it happened? When you were attacked I mean." Hodge leaned closer. "Seems to me a man gets worked over the way you did, knocked unconscious and all, getting in touch with us would be the first thing on his mind."

"He doesn't carry a phone," Becky said, staring out the window. "Doesn't think he needs one."

"That true?"

Mike glared at the detective. "Is there a law against not having a cell phone?"

Hodge leaned back. "Okay, just trying to get the whole story. Tell me one more time, from the top."

"I told you. I stopped to help someone…Missy, who was stranded on the side of the road. She asked for a ride home, and I said yes."

"Why did you feel the need to walk her inside? Anyone suspicious hanging around the parking lot? She mention being afraid of someone, ex-boyfriend maybe?"

"No. No one suspicious."

"Then why were you in her apartment?"

Becky walked back to the sofa. She didn't speak though both Mike and Hodge looked up to her. Mike smelled burnt meatloaf, but it didn't matter, he wasn't hungry. She glanced first at her husband then the detective. "He was there because I asked him to talk to her."

"That so?"

Before Mike could answer, Hodge's phone buzzed from inside his coat. He held up a finger, got up, and walked to the kitchen. Mike couldn't hear the brief conversation, but it was obvious the call concerned the case.

When Hodge returned to the sofa he had the notebook in hand. "That was my partner. Missy picked up her car from the wrecker company around 4:30 this afternoon. The owner wasn't sure how she got there, but insisted to us everything checked out fine with it. Perfect working condition. Said she was in a hurry, didn't even wait for change from the hundred she threw on the counter." He paused to scan his pad. "Thirty minutes ago she used a credit card for gas near Macon. Description the clerk gave matches Melissa Mosby. Sounds to me like a woman scared and on the run."

"Look, I told you what happened. I didn't see anything. They got me from behind." Mike tried to hide his trembling left hand. He hadn't seen anything, that much was true, but he had felt something. Something cold and dead. "When I came to, Missy was gone, I got in my truck, and drove to the library. Danny wasn't there so I came home, and when he wasn't here we called the cops."

Becky sat down beside the detective. "Just find my nephew."

Mike started to get up, but she motioned for him to sit, and he looked back to Hodge. "Please. Tell me what you know about Danny."

He sighed and sat his notepad down. "Okay. It's not much. White male, maybe thirty, forty years old, she said she wasn't good with ages. Short blond hair, driving a white van with 'Two Brothers Plumbing' printed on the side." Hodge stopped and asked Mike if he had seen a van matching that description in the apartment parking lot. When Mike said no, he continued. "Anyway, we tracked the company and it was a one-man deal, no two brothers about it. The owner, Jose Ruiz didn't give us much. Same basic details as Mrs. Walsh. Got a name, but we're almost certain it's an alias. Either of you know a George Gregory?"

Mike and Becky said they didn't.

"Didn't think so. Like I said, probably an alias but we're checking it. We're chasing one more lead but I don't figure it to amount to much either."

"No tag number?" Mike asked.

"Nope, but it probably wouldn't matter. Guys like this might go through three or four plates a day."

Becky sat down by Mike and took his hand. "Detective," she paused, "may I call you James?" Hodge nodded patiently. "James, I know you're doing what you can, but promise me even if you don't think it's important, you'll check it out."

"Mrs. Hill, I assure you-"

Becky held up her hand. "I know, and thank you. I had to say it. Now, please, what's the other lead?"

Hodge hesitated, then relented. "Mr. Ruiz said the guy was upset, real nervous, so he asked if he was alright. Our suspect mentioned that his son was in the hospital. Had some kind of camping accident. Chances are it's a wild goose chase, but we've got officers there now and we're reviewing 911 calls."

Becky clamped down on Mike's hand and said what they both knew. "Ben."

***

DANIEL HAD A plan, all he needed was opportunity and a little luck. Mr. Johnson kept his word about cutting the duct tape from around his ankles, though Daniel couldn't help but focus on the knife he used. At least a foot long with a handle made of some sort of white stone. The slightly curved blade had odd symbols and shapes etched into it, and Daniel thought back to the towels, trying not to imagine their purpose.

Although Mr. Johnson had freed his feet, part of the deal was he had to lie in the floor. From his vantage point, he had a clear view out the front, but he saw only trees on either side.

Daniel decided to take a chance.

"Mr. Johnson, I have to go to the bathroom." A lie, but he thought God would forgive him.

"Here, use this." An empty water bottle landed in front of him.

"No, not that one. I need to do the other."

Daniel heard a sigh from the front.

"I promise I won't try to get away. I really have to go."

Mr. Johnson pulled the van off the road, and they came to a stop on the shoulder. Preston's dad turned around and looked at him.

"Here's the deal. Your hands stay tied and you go by the van. On the shoulder. I'll give you privacy, but I'm going to be standing outside. If you try to run, I'll shoot you. Understand?"

"Yes sir." Daniel hesitated, "Do you have anything I can...um...you know?"

"There's some napkins in the box. Not the towels."

Daniel grabbed a pile of napkins, searched the bottom of the box, and found the nails. He lifted one and folded it into the stack.

A few seconds later the side door slid open, and Mr. Johnson grabbed his ankles, yanking him to the edge. He looked mad and waved the gun toward the rear of the van. "Remember, you take off on me and I'll put a bullet in your back."

Daniel didn't waste time. He squatted in the proper pose next to the rear tire and slipped the nail out of the napkin. He glanced toward the front of the vehicle, then wedged the nail between the ground and the tire. It might not work, but at least it was a plan. Best case, the tire would go flat in the middle of city traffic allowing him to make a run for it. Worst case, the nail would slide out of the way, no damage done. Or the tire goes flat on deserted stretch of highway, and he would regroup.

Daniel prayed as he set the nail in place. "Please Lord, let this work. I don't know what else to do." Positive he had secured it at the proper angle, he went through the motions of finishing up his business, then, hoping Mr. Johnson bought the act, wadded up the clean napkins, and threw them under the van. The whole charade took less than five minutes.

As the van pulled onto the road, Daniel worried the tire would pop on the first turn of the wheel. Thirty minutes later, according to the dash clock, Daniel thought maybe the nail hadn't punctured the tire at all. Five minutes after that, Mr. Johnson cursed and pulled onto the shoulder of the same deserted road.

30

After re-taping Daniel's ankles, Ben slammed the driver door shut, walked to the rear of the van, and cursed the flat.

He bent down and ran his fingers across the tire, locating the culprit almost immediately. His head hurt, he was sick to his stomach, and now his back ached. Backaches were for people over forty. Or people who had been hurled into a wall. The thought refocused Ben, reminding him of the consequences if he failed.

He found the spare, jack, and crowbar, then went to work and thought about his luck. Of all times to catch a flat. He couldn't remember the last time he'd changed a tire. Jill, she ran over random crap all the time. Roofing nails, bits of scrap metal, even a glass jug once. Thank God for the auto club. A rustling from inside the van caused him to flinch and jerk the crowbar from its slot, which sent him sprawling backwards. He landed hard on his butt, scraping both palms in the process. Stupid kid. For a moment he considered forcing the brat to sit outside so he could keep an eye on him but changed his mind. He didn't have the energy to haul him out of the van, much less help him back inside.

The lug nuts took longer than expected, but he had time. After he tightened the last one, lights lit up the night. Ben hurried around the bumper and peeked up the road. Headlights from the opposite direction cut through the dark, but on this particular remote straight-way they were still a few seconds away. Ben prayed it wasn't a Sheriff's car. Crowbar in one hand, he patted his jacket pocket with the other, searching for the .38. Still there.

He cracked open the rear door. "Kid, you so much as make a sound, and I'll kill whoever's in this car, then you." He slammed the door shut and paused. The kid looked guilty. "Guilty as sin," his dad used to say. He grabbed the handle, wanting to ask the boy what he had done, or what he was planning, but the red glow of brake lights stopped him. At least until he dealt with their guest.

The car pulled onto the opposite shoulder and came to rest. Ben recognized it as an older Buick Regal. He guessed a maroon mid-seventies model, difficult to tell in the dark, but it definitely was not a cop. The driver, also mid-seventies, leaned out the window. "Need some help son?"

He relaxed his grip on the crowbar.

"No, I think I'm good. Had a flat, but I got it fixed. Thanks."

Ben waved and turned to retrieve the flat tire, leaning it against the bumper. Light bounced off the head of a nail, and the truth of its origin came to Ben at once. Heat rushed to his face. Stupid, idiot of a kid. He was going to get his wife and son killed.

"Sir, you sure you don't need some help? It's no trouble."

When the old man reached to unfasten his seatbelt, Ben realized it was time to go, but he couldn't risk opening the back door until these idiots decided to move along. One close call was enough for tonight. The next car that came along might be the kind equipped with radios and shotguns.

"Really, I'm good. Thanks though." Ben waved then turned to the van, trying his best to end the conversation.

The man from the Buick called after him. "If you don't mind, me and my friend need a little help. Seems we got ourselves turned around."

Ben took a couple of deep breaths to relax and called over his shoulder. "I'm really sorry, I'm not from around here myself. Don't think I'd be much help."

"What's that? Getting a little soft on the hearing. Walter here says if I'd trim my ears every once in a while, it'd do wonders."

Ben imagined walking over to the car and sending the pair off with a couple of quick shots. He palmed the grip of his revolver, felt its weight, its power. Not a murderer. He would have to remember that when he confronted Daniel about the nail.

"You are a murderer." He heard the voice clearly. "A murderer, a pervert and a thief."

"What did you say?" Ben yelled and moved his finger from the guard to the trigger.

"I said I don't hear too good. We need a little help getting back on track, and since you came from that way," the man pointed down the highway, "I thought you might be able to help."

Don't lose it now Ben. You're almost there. Help the old man and don't make any more of a scene than you already have. Don't give them any more of a reason to talk about the jerk on Highway 64 that wouldn't take the time to give directions to a couple of lost senior citizens.

Ben relaxed his grip on the gun. "Sure, what are you looking for?" He said, and walked across the road.

"We're headed to a tent meeting. Heard of one getting ready to happen tomorrow evening," the old man laughed and looked at his friend, "only they say it's not under a tent, but in a barn. You know what that is son? A tent meeting?"

Ben stiffened. "Yeah, been to a few myself."

"You don't say."

The friend, Walter, leaned across the seat. "Do you know The Lord, son?"

Ben's grip on the pistol tightened again. What kind of lunatic goes around asking complete strangers if they knew The Lord, on deserted roads, in the middle of the night?

"Yeah, I know who he is." Ben scanned the road and once again debated killing the men and getting on with the plan. Easy shots, couldn't miss at this range. Might even be tomorrow morning before someone came along and decided to investigate the Buick stranded on the side of the road. The thought startled him, and he released his grip on the revolver. Not a murderer. "Listen fellas, I've got to get going. Sorry I couldn't help."

He started to walk away when one of the men called after him, "Knowing who He is isn't the same as knowing Him. Whatever is troubling you, don't worry. He has a plan. He's the One in control. He knew the end before He began."

Ben stopped but didn't turn around. "Yeah, thanks. I'll remember that." Then, without thinking added, "Hope you find your barn meeting."

"We will, and you never know, maybe we'll see you there."

Not likely, Ben thought as the car pulled away. Not ever again.

***

DANIEL SAT MOTIONLESS until the jack did its thing, then he slid the box to him, reached in and pulled out a bottle of water. With his hands tied in front, twisting the cap off wasn't difficult. The water was lukewarm but refreshed his parched throat. He drank half before forcing himself to stop.

The hair on Daniel's arms tingled to life, and he lifted his eyes to the roof of the van. "Father, I need your help. I don't know what's going on. All I know is I'm scared." The familiar feeling of dread mingled with hate was distant but unmistakable. He sensed it like someone would sense an ocean over the next hill.

Daniel gasped as light filled the van. It took a few seconds for him to recognize the source, headlights of an oncoming car, and it was slowing down. He held his breath when the back doors cracked open and Mr. Johnson threatened him if he tried anything.

From his position on the floor he couldn't see much, so he slid to the rear driver side window. The blinds were closed and he didn't dare pry them open, but if he scooted right up against them he could see a car idling on the other side of the road. Inside he saw two people, an old man and someone in the passenger seat. Mr. Johnson was out of sight, but he heard him behind the van.

"Father, please, is this it? Is this your answer? Should I run?" He peered out the blinds one more time, muscles tense, ready to fling the door wide. Every sound, the running motor, crickets singing in the field, the old man offering assistance, seemed clearer. Even the constant ache in his foot vanished.

He inched to the side door, gripped the handle and weighed his two options. Either take his chances with the people in the car or try to sneak away into the field and find a house before Mr. Johnson could find him. Both offered advantages and disadvantages, but the field won the toss up. At least the Good Samaritans in the car might not have to take a bullet meant for him. He held his breath and turned the handle.

"No, son." The voice came from inside the van.

Daniel jerked his hand from the door hard enough to send him tumbling into the back of the driver's seat. He scanned the van knowing he wouldn't see anyone. "No?"

"No, my child." He heard the man's voice from behind and spun, expecting to see Mr. Johnson aiming his gun, but the van was empty. The conversation continued outside, though the voices faded into the background. Daniel's eyes darted back and forth, searching, listening, but the voice went silent. He considered going ahead with the plan, dismissing what he heard to adrenaline and an overactive imagination, but the voice was clear, and he knew its source. Daniel slumped against the window and fought the urge to cry. He wouldn't let the man see him cry. The sound of an engine kicking into gear told him time was up, the man was coming, and any chance of escape slipped away with the car he thought was the answer to his prayers.

***

BEN SAT BEHIND the wheel and stared at the deserted road ahead. He hadn't killed the old man or his friend, though for a moment he thought he should. He even rested his finger on the trigger during most of the conversation. Standing two feet away, hand in his pocket with the .38 chest level of the man in the old Buick, it would have been easy. But he didn't do it. He wasn't a murderer.

Yes you are. You are a murderer, a pervert and a thief. And you're mine.

Ben shouted into the darkness of the van, "No, I'm doing what I have to for my family!" He glanced in the rearview mirror. Daniel stared back, eyes wide.

"You did that didn't you? You put the nail under the tire."

The boy blinked but nothing else.

"Answer me!"

Daniel nodded, began to speak, but stopped.

"You got something to say?" Ben sprang from the seat and jerked Daniel to him. "Say it."

The boy met his shout with silence.

"Say it!" Without thinking, he drove his fist into the boy's face, knocking him sideways into the blinds. A gush of blood poured from Daniel's nose and found a home in the gash that had opened on his lip. He debated tossing the kid a napkin, but decided if he wanted to sop up the blood he could find one himself. If not, let him bleed.

His fury spent, Ben wiggled his way back to the front, turned the ignition, and pulled onto the highway. Less than a mile down the road Daniel finally spoke, no louder than a whisper, but Ben heard.

"Father, please forgive him. He doesn't understand The Darkness."

31

Mike sat behind the wheel of his truck watching a crow peck at the splattered mess on the asphalt. Probably a possum, usually was.

After all night on the road, he had passed a sign proclaiming his 'Welcome to Olive Branch', and this gas station looked as good as any for a quick stop. Halfway there and not a bathroom break.

Over the past few hours he had wondered if he was doing the right thing. Probably not, but when Becky leaned into his chest, sobbing and pleading for him to "find our boy", he knew he had to go. Besides, the cops knew who they were looking for and had a general idea of where he was headed. They would do their thing, he'd do his. When Mike noticed the Amber Alert, posted on a digital interstate sign somewhere outside Chattanooga, Tennessee, he called Becky and told her not to worry, they'd find him.

Apparently Ben knew his way around technology, but a ragged piece of notebook paper and hand written Bill of Sale made out to George Gregory, tossed casually in his kitchen trash, proved his undoing. Several routes, scribbled in red ink, each with mileage and times, all leading to the same place, Walker, Texas.

The police didn't know an exact location. He told him about his hunch, but without an address he wasn't much help. They would cast their net wide, over several counties at least, and they would catch him. Rangers are good, and like they say, don't mess with Texas.

The Voice hadn't been this clear in years. He had heard it as a kid, a soft whisper calling out to him, beckoning him to draw near. Now, after years of turning a deaf ear and alcohol-induced silence, it was back. Distant, but unmistakable, calling like a Sparrow's song, carried along by the wind.

He knew their destination. No street names or numbers, nothing solid, he'd have to wing it when he got close, but he knew the place. A place he had been before Becky and Emily, when he was young. It was the last place he had heard The Voice, and the only time he saw the Others. That's what his big sister called them, though he didn't understand the term until that evening. The moment he saw them was the most terrifying moment of his life.

He was seventeen when he witnessed the cowboy preacher fall to the stage. He didn't remember much about the revival, only a few fuzzy episodes and one vivid image. He remembered the oppressive heat while he and Rachael listened to some pregnant girl complain about her boyfriend leaving her in a bad way, and he remembered people cheering when the woman in the wheelchair got up and walked. But he'd never forget the look on the preacher's face as one of the Others, a bright one, hovered over him. For months when people around town told the story they focused on the words (some called it a prophecy) that came from the preacher before he fell, but what kept Mike up at night was the horror in the preacher's eyes. The horror and the Dark One standing beside his sister. In the memory Mike thinks he screamed.

He turned the key, sparking his truck to life. With six or seven hours of highway in front of him, he hoped to drive through without stopping for sleep. He didn't have a solid plan if he did catch a break and find Daniel. Call the police for sure, but he doubted he'd wait for them. Of course, Mike Hill rarely caught a break. Not a great position for a guy following a hunch and a Voice he hadn't heard in years.

"Lord, if you're real talk to me. Danny needs help."

Mike waited for an answer. He waited while a teenager drove up to a pump, filled his Jeep, and drove away. He waited while an elderly man pulled into the handicap spot by the front door, inched his way inside, finally exiting with a gallon of milk. He waited.

Nothing. Only the occasional hum of tires as cars zipped past the station. Figures. Where's God when you need Him, right Jim? Certainly not here in Olive Somewhere Mississippi, or Monroe's Kwik-Shop, huh buddy? If God wasn't taking calls, maybe Becky would. Time for him to check in anyway. He studied the phone, trying to remember her instructions. Phone, contacts, home. Simple as touching the glass. When his finger landed on the surface, the screen went dark. Mike pushed every button he could find but nothing brought it back to life.

The charger. He had forgotten the stupid cord that plugged into the truck's cigarette lighter.

Frustrated, he slammed the wheel. Why not walk into the store, grab a six-pack, and forget the whole mess? Because his boy needed him. Something had him. Something evil, and if God wasn't answering prayers tonight, he'd take care of it himself. He was a man and that's what real men do. They take care of business themselves.

Mike shifted into drive, rolled past the crow and its breakfast, and headed west.

32

Ben studied the map, a low-tech necessity, as the boy slept. Perhaps a bit overcautious, but exposing his phone to cell tower pings was out of the question. A hassle, but he would rather go old school than spend thirty to life showering with a dozen other guys. No thank you.

According to the map, he had taken a right onto Highway 53 when he should have turned left, meaning another gas stop. The van sucked juice quicker than he'd planned. Ben pulled a U-turn on the deserted road and headed south. He would lose two hours at most. No big deal.

Thirty minutes later, Ben pulled into a gas station that looked safe enough. The boy was still asleep and bound, so Ben let him rest. He surveyed the outside of the building before getting out and decided it would do.

A lone truck, as neglected as the building, sat in the gravel lot. An old tin sign, advertising some kind of oil Ben had never heard of, covered the lower half of the window that looked out over the pump. He could see the top half of someone's head, most likely the owner of the truck, but the sign hid their face. Predictably, he didn't spot security cameras. His overall impression of the place was that technology had passed it up during the time of bell-bottoms and love beads.

The man leered out the window, so Ben threw up his hand in a friendly wave. The man didn't wave back.

Inside, the smell of wood and tobacco overwhelmed him. The man behind the counter wasn't smoking, but the overflowing ashtray gave his habit away. A TV, plain and bulky, blared from the end of the counter.

"Just need some gas," Ben said, and laid down a twenty.

The clerk grunted and took the money. His hand covered half the width of the counter as he picked up the bill. He never took his eyes off Ben.

"May grab a candy bar too. Give me a second before you ring the gas up."

The man behind the counter, Larry according to the patch on his shirt, dipped his head without breaking eye contact.

Ben wished he hadn't stopped. He didn't like the clerk, never did trust a man with long hair, especially ones with beady eyes and brown teeth. He glanced at the sign over the dirty man's head, "God, Guns, Granny. I luv 'em all," and instinctively felt for the .38. Touching it offered immediate comfort. He turned down the candy aisle, and the clerk's eyes followed. "You're being paranoid," Ben mumbled to himself. "This idiot has no idea what you've done or who you are. You're an outsider. Places like this don't trust outsiders."

"He may not know who you are, but I do. You're a murderer and a thief," the voice whispered again.

Ben decided on a Bear Claw and Coke, then grabbed the same for Daniel. They were Preston's favorite, why not give the boy a last meal. He tossed the pastries on the counter, expecting change. Instead, the clerk raised a shotgun, his eyes nothing more than dark slits. Two dull thuds echoed off the paneled walls as the Coke cans slid from his hands and bounced off the wood floor.

"I know who you are. Seen you and the van on the TV. You stole that boy from Georgia. Got one of those Amber Alerts out."

How? He'd been careful. He'd planned. They were three states away. Ben grabbed the counter as the realization hit him. He didn't know how he'd been identified, but it didn't matter. They knew. His life was over.

"Go ahead boy, make a move." The black barrel, less than three feet from his head, stayed steady. "Ain't got no use for queers." He spit the words out like a stream of tobacco juice.

He'd go to jail, and Preston and Jill would end up dead. A couple of weeks ago the most he worried about was losing his business, maybe his home. Look at him now, roaming the east Texas backwoods trying not to stare at Clerk Larry's soiled teeth. He hated clerks.

Ben raised his hands. "Go ahead. Do it."

Larry didn't move, except for his eyes. They flicked back and forth between him and the van. Cautiously, the man reached back and grabbed the phone off the wall.

"Gonna call the Sheriff. You sit tight."

Ben knew it might be the last move he ever made, but when the man looked down to punch the first number, he swung at the barrel and ducked right. A blast rattled Ben's teeth, and somewhere in the back of the store glass shattered and plinked off the floor. Dazed, Ben groped for the counter, but before he regained his balance, a crushing pain exploded in his jaw. The blow from the man's fist sent him sprawling into a magazine rack and onto the floor. Copies of Guns and Ammo, Prepper USA and Sports Illustrated, skidded down the candy aisle. The man slid around the counter and stood over him. Before he could raise the shotgun, Ben delivered a well-placed heel to his crotch and Clerk Larry doubled over.

Ben staggered to his feet and fished the pistol from his jacket. The two men's eyes met and Ben stopped. He wanted to squeeze the trigger. His finger trembled, anxious to do its job, but the look on the clerk's face made him pause. The memory of a man in Atlanta, begging for his life, came to him. I got kids man, a little girl. Alice, he thought. Little Alice.

"Where's your phone?" Ben asked.

The clerk, still doubled over, hands on his knees, pointed to the counter without moving his arm.

"No, your cell."

"In my pocket."

"Toss it over. By my feet."

He did, and Ben stomped until he heard nothing but crunches. In the background a news anchor mentioned his name, but he didn't turn around. No need. He knew the story. The counter was to his left, and he blindly searched until he found the Bear Claws. He stuffed them into his pocket, the .38 trained on Larry. The lust to kill surged through him, and with the anticipation of an addict heating a pipe, he moved his finger to the trigger. At the last moment, he exhaled, shifted the gun away from the clerk, and fired twice.

The wall phone behind the counter splintered, and Ben stepped around a stunned Larry and out the door.

***

BRANCHES SCRAPED THE sides of the van as Ben pressed deeper into the woods. He had turned off the main road onto the dirt path a hundred or so yards back. Barely wide enough for the van to squeeze through, the old trail probably hadn't hosted a car in years. He wanted to go deeper. He wanted to make sure a passing car on the highway wouldn't spot him, but the trees didn't offer much cover. The white would catch the sun like a beacon, and East Texas wasn't exactly the snow capital of the world. No camouflage today. It didn't matter. They were close, fifteen miles or so from the old camp meeting site, and he was tired and needed to think.

He could finish this and head for the coast. He always wanted a place there. A nice vacation house, steps from the beach, where he and Jill could drift off to the sound of waves crashing to shore. Maybe teach Preston to fish the surf and grill their catch on the deck.

He pulled out a Bear Claw and tossed it to Daniel.

If he ran they'd catch him. Probably holed up in the best one-star motel Panama City had to offer, and he would certainly be alone. He would never go back to the life he had. Never go back to his office, never shoot hoops with Preston in the driveway, never spend another night with Jill. At least he wouldn't have to bother wiping the van for fingerprints once it was over. He had that going for him.

Ben killed the engine and peered back at Daniel. The swelling in his lip had spread to the side of his face, and a pool of blood had settled in the corner of one eye. He was weak, frail, even for a twelve-year-old. Nothing like his son, an early bloomer Jill called him.

"So, you and Preston are in the same grade?" Ben knew how absurd that must have sounded to Daniel coming from him.

"Yes." The voice from the back sounded weak.

Ben slid out of his seat, moved to the center of the van, and sat crossed legged in the floor. If he couldn't talk to Preston, he'd talk about Preston.

"Getting cold in here huh?" Ben tried to think of a way to ease into the conversation, but the question sounded forced- an awkward olive branch. "Thought you might be hungry? Is the Bear Claw good?"

Daniel nodded, forced another bite and stared at him with sleepy, swollen eyes.

Ben opened the other pastry. "Tell me some stories from school. Are you two friends?"

Daniel averted his eyes and lowered his head. Ben knew he was uncomfortable. Why wouldn't he be? This wasn't the type of conversation that usually happened between abductor and abductee. "It's okay. Chances are I'll never sit down with him man to man and talk. Either I'll be in prison or he'll be..." Ben couldn't finish. "Please talk to me about my son."

"We weren't close. I mean we had some classes together and I saw him around, but not friends. I got to know him some on the camping trip though, and I guess we got along okay."

"Surely there's more. What about his girlfriend Nichole? Do you know her? From the way he talked she was friends with everybody."

Daniel didn't respond, but forced a smile.

"You were friends with Nichole?" Ben asked.

"Yes."

"So you've got to have a story."

"Mr. Johnson really, Preston didn't talk to me much. He and Nichole broke up, and I think he thought she was my girlfriend and well..."

"Well what? He get jealous? No offense, but you don't have the look of a ladies' man."

Daniel looked away, and the truth pierced through Ben. This was the kid Jill told him about the morning of the meeting. Daniel was the boy that Preston had bullied. An overwhelming feeling of guilt swept through him. "He bullied you didn't he?"

Daniel lowered his head, wiped his mouth, and grimaced; a smeared patch of red visible on his sleeve.

Ben found a napkin and tossed it over. "You opened it back up."

Daniel took it and gently dabbed at his face.

"Sorry for that. Guess I lost my temper." He finished the last of his pastry, then continued. "Sorry for all this kid, but you have no idea what I'm dealing with. I don't have a choice." He reached out to comfort Daniel, but recoiled as a drop of blood trickled down the boy's chin and fell to the floor, barely missing his hand.

"You're wrong. You do have a choice," Daniel said without looking up.

33

Mike first heard the noise about two hours outside Olive Branch. By the time he crossed into Texas, his truck slowed, then lurched forward before losing power. He pulled hard on the wheel and guided it to the shoulder. "Ain't that about the way it goes."

Traffic on I-30 was picking up which meant evening rush hour. Ordinary people scurrying home from work, thinking about what to grab for supper or wondering if the kids had finished their homework. Mike reached into the back floorboard and snatched the small tool bag he'd thought to carry along. Prepare and you won't despair. Another one of his papaw's lines. He checked the rearview mirror, and when the last in a line of tractor trailers passed, stepped onto the shoulder.

He made it to the front without incident, propped the hood and leaned over. Deep orange and red light peeked over the western horizon, not much but enough that he might be able to find the problem. A simple problem he hoped.

He went through the checklist of possible culprits; fan belt, radiator hose, battery cable. No luck. Mike slammed down his wrench, cut his knuckle in the process, and sent a stream of profanity to the heavens.

"I don't think it's His fault." Mike looked around the hood and saw an old man pointing to the sky. "Need some help?"

The man's Buick was parked a few feet behind the truck. He could make out a figure in the passenger seat but no details.

"Might need a phone to get a tow. You don't happen to have one do ya?"

The stranger, already beside him, leaned over the engine. "Nah, don't trust 'em."

Mike studied the man with a bit of amusement. If he had been a mechanic, he would have retired about the time the truck's odometer rolled its first thousand miles, and it read over a hundred thousand now.

"Where you headed?" The stranger asked.

"Down the road a couple of hours. Walker, Texas."

He nodded like a man in the know. "Need a ride?"

Mike wasn't sure if he heard right. "What's that?"

The old man considered him, squinted his eyes against the sun, and repeated his question. Mike didn't know how to answer. Of course he needed a ride, but he wasn't about to hop in a car with someone straight from the nursing home. Especially someone he didn't know.

"What I really need is a tow truck. Know any good garages that'll work fast?"

"No, not from around here. Neither are you, saw the Georgia tag." He patted the roof. "Tell you what young man, we're headed in your direction and there is a garage up the road a little way. We'll call you a tow from there. If they've got to keep your truck for a few days you can keep us company on our trip, at least to Walker. Worst case, you get to where you're going and take the bus or a cab back here when it's ready."

Mike considered the awkward proposition. Spending several hours cooped up with an old man who might or might not be slightly touched in the head didn't sound remotely appealing, but it beat sitting around a motel doing nothing. Besides, Jim was more than a little off and he loved that man. "Why?"

"Would you believe me if I told you it's what God wants?" The man's eyes sparkled when his wrinkled face scrunched into a smile.

Yep. This one is touched. "Mister, I really don't know what to believe, but I think I'll take you up on the offer. Name's Mike."

The man stuck out his hand. "Walter. Nice to meet you."

34

Though hidden under the horizon, the sun painted the sky a montage of burnt orange and deep red, colors that matched the landscape of late November in East Texas. Mr. Johnson kept the van at a crawl, and from the crunching sound underneath the wheels, Daniel guessed they were driving through a pasture. Before they'd turned off the main road, he had heard the faint sound of music and people laughing. Mr. Johnson cursed and mumbled something about a stupid festival. Daniel could make out the roof of an old barn, but not much more from his position on the floor. A yellow balloon, liberated from the grasp of its owner, floated above the tree line before drifting out of sight. Daniel closed his eyes and thought of Jim.

The van slowed to a stop, and Mr. Johnson killed the ignition and stepped out. He hadn't said much after their conversation about Preston, but Daniel could tell it bothered him. Not enough to let him go, but he seemed different. He looked tired. Daniel could empathize. His muscles ached, and he could no longer see through the watery haze of his right eye. At least the constant stinging in his lip had subsided to a dull throb.

Mr. Johnson returned and pulled the van into the old barn. "We're here."

He felt The Darkness before the side door opened. The air had weight and bristled with energy. That's the best way he could describe it. The first thought that occurred to him was the air seemed alive, but he knew alive wasn't the right word. The Darkness was the opposite of life.

Mr. Johnson helped Daniel out of the door, and after the long drive, he stumbled like a newborn fawn when his feet hit the dirt. Preston's dad picked him up and dusted off his shirt. "You good?"

"I'm fine. Just lost my balance."

Mr. Johnson nodded and searched the interior of the barn. "Get over by the wall and sit down. I've got a couple of things to take care of."

His shaky legs took him to the spot, where he eased to the dirt.

"Stay there until I tell you to get up. Don't move. Are we clear?"

Daniel spotted The Darkness standing by a wooden ladder that led to the loft. He could see its features, not just a vague figure. It was black, though not the color of its skin. It simply absorbed any light brave enough to peek through the plank board walls. At first Daniel thought it might be a tall man hiding in the shadows, then he saw the solid white eyes. It smiled, and a pair of wings rose over its shoulders.

"You're not going to piss yourself this time are you?"

Daniel instinctively covered his throat, and it laughed.

"Though we've met, I don't believe formal introductions have been made. I am Prince Araphel, commander of twelve Legions."

Mr. Johnson didn't seem to notice the monster standing less than twenty feet from them as he struggled to close the doors, shutting them in.

"He can't see me or hear me yet. He knows I'm here though. We have a...connection you might say. Not much different than you and I. Am I right?" Araphel stretched his wings toward the roof and fluttered them in a slow, fluid, motion, sending a small pile of hay skidding across the ground. Daniel heard the wood doors thud together and began to pray.

The corner of the monster's mouth crept upward. "Do you really think I haven't thought about that?" Araphel said, and glanced up.

Perched on the rafters and clinging to the ceiling around the inside of the barn, waited an army of them. Several more walked to the edge of the loft above Araphel. Daniel couldn't count them, but he guessed they numbered at least twenty. Some smaller than the Prince, several larger. Most didn't have wings, at least that he could see, but a few displayed two or three pairs. An army of darkness stared at him with marble white eyes.

"Pray on young man, but you should know you are outnumbered. Why don't you relax for a bit? We'll get started shortly."

***

DANIEL ROLLED OVER on his side and tried to get comfortable on the dirt floor. It didn't work. His fingers, nearly numb from the cold and Zip Ties, cried out in protest when he clutched the blanket close to his body. Across the barn, boards slammed together, followed by an outburst of obscenities. Daniel lifted his head and glanced over his shoulder. It was dark along the walls, but a lantern bathed the center of the room in a faint yellow glow. Mr. Johnson, Ben, struggled to place a large plank on a pair of sawhorses.

In the cold dark prison of the van, Daniel thought he might die. Now here, wrapped in a blanket, under the watchful eyes of an army of darkness, he knew he would. His mom and dad weren't coming to rescue him this time. Sure, God could swoop in at the last moment and snatch him from the edge of eternity, but would He? Probably not.

A war swelled up within him. Everything he ever knew about The Author couldn't be a lie could it? What if He wasn't The Author, only a character, driven by the whimsy of some natural force or His own amusement? His mom and dad lived good, wholesome lives and look what happened to them. Jim devoted his life to teaching others about The Author, and He didn't magically appear and snatch the bullet away before it slammed into his friends face. If The Author conceived and penned the story, how could He be good? Logically, The Author was either indifferent to His work or not the final authority.

But that couldn't be true, and he knew it deep within his soul.

Daniel sobbed, "Please God, help me. Show me the truth." A line from one of the Gospels, Mark he thought, came to mind. "Please Lord, I believe. Help my unbelief."

The sounds of hammering and slamming boards faded as his view of the room distorted. Through his tears, the image of Mr. Johnson and the construction project blurred. Daniel rubbed his good eye in an attempt to focus. He wondered if the damage to his right eye had spread to his left but quickly dismissed the idea as impossible. Almost as impossible as the scene unfolding before him. The space between him and the middle of the barn shifted...shimmered. The effect reminded Daniel of waves of rain rolling down a clear window, the scene on the other side visible but hazy.

He sensed motion, and his eyes followed an unseen figure step through the shimmer and sweep across the room toward him. The familiar sensation of close proximity to spiritual power overwhelmed him, but this felt different...safe.

Lying on his side, in a semi-fetal position, Daniel felt movement across the top of the blanket, then a light pressure on his leg. The sensation didn't register. It wasn't natural. Terrified, he looked down and saw the indentation of a hand above his knees. That's what it felt like, what it looked like, a hand. The touch sent a rush of peace through him. His body lit up with life. Waves of energy flowed through him, sending tingling currents pulsating through his limbs. The sensation kept rhythm with his pounding heart, each beat intensifying the feeling then subsiding.

From the darkness a voice spoke. He didn't know if audibly or silent, but it didn't matter, he heard.

"Soon my son. Soon."

35

Ben considered his workmanship, crude but sturdy. Utilitarian was the word that first came to mind, but even that was flattering. Eight rough wood planks of various widths and lengths, set neatly side by side on homemade sawhorses. He pressed the center, and the dry boards bowed but didn't snap. It should hold. From behind he heard a familiar voice and swung around.

"Not as spectacular as the Roman way, but it will do."

Startled, Ben grabbed a sawhorse, disturbing several boards but not collapsing the makeshift altar.

"Don't look so surprised. Surely you knew I would attend the finale." Richard closed the gap between them in an instant. He struggled to hold the thing's stare. Eyes filled with nothingness. Not even evil, which surprised him.

Richard cocked his head and smirked. "Evil is relative Benjamin. For instance, you might say the man who accosted you in Atlanta is evil. Alfred Brown, but you already know his name don't you? A vile man who preys on the innocent. However, Alfred's wife might argue he is a good man who does what he must to put food on the table. A table, mind you, that sits on worn linoleum in a roach infested kitchen. She might also say the man who split her husband's head open and left him a drooling invalid, unable to read his little girl stories at bedtime, is the evil man."

Ben took a cautious step back, and Richard took a step forward.

"Some, many in fact, label me and my kind as evil, but few throw that accusation in the face of The Author. Yet, it is He that refuses to show mercy and forgiveness to my kind. A cruel master who favors one slave over the other. Or, if you prefer, a heartless father who disowns one son yet loves the other, though both rebelled. I would argue that is evil. You see it's all about perspective."

"I don't know if I can do it."

"You will do it, and to prove my point, you will be rewarded." Richard didn't break eye contact but stepped back, offering relief from the stench expelled with each syllable.

"What?"

"Right now your son is fighting for his life, your wife is packing her bags to leave you, and every law enforcement agency in the area is searching for you. They know you took him. They don't know why, but you should hear the theories. Most of them involve little boys in cheap motel rooms." The man's voice was void of emotion, but the crooked smile remained. "I can make it all go away. Give you back your family, your money, your freedom. Everything you have lost."

"Why?"

"You tell me."

Ben couldn't answer. He had no doubts Richard could follow through on his promises. If he had a chance to get it back, to hit the reset button on his life to a time before Richard, or the boy, he'd be a fool not to take it.

"Are you saying you'll give me back my life, my family, if I go through with this?"

"To a point, yes. You will come through with no legal ramifications, and I can arrange things so your financial situation improves dramatically. That should be solid ground for you to begin repairing your relationships."

"My son. What about Preston?"

"As I told you before, my forte is taking life, not giving it. All I can promise is I will not hinder his recovery. Nor will I harm your wife. Do we have a deal?"

The answer flowed out of him as naturally as anything he'd ever spoken. "Yes."

"Good. Now back to my previous point. From your perspective, am I evil?"

Ben thought about the task ahead of him but shook his head no.

"But you still stumble over what is required of you?"

"He's just a boy."

"The Rules dictate that unless the boy is willing to take your place, I cannot be the one to handle this. Unless of course you've changed your mind and prefer one of the other two options. Someone has to pay the debt you owe."

"No."

"No what?"

Ben dropped his head. "No, I don't think you're evil." He couldn't look at the thing when he said it.

"It seems to me The Rules have you cornered wouldn't you say? So, tell me friend, what do you think of The One who made those rules?" Richard reached out and gently lifted Ben's chin so their eyes met. "You see, it's all about perspective."

36

Daniel didn't struggle when Ben carried him to the altar. The fear was gone. God was in control. The boards, cold and rough against his flesh, groaned as they absorbed his weight. A flash of pain spiked through his back when he slid across the nail embedded wood, and he forced himself not to cry out.

To his right he saw a large, dark haired man standing, arms at his side, alternating glances between Ben and Araphel. He wore a garment that resembled a white silk robe, but Daniel couldn't be sure, because the light surrounding the man enveloped him in a way that obscured all but the most obvious details. Daniel let his head roll to the left and saw another man he didn't recognize, dressed in similar fashion to the first, wrapped in the same warm light. They made him feel safe.

He forced his head back to center and scanned the ceiling of the barn. A hundred white eyes stared back. The creatures formed a semi-circle along the rafters and perches, surgical students eagerly awaiting the operation to begin. Hot streaks of pain radiated through his torso;

his wet back unable to quench the fire. The Darkness stood at the foot of the altar, and he sensed Mr. Johnson standing behind him, out of view.

"It's time Ben," it said in a voice that sounded calm, professional.

The Darkness began to speak a language Daniel didn't understand, and out of the corner of his eye he saw the dark haired man to his right lunge. The one to his left yelled, strange words born from that same unknown tongue, but The Darkness flicked what might pass for his wrist at the attacker. The man in white recoiled as if he'd run head long into a granite wall. The Darkness never broke the rhythmic chant, while the audience above moved in unison to the cadence of his words. Vultures anxious for a meal.

The order from The Darkness came hard and in English. "Now!"

A ray of moonlight glistened off the edge of something silver and sharp as the object arched into Daniel's field of vision. The men in white strained against invisible chains that bound their movement, looks of desperation etched into their faces. A guttural wail rattled the walls as the audience above anticipated the climax.

Daniel heard a dull thud when the blade sank into the wood beside his head.

"I can't do it. I won't do it," Mr. Johnson said from behind him.

Hate saturated the room. "Coward, do it now!" The words split the air like a steel hammer, throwing Daniel and the altar to the ground. He heard the crack of boards off to his right, followed by a sharp cry. Daniel pushed a board off his leg and scrambled to his feet. The Darkness glared at him from the other side of the fallen altar with eyes the color of dirty cotton. Mr. Johnson's screams hadn't stopped from behind him. Daniel stumbled backwards, toward the sound, feeling for the wall.

The Darkness stepped forward, deliberately, carefully. The chorus from above roared its approval of their Prince. The cries from Ben morphed into moans.

Daniel's heel caught on a fallen plank and he toppled back and to the dirt. Fire shot up his right arm as his hands absorbed the fall. A rusted nail pierced his palm, its tip driven clean through by his weight. He wanted to scream but his throat locked. He wanted to inspect the wound, but couldn't pull his eyes away from the encroaching darkness. It drew closer, absorbing any light in its path.

"Daniel?" A weak voice called from underneath the rubble behind him. "My leg."

Daniel was too terrified to reply. He couldn't see Mr. Johnson, but he could feel him. "Mr. Johnson, he's not The Author."

"Shut up you little-" The Darkness lurched forward.

The balcony crew grew louder, individual sounds morphed into a synchronized roar. A sea of darkness whipped to a frenzy and crashing to shore.

The men in white moved fast, taking up position in front of The Darkness. The brightness radiating from them fought the dark, creating a swirling vortex of shadow and light.

"What?" Mr. Johnson said, his voice barely a whisper.

"He's not The Author. I don't know what he told you or what he did to you, but he's not the one with the power. There's only One who knows. The One who knew the end before He began."

"It's a lie," Ben said, mindlessly examining the fresh blood stains on his pants leg. "A scam. I know, grew up knowing."

The light held The Darkness at bay, but Daniel hardly noticed. "No. You saw the truth that night. The same night your father saw it. It destroyed him. You still have a chance."

"No. I can't. It's…it's too late."

The light faded ever so slightly, and Daniel experienced momentary weightlessness as his body flew through the air. He landed on the other side of the barn. Boards rained down beside and in front of him, missing by inches. The two men embraced in light, the safe men, remained firm beside The Darkness, while the balcony audience screeched with voices that might be mistaken for wild animals.

The Darkness darted toward Mr. Johnson, screaming in the unknown tongue.

"In the name of Jesus leave him alone." The words flew from Daniel without thought.

The demon recoiled and sailed backwards into a pile of hay across the barn. Mr. Johnson gasped.

Araphel stood and unfurled two pairs of mammalian wings. His roar initiated a shower of old dust and dirt from the rafters. One set of wings came down, sending loose bits of hay into the air, and the demon prince landed two feet in front of him and stopped. Daniel didn't move. Their eyes locked, and for the first time

Daniel understood the evil. He saw emptiness where passion had burned, hate where love once flourished, but most of all, he saw envy. A raging jealousy of those who had rebelled against The Author but were given a second chance.

From behind, Daniel heard the creak of the doors. The Darkness broke his stare and looked past him to the sound. The crack of a gunshot rang in Daniel's ears.

***

THE SMELL OF hay and manure assaulted Mike the moment he stepped into the barn. He didn't recognize the man standing in front of Daniel, but he knew from the look in his eyes the guy intended to kill his nephew. Pure instinct drove him to pull the trigger, years of country living steered the bullet into the man's forehead. The man in the suit dropped into a heap with a dull thud.

Daniel spun toward him, a look of horror on his face. For an instant Mike second-guessed himself, the boy had seen enough killing to last a lifetime. They all had.

Blood poured from the hole in the back of the man's head, the memory of his friend, sprawled out behind the counter of a little country store, flashed through Mike's mind. Sickened by the thought, and what he'd done, he let the pistol slip from his fingers. "Don't look at it Danny." The words seemed to come from someone else.

But Daniel wasn't looking at the body or the pool of blood under its head. His eyes were locked on the empty air above him. Nothing but wood rafters and an old tin roof in need of patching. Except...moonlight seeping through a hole, flickering out, then pouring through again. Bits of dust and hay rained down from the loft, then the illusion of movement again. Light. Dark. Light.

Mike was still trying to understand the sight when Daniel spoke. "You can't kill it."

***

DANIEL WATCHED THE Darkness leave the dead man and soar toward the roof. If it had gone straight for his uncle he wouldn't have made it, but it didn't. Instead, The Darkness hovered ten feet above them, it's wings covering half the width of the barn.

He took a cautious step back, shot a quick peek at his uncle, then another step along the wall. "You can't kill it."

Both men in white held their place twelve feet to Daniel's right, his uncle less than ten feet to his left. Araphel flipped one set of wings, spawning another debris shower. Streaks of red appeared in the demon's lifeless white eyes as it curled its lips back into a snarl and hissed. Its head, the details clearer now than ever before, swiveled first to the Guardians, then to Ben, before settling on Mike. In that few seconds, Daniel comprehended the truth. He knew his purpose.

"You lost." Daniel's voice didn't falter. "I know what you wanted and you lost." He glanced at a confused Mr. Johnson, still sprawled out against the wall, before turning his attention back to the demon.

The Guardian to Daniel's right didn't flinch, though the intensity of a thousand battles showed in his face. Daniel started forward then hesitated. The Guardian nodded, and Daniel stepped between Araphel and his uncle.

"Do you see it?" Daniel asked without looking behind him.

"I don't know." His uncle's voice faded to a whisper. "I...I think maybe. I don't know."

Araphel drifted down six feet in front of Daniel. "Do you really think you can stop me?" He pointed to the two Guardians. "You think they can do anything against me? Messenger boys against a Prince?" An oily green liquid slid from the corner of his mouth.

The Guardians didn't move.

From behind, "I hear him. I hear him." Daniel turned to his uncle, who had his hand over his mouth, face white.

"Shut up!" Araphel pointed at Mike, sending him soaring into the corner and crashing into the pile of boards next to Ben. "I'll deal with you in a moment." Then to Ben, "and I'll keep the promise I made you. Your son, then your wife." He turned back to Daniel. "But you're first."

Daniel stepped toward the monster. "You can't do anything unless The Author allows it. The Rules, remember?"

Araphel winced at the mention of The Rules but regained his composure, spread his hands, and looked around the room. "Where is He I ask? Is He here? He abandoned you. Just like he abandoned me."

"You abandoned him." A surge of electricity pulsed through Daniel. Every hair, every cell, bristled with energy... with life. "He created you, and you abandoned Him."

Drops of rancid smelling bile dripped from the demon's mouth. "You have no idea what happened."

"I know what He did."

"You know nothing."

"I know He gave his life for me."

"FOR YOU!" The whole structure shuddered with the demon's words. "Not for us. Not for me."

Mike sobbed in the corner. "Oh God. Oh God, I'm sorry. Please God-"

"I said shut up!" Araphel lunged at Mike, talon raised and crimson streaked eyes wide with fury.

"Wait!" Daniel shouted.

Araphel froze mid-flight, his claw inches from ripping into Mike's throat. He rotated his head to Daniel. His upper set of wings arched wide, the lower set flowed behind him.

"Take me," Daniel said.

Araphel cocked his head and studied him. The look of a predator sizing up its meal.

"You can have me."

Boards shifted in the corner, and Mike cried out. "Wait, what? Danny no."

Daniel thought of his uncle and Aunt Becky. He wondered if he was doing the right thing. Then he thought of the little girl from his dreams, Hannah.

Ben shoved a board off his leg and started to stand. "What's happening?" Araphel silenced his questions with a flip of his hand, sending Ben crashing back against the wall. Mike looked too frightened to say more.

Araphel motioned to Daniel. "Go ahead, as you were saying." The look on his face was curious but cautious, hard things to discern when describing a demon, Daniel thought, but he noticed them.

"The Rules say a substitute can offer to pay a debt." Daniel raised his head and locked eyes with the Prince. "I offer myself as that substitute."

"Danny no." Mike's words came softer this time, and neither Daniel nor Araphel acknowledged them. Neither Guardian flinched, faces firm, eyes on the demon.

"My life for theirs as a substitute bound by The Rules. This settles the debt in full."

Along the wall he heard a gasp, and through sobs. "Help me. God please help me."

Daniel glimpsed a flash from his left, and his mind jumped to the lunch room at Pine Creek, a day that seemed so long ago. Part of him expected to feel a cold tile floor against his cheek, Nichole's pink toenails inches from his face. Instead, a slight sting on the side of his throat, and an instant later a flood of warmth across his chest. The strength drained from his legs, and he crumbled to the ground. He felt the blood leaving his body but didn't care. Somewhere in the distance, it seemed so far away, he heard Mike scream. In his peripheral he saw a Guardian, he thought the one closest to him, pass by and take up position beside his uncle. The two, Daniel and Mike, locked eyes, and Daniel saw the anguish. He didn't understand, but one day soon he would. He was okay now. They both were.

Mike held his head in his hands; his lips moved without sound. An explosion of light permeated the air with energy, and the two men in white bowed in place. Another Man knelt in front of his uncle. The Author.

Time lost all meaning, a cessation of all, save the fellowship between his uncle and The Author. The

Darkness, all but swallowed by the light storm, cowered by the wall. The Author leaned forward, whispered in his uncle's ear, then rose. Daniel tried to move but couldn't, he was so tired. Out of the corner of his eye he saw the two Guardians that had fought The Darkness, their faces hovered inches above the dirt.

"Look at me my son." He knew it was The Author who spoke, though Daniel was sure no one but him heard.

Daniel lifted his eyes.

"You've fought well, and it's almost over. I'm with you, I always have been."

The barn grew silent except for his uncle's sobs. Even the hungry flock from above hid from the penetrating light that radiated throughout the barn.

Daniel shifted his eyes to Araphel, but the demon hadn't moved. He smiled and mouthed "You lose." He didn't know if the demon heard, but he saw.

Dust coated his tongue when he opened his mouth to speak, to tell his uncle it was okay, this was his purpose, but his voice failed him. The barn started to fade, and Daniel knew it was almost time.

The creaking of old hinges brought him back. The barn doors opened, revealing the silhouette of a car, Daniel didn't know what kind. He would miss Uncle Mike trying to teach him those things. Two Guardians walked through and bowed to The Author, who was once again kneeling by Mike. After a few moments The Author nodded, and they continued toward him. Coming to take me home, Daniel thought.

His eyes scanned the portion of the barn visible without moving his head. He was so tired, so cold, but what he saw brought another smile to his lips. Guardians covered the room. All of them, except the two coming for him, bowed prostrate, heads pointed toward the Man kneeling with his uncle.

And The Darkness was gone.

The last thing he remembered from his life on earth wasn't the cold dirt against his face or the smell of mildewed hay. It was the words of the Guardian that knelt beside him. "It's time to go Daniel." He looked to The Author, still welcoming Mike. "He wants to take you in Himself."

37

Daniel heard music coming from somewhere. Every-
where. The melodies called out to him, surrounded him,
soothed him. A swarm of beautiful voices sliced through
the air. He realized someone was carrying him, and he
looked into the face of the Man from the barn, the One
that knelt with his uncle. The Author. The King. The
sights overwhelmed his senses, making him grateful to
be a passenger on this ride. From behind The King,
Daniel heard voices, and he peered over His shoulder.
The two Guardians that drove his uncle to the barn
followed close behind.

"Normally it's our privilege to escort His children
home," the taller, dark haired one said.

The King looked into his eyes and smiled. "You'll
be strong enough to walk on your own shortly."

Daniel wasn't sure he wanted to walk on his own.
He had never felt safer than he did in those arms.

A chuckle escaped The King. "It's okay son. But I
created this for you. An eternity of exploration,
discovery, and fellowship await. Besides, there are those
who've been waiting for you."

With each step Daniel perceived more color, heard more notes, became more alive. Fragrances, so magnificent he could taste them, drifted through the air. He grew stronger and began to hear more voices along with the music. The street was alive with people. Some walked alone, others in pairs. To his left, a man talked to a large group gathered by a stream. "That's Peter. People love to hear his stories," The King said, laughing.

"You mean?"

"There's so much to learn. So many people to meet, but first there's a group that wants to say hello."

A noisy crowd had gathered outside a small marble building. "That's your welcome party. The rest are inside." The King sat him down, and as one the group bowed to the ground.

Daniel turned to The King.

"Well done, my good and faithful servant." Daniel fell to his knees. He had never experienced such joy, such peace. The King lifted him up and embraced him. "Welcome home son."

Daniel gazed at the group as they stood to their feet. Then, from the sea of people, a yellow balloon sprang up. Jim stepped to the front, waved, and released the string. The balloon floated out of sight. Daniel smiled and waved back.

The King put his hand on Daniel's shoulder and laughed. "That was his idea."

Through watering eyes, Daniel scanned the crowd, searching for the two people he longed to see most. Sensing his need, the sea parted, and his mom and dad stepped forward. He started to run to them, but after only a few strides, hesitated and looked back at The King.

"Go to them. They've been waiting for you." He reached down, put His hand to Daniel's face, and Daniel saw the scar. A horrible wound inflicted on the hands that molded the universe. Tears gathered, ready to pour down Daniel's cheek, but The King brushed them away and lifted his chin so their eyes met.

"I would do it all again. You are worth it."

38

Ben shifted in the hard plastic chair, waiting on guards to escort his visitor to the room that provided his only contact with the outside world. Mike's trips to Hays State Prison started a few months after his sentencing. The initial meetings proved awkward, but Ben understood. Four years ago, he had pled guilty to the assault, kidnapping, and felony murder of Mike's nephew. No, he didn't cut Daniel's throat, but he played a role. The choices he made over those few weeks had sealed his fate. He understood, and he was okay. He had pled guilty to all counts, and in return, the D.A. offered life instead of death. He would die in prison, and even that was okay.

In the beginning, probably the first three months, he spent his days learning how to survive and his nights agonizing over a single question. Why did Daniel choose to sacrifice himself for a man like him? He spent many sleepless hours searching for understanding.

The night his lawyer handed him the divorce papers, he decided to end the constant torment. The certainty of never holding Jill again, or seeing Preston off to college, tore into his heart, and the image of that little boy, pale and covered in blood, never left his mind. He had tied one end of his bedsheet to the window bars near the ceiling, slipped the other end around his neck, and tightened the knot. Then he remembered the words Daniel spoke to him in the barn. "There's only One who knows. The One who knew the end before He began." The same words an old man told him on the side of the road somewhere between Georgia and Texas. That night, teetering on a stool, homemade noose around his neck, he met The Author. God had worked in him, drawn him, loved him, forgave him. So had Mike and Becky.

Jill took Preston and moved to Atlanta. It hurt, but he understood that also. At least Preston was recovering. He started walking with a cane last year, and she had even brought him to visit a few times. He'd never take him to another ball game, but at least he was safe. He and his mom were alive.

Most lifers struggled with a single repeating thought. No hope. No hope for that father son moment, no hope to hold a woman and whisper, "I love you" in her ear, no hope to watch the sunrise over an ocean. In here, behind steel and concrete, there was only fluorescent light. A poor imitation of the original. Artificial. Darkness. Ben was determined to change that, and Mike had agreed to help.

The door opened, and his friend dropped into the chair on the other side of the glass. Each picked up the phone in front of them.

"Hey brother," Mike spoke into the handset.

Mike had managed to avoid the wrath of the Texas court system. He freely admitted to killing Richard Corradetti, and the D.A. thought it justifiable. Especially once they matched his DNA to samples found in Kat's car. Southern justice at its best.

"Thanks for the literature," Ben said, "the group loved it. Even had two recommit their lives to Christ when we taught it."

"Great. Tell Chaplin Jennings we've got plenty. I'll need some for the revival in Cartersville next week, but we can always get more."

"How's the family?" Ben asked.

"Good. Becky's as feisty as ever. I guess having a three-year-old at home kinda forces you to be."

Ben laughed. "I remember. Preston was a terror at three. Into everything and doing it at ninety miles an hour." The thought of Preston hurt, but he wouldn't trade the memories for anything.

"Yeah, Hannah's the same way. Smart as a whip and cute as a button. By the way, I brought the picture for you." Mike fished in his shirt pocket and pulled the small photo out. "Guard said he'd make sure you got it."

"Hold it up so I can see."

Mike held up the picture. It showed Hannah sitting on a rocking horse surrounded by stuffed animals, fake fence and pasture scene serving as the backdrop. She looked beautiful in the pink dress and big white bow propped on the side of her head. "She's beautiful," he said. "And her eyes..." Ben had to take a breath so he wouldn't break down, "she has Daniel's eyes."

Mike nodded and flipped the picture so he could look at it. "She does. And her Aunt Rachael's."

"Is she...I mean does she...?" Ben didn't have to finish.

"We think so. She talks to her invisible friends and is always pointing and staring at nothing. I know, lots of kids do that. I guess what got us was when she told me she didn't like the black ones. At first we thought she meant people. You can imagine how horrified Becky was, but when we asked she said no, 'the kind with wings, like a bird.'" Mike shook his head and looked away. "We've figured out when she's talking to them. No smile or giggles. Just stares at nothing and starts talking about Jesus. Gives me the willies."

"Is she scared?" Ben thought of Richard and whatever else was in that Texas barn.

"That's the thing, she's not. Not at all. Matter of fact, she usually tells us not to worry, it'll be okay, she knows what she's doing. I'm telling you, it'll make your hair stand straight up."

Ben agreed, and the two sat in silence for several seconds. Ben thought about the conversation he heard Daniel have with an unseen creature in the barn and shivered.

Mike finally broke the silence. "Tell me the latest on the Bible Study."

The visiting area started to fill up, so the two spent the rest of their time talking about the ministries, Ben's new role in the prison Bible Study and Mike's growing responsibility as an evangelist. God was using them, and before ending their time together prayed He would continue.

"Well, I better get back to the girls. Becky's helping with Pastor Middleton's retirement party, so I'm watching the little one. I'll leave the picture with the guard and see you in a few weeks. Take care."

Ben told him to do the same and hung up the phone. The Study group met in a few minutes, and he didn't want to be late.

When he opened the door Ben saw Mr. Clarence holding a bible, his grey hair neatly combed- a new development. He wasn't sure if the old man could read, but he and Chaplain Jennings had given it to him after his first meeting with the group three weeks ago. Two rows behind Mr. Clarence, sat three young men covered in tattoos. Ben knew them as Marcus, Antonio, and Travis, three ex bangers who never missed a study. He waved, and the three waved back.

He made it in time and searched the crowd, letting them settle before starting with prayer and turning the study over to Chaplain Jennings. He tried to note any new faces for follow-up, but the task was becoming more difficult as the crowd grew. Along the back wall he spotted a newcomer and jotted a quick note. "Tall, short brown hair, smooth complexion, standing with Douglas Sanders from Cell Block B." He'd spoken with Douglas on several occasions so follow-up should be easy.

Ben scanned the crowd one more time before opening the study, and his eyes caught on a young man sitting on the front row to his far right. Another visitor, though something about the man gave Ben pause. Mid-twenties, short cropped blond hair, bad case of acne. He couldn't place it, but this particular visitor unsettled him. Unsettled him because he was…familiar.

Ben waved Chaplain Jennings over. "Do you know that guy? Front row, to the right."

Jennings glanced at the man. "I met him on his way in tonight. Says he was transferred here last week. Why? Do you know him."

"I don't think so. He tell you his name?"

"Yeah, Billy, but said some people call him Bama."

Ben turned back to the crowd, the feeling of familiarity still lingering, and noticed Bama Billy strumming his fingers on the cover of his bible, cocked head and half smile. They had met before- he was sure of it.

I

Author's Note

Dear Reader,

I hope you thoroughly enjoyed Darkness Watches. I know I enjoyed writing it. I'll certainly miss Daniel and Jim, but who knows, maybe we'll see them again somewhere down the road. More than that though, I pray these words, these characters, somehow drew you closer to The King, The Author of creation, Jesus Christ.

Several people have asked about my favorite character. I honestly don't know. I can tell you which characters I enjoyed writing most (and least) and which characters where the easiest (and most difficult) to write.

Araphel/Richard/The Darkness was the easiest to write. He was also the most fun. I know, I know. That's horrible, but it's the truth. Bad guys are usually like that, and I think Richard made a pretty good bad guy. Ben was also easy to write, but not as much fun. I think he forced me to look at myself and where I might be without Christ.

The most difficult character to write was Daniel. I don't know if it was his age or innocence. Probably a little of both. I can tell you, that as a loose type of Christ, he also forced me to look at my life and what I hold dear.

For His Glory,
Jason Parrish

ABOUT THE AUTHOR

Photo by Alexis Jones

Jason Parrish is a teacher of Theology, Leadership, and Biblical History. He enjoys collecting ancient artifacts and is a notorious book hoarder. A lifelong resident of The South, he lives with his wife in Northwest Georgia.

Made in the USA
Middletown, DE
10 May 2022

65609084R00168